Cabbagetown Diary

Cabbagetown Diary
A Documentary

Juan Butler

WILFRID LAURIER
UNIVERSITY PRESS

Wilfrid Laurier University Press acknowledges the support of the Canada Council for the Arts for our publishing program. We acknowledge the financial support of the Government of Canada through the Canada Book Fund for our publishing activities.

Library and Archives Canada Cataloguing in Publication

Butler, Juan, 1942–
  Cabbagetown diary: a documentary / Juan Butler.

Also issued in electronic format.
ISBN 978-1-55458-830-5

  I. Title.

PS8553.U7C3 2012   C813'.54   C2012-904274-9

——

Electronic monograph issued in multiple formats.
Also issued in print format.
ISBN 978-1-55458-854-1 (PDF).—ISBN 978-1-55458-855-8 (EPUB)

I. Title.

PS8553.U7C3 2012   C813'.54   C2012-904275-7

Contents

Juan Antonio Butler: A Biographical Sketch
by Charles Butler Mackay   vii

CABBAGETOWN DIARY: A Documentary   1

"Thread Gathered and Tightened": An Afterword
by Tamas Dobozy   203

Juan Antonio Butler: A Biographical Sketch

Writing in the November 1970 edition of *Saturday Night* what is a nicely concise description of the 1960s anglo-Canadian literary world, editor Robert Fulford explains why Juan Butler's first novel, *Cabbagetown Diary*, had failed to appear in bookstores following that magazine's review of the work nine months earlier. Explaining that the reviewer, Eldon Garnet in this case, had worked from the manuscript, Fulford goes on to list the encumbrances encountered by the publisher, Peter Martin Associates, in getting this novel on the shelves:

A printing company, asked to estimate the job, quoted an outrageously high price. The salesman, under pressure from Martin, finally admitted he had quoted high so that his company wouldn't have to print all the dirty words in Butler's manuscript. (It is, as Garnet suggested, a very realistic account of Cabbagetown life.) A second printer accepted the job at a reasonable price, set the type, and then tried to censor the contents. The fictional characters in the book made comments about various public personages—I believe the mayor of Toronto, Prince Charles and Ted Williams were among them—and the printer felt this might be libellous and in any case was unsuitable. Martin argued, fought back, finally lost. He became involved in other matters and the book slipped out of sight.

Finally Martin, who had his own printshop, decided to make the book himself. So, nine months after it was reviewed, the book finally appeared. I wish it well.

How Juan Butler (1942–1981), with the inestimable collaboration of Peter Martin, came to be the writer that broke down this barrier of politeness constitutes an interesting comment on the times in which he lived—a historical moment in which content could refreshingly trump technique and in which ambition and self-destructiveness were widely considered to be attributes essential to artistic relevance and not mutually exclusive traits. Juan's life, at least the patchwork version that any one person can know of a man who lived in so many different places and maintained so few lasting relationships, looks like a highlight reel for the ethos of the naive anti-hero.

Juan was the first child of the improbable marriage of a woman of the class usually known as "landed gentry" from an out-of-the-way mountain town in northeastern Andalusia and the eldest son of a well-to-do, at least until the 1930s ended that, London commercial family. When the Spanish Civil War broke out following Franco's failed coup, Juan's maternal grandfather decided to remove to his native Tenerife those of his six daughters who wished to leave. Except for the inconvenient fact that the Canary Islands, having never been involved in the civil war, was behind Franco lines from the very outset, this would have been a simple proposition. Instead the voyage from Madrid, where most of the family then lived, involved the securing of a safe conduct (not a problem, seeing as the head of the household was by then a high-ranking civil servant) and a passage via France to Great Britain, where berths could be had for their destination.

The escape itself took place under the circumstances of ongoing conflict within the family itself. The principle protagonist in the dispute was the daughter who was to become Juan's mother, and the resolution that was reached was to leave Elena, then twenty-seven years old and still unmarried, in London with the family of a trusted business associate of her father's brother. In 1940, she wed the eldest of that family's sons, the RAF pilot James Roland Butler. Juan was born at Stansted on July 4, 1942.

When the Second World War ended and Roland was demobilized, it was decided that the family should go to Spain to introduce the grandson (not to mention the husband himself) to his forebears and see if a living could be made in the town of Cazorla. The result of this latter proposal was negative. Whatever hopes Juan's father may have had of garnering some financial support from that very well off family—his mother-in-law's father had been the wealthiest man in the province of Jaén in the late nineteenth century—were probably replaced with a creeping suspicion that he was out of his element in the toxic family politics so characteristic of the Spanish upper class. In any event, after taking two and a half years to figure out that he would never be seen as anything but a carpetbagger and interloper by the iron-willed mother-in-law who controlled the household purse, he returned with his family to London with the economic assistance of the same uncle who was responsible for their introduction. Before long, they were making their way to what they certainly were to have considered the colonies.

It is hard to imagine what a shock the Canada of late 1948 might have been to the Butler family. Armed with a promise of employment earned when his flying skills saved the lives of various RAF brass from a manufacturing defect in a latest-model Malton-built Lancaster bomber that he was charged with demonstrating, Juan's father took his position on an aircraft assembly line at A.V. Rowe. His wife, in the meantime, discovered that she was all of a sudden married to a factory worker, that she had been transformed into a North American housewife after having never been assigned a domestic task in her entire life, and that she had been unceremoniously demoted in class from *gente de bién* to displaced person—one of the uncouth refugee pariahs, referred to as DPs, that all people speaking broken English were assumed to be in postwar Toronto. The seven-year-old Juan, for his part, embarked on this adventure with a really odd first name in a very provincial city and was further encumbered by his having to resume learning English, a language he hadn't used since he was three years old and his family left England.

That Juan's father quickly returned to the insurance business that had been his livelihood prior to the war and moved the family into the southern Ontario middle class was some, but not much, relief. These were not the immigrants who were later to find themselves lauded and protected by the ideology of multiculturalism. They were merely fish out of water—without any supporting community and too poor to impose their self-images on the rest of the world—who ended up laying much of the burden of maintaining their dignity on their son.

Juan was having none of it, though, and clearly began placing his bets on the alien culture within which he saw himself as little better than a freak. When he was twelve, he assigned himself the name Johnny and soon after, much to the chagrin of his besieged parents, set about emulating those American white-trash anti-heroes of the mid-1950s—Billy the Kid, James Dean, Elvis Presley—who were delivered, as if some sort of free bonus promotion, to the household in the same box as its first television set.

Buffalo

Exactly how serious he was to assume his new identity became evident in the summer of 1957. Transfixed by the possibilities offered by the unserviceable America Civil War–era revolver his father had recently bought, Juan took advantage of his family's absence one August day. Removing the curio from its place in the living room showcase, the fifteen-year-old writer-in-waiting made his way from the Butler's Glen Park Avenue bungalow to the Toronto bus depot and spent his allowance on a Greyhound ticket to the city that was the source of all this televisive potential for personal fulfillment—Buffalo, New York. About three hours later, he was arrested for having attempted to rob at gunpoint a restaurant of the contents of its till.

Uxbridge

The humiliation accompanying the utter failure of the grand plan of this optimistic and determined kid might have been punishment enough (the cashier took one look at him and his weapon and, likely stifling a laugh, disarmed him and called the local police), but the result of this foray into the headwaters of new-world manliness was one year of residence at St. John's Training School for Boys in Uxbridge, Ontario. It is little wonder that his twelve months at the mercy of the tough love of the Christian Brothers diminished his desire to return to their high school upon release. He never went back to De La Salle—which, to the temporary joy of his parents, had awarded his marked grade school intelligence with a full scholarship—or to any other formal education. On the other hand, it also was the end of his career as gunslinger, if not as outsider.

Cazorla

In the acrimonious aftermath of Juan's adventure across the border and a possibly related family move to way beyond what were then the suburbs of Toronto, it was decided that the most appropriate course of action would be to reacquaint him with his roots—or, in the finest of Iberian traditions, fob off their sulking and aimless juvenile delinquent on the grandparents before the biker town of Richmond Hill sunk its hooks into him.

Among the first things to be accomplished upon his arrival in Cazorla was to reintroduce him to the Spanish language. To this end, a local schoolteacher was enlisted. Juan's contribution to the folklore of the town, aside from tales of the fool the locals made of him by teaching him how to drink to excess, was the scandalous affair in which these two were said to have engaged. He was sent packing back home two years later.

Puerto Vallarta

When Juan became politicized (in the radical-left sense of the word, given the times) in his early twenties, serendipity handed him an unrefusable offer. Armed with an entry that his tremendous natural charm had earned him into the inner cabal of the Canadian Nazi Party, he approached the RCMP and offered to engage in espionage on their behalf. The two thousand dollars he earned by selling that group's strategic plan to the Canadian Jewish Congress, rather than delivering it to the Mounties, bought him a ticket to Mexico. Clearly, his specific destination of Puerto Vallarta indicates that he had already set his sights on being a writer. The year was probably 1963. He returned six months later toting a dozen jalapeño peppers, a bag of pot, a .22-calibre revolver, and some familiarity with the writings of the likes of Hubert Selby, Jr.

Saint-Jean-de-Luz

Juan returned to Europe in late 1964. A short stay in Cazorla. A period raising money smuggling kef from Tangier to Algeciras. Three months in Lisbon. Then Madrid, where he wrote, and later destroyed, his first book—something based on the political hothouse that was the capitol in the early waning days of the Franco regime. Then Barcelona. Eventually he found himself in Saint-Jean-de-Luz in the French Basque Country, where he took up with an ex-intimate of Albert Camus—and was introduced to the writings of Jean Genet. Penniless, and thanks to the good graces (later billed to his parents) of the Canadian embassy in Paris, he returned home in 1966.

Toronto

This was the beginning of a run of pretty good years for Juan. Working fairly regularly, albeit in a near endless series of clerk positions that saw him behind the cash in almost every bookstore in central Toronto at one point or another, he wrote *Cabbagetown Diary*. More importantly, he liked what he had done enough to submit it to potential publishers. Signing that first contract with Peter Martin Associates, seeing the book in print, and reading all the reviews that, if not utterly convinced by the work, were nearly unanimous in insisting that he continue to write—these were what he needed to sustain him, although they did not change his nature. His eventual complete refusal to contribute in any way to the marketing of the book was presaged by the fight he got into with one of the invited to its publication party.

In 1972, to reviews ranging from unconcealed revulsion to near adulation, *The Garbageman* was published. Its combination of extreme, close-up, first-person violence and utterly alien anarchist politics placed its writer far to the outside of any position previously occupied in Canadian literature.

Then *Canadian Healing Oil* in 1974, his elegant and compelling surreal journey through the surfaces that might be the reality of someone who is doomed to always be somewhere but not from anywhere. *Cabbagetown Diary* had sold five or six thousand copies (making it a near-bestseller in the parsimonious market for 1970s Canadian fiction). *The Garbageman*, maybe two thousand. Sales of his third totalled far closer to zero than either of those two figures and Juan's conviction that he had written the important work he had truly wanted to was categorically not shared by the press, literary or popular. He did not take this well.

The End

One of the notable events of that five- or six-year period in which Juan, in his manner, had managed to pull himself together was the appearance of his first long-term and stable sentimental relationship. Neola—native of St. Kitts, with dark, dark skin on oriental features to beautifully complement Juan's most remarkable handsomeness—and he were truly happy together. She saw him through the writing of *The Garbageman* and probably accompanied him (if not physically, certainly in spirit) on the Canada Council–sponsored 1973 trip through the Caribbean that produced *Canadian Healing Oil*, providing the model for the novel's St. Pat in the process.

But one day that same year she was gone.

And there was someone else.

And Juan and she got married.

And the next book didn't materialize.

And they moved to Montreal.

And the book continued to fail to be written.

And in early 1975 a call is received that informs that Juan had been forcibly committed to the psychiatric ward of the Royal Victoria Hospital.

You hug him and note, frightened, that the barbiturates have vulcanized his skin. Sitting beside him on the bed, you try to understand what had transpired. But the medication causes the words to fall, dry and only tenuously connected to one to another, from his mouth. Approximately reassembling the pieces ... she had left him, possibly aborting her pregnancy. Juan had gone nuts in a barroom.

They let him out a couple of months later and he returns to Toronto. It is 1976. Juan is now a day patient at the Clarke Institute, constantly medicated and living on welfare. Economically reduced to ballpoint pens and yellow draft paper, he writes a novella. It disappears.

Despite, or even due to, his by then irremediable condition, Juan announces in 1977 that he is moving to the city to which Canadians go when they run out of options but insist that there is a future— Vancouver—accompanied by the pathetically simple female outpatient who he is at that moment presenting. His "girlfriend."

Then, without warning, it is five in the morning in the winter of 1978 or 1979 and a there's a knock at a west-end Toronto door. Beard and hair untended for months, three overcoats, and the word *love* tattooed back to front under one eyelid, Juan steps in fresh off four delirious days and nights on another Greyhound bus. Bulldozing his way through a bottle of liquor, he rants about the intimate connection his father had had to the death in 1942 of his wife's sister. Everything—the people, the places, the events, the dates—is all mixed up. The wafer-thin, hyperreal characters of his fiction, all composites of aliens he had known but could never get inside and only negotiate his way around with difficulty, had now populated his own narrative.

In June of 1981, Juan strung himself up from a basement rafter in the Lauder Avenue halfway house in which he lived.

Charles Butler Mackay
Cazorla
May 2011

A Note on the Text

This reissue of *Cabbagetown Diary* reprints the text of the novel as it appeared in its first printing. Typographical and formatting errors have been silently corrected.

Cabbagetown Diary
A Documentary

Dedicated to "the gang"
Elena, Charles, Roland, Lucienne, Jack
and George (who helped me with the big words)

Allan Gardens, a downtown oasis

There's a jungle in the heart of Metro's high-rise desert.

It's called Allan Gardens—12 acres of pathways, flower beds, fountains and trees—bounded by Carlton, Gerrard, Jarvis and Sherbourne Sts.

The gardens have been there in the city's core since 1860.

There are a number of greenhouses visitors can walk through free of charge including a Palm House with varieties of palm trees, tropical plants, orchids and orange trees.

—*The Toronto Telegram*

July 4

It's my birthday today and it's Sunday too, so I'm celebrating by lying in bed at eleven o'clock in the morning, drinking a coffee, smoking a cigarette, and opening presents nobody gave me. Which is okay by me, since nobody knew it was my birthday today anyway. And besides, the friends I've got wouldn't send me a present if their lives depended on it.

I can see it's going to be hot as hell because already I'm starting to sweat, so when the radio announces it's twelve o'clock, I decide to get up. Half an hour later I'm dressed and by that time I'm really sweating. What did the radio say, 85 to 90 degrees? I know if I don't get out of here soon, I'll melt like a spoonful of sugar in a bowl of cornflakes because even though it's an $8 room, which is pretty cheap even for Cabbagetown, and the toilet down the hall doesn't flood over too often, it's not meant for living in in the summer. Christ, that old sun, as soon as it warms up, turns all these rooms into blast furnaces. You just won't find anybody inside on a hot summer day.

When I step out onto the porch, there's Mrs. Himmel, the landlady, who's about thirty-five years old and looks about sixty-five. She's sitting on the steps with her latest lover, if that word can be used to describe the fat carcass sitting beside her. Between them rests a twelve-pack of beer with ten bottles drunk out of it already. Not bad, considering it's only one o'clock. I step over them and walk up the street. Then I remember my manners and call back "Lovely day, isn't it Mr. and Mrs. Himmel?" which gets a rise out of the old lush, since I know damn well that he's only been shacking with her for a couple of days and will probably dump her by next week. Not that I blame him. The original Mr. Himmel must have really loved her, though. Not only did he marry her, he stayed with her for a whole month before her boozing and yelling and fighting drove him off. That was five years ago, and no man has beaten that record yet, although enough guys have tried.

It's funny that I'm not hungry yet. Hell, I haven't had a bite to eat since last night. I figure it's the weather, so what I'm going to do is take a stroll over to Allan Gardens and see what's happening there. It should take me about an hour to tour the park and by that time my gut should be kicking for a good meal.

Allan Gardens—quite a place to go if there's a lousy show at the movies. It's a slum park, and by that I mean a city block of grass, trees, benches, a drinking fountain and a hothouse beside the public toilets, full of plants and flowers—all that right in the middle of the worst slum in Toronto. The people in Cabbagetown (they say Cabbagetown got its name because the first people to come here were Irish, whose love of boiled cabbage and potatoes is second only to their love of booze) all flock to the Gardens when the midday heat starts driving them out of their grimy little rooms, and by one in the afternoon the place is so full you can hardly see the grass you're stepping on. But even so, it's still better than sitting in some greasy restaurant or frying your feet on the sidewalk.

I live only about a block away from the park, but by the time I get there, my forehead is covered in sweat and fishes could swim in my armpits. Jesus, now I know what Lawrence of Arabia felt like!

And then, what should I see parked on this side of the Gardens but an ice cream truck. I think of cold, creamy Eskimo Pies, and realize that I'm damn thirsty. But when I get there, the truck is surrounded by about ten million dirty kids all yelling at the same time at the driver, who's going mad handing out ice creams as fast as he can scoop them up. Oh well, water's better than nothing. If I don't die of sunstroke on the way over to the fountain.

"Yes, I have sinned, brothers and sisters." That must be Preacher Mouth over there. Hard to tell, though, until I get closer cause there's quite a crowd around him today. "I have drunk myself stupid with cheap red wine …!" It's the Mouth all right. Nobody else has that booming voice, that face like a slab of raw meat, or that belly the size of a barrel. "I have taken God's name in vain—"

Behind him, his wife, a tall, thin woman with shadows under her eyes and a little pot gut, stands glaring at the sinners, holding a placard above her head which reads:

REPENT NOW
BEFORE
IT'S
TOO LATE

If you turned her sideways, she'd look like a pregnant twig.

"—and fornicated with evil women—"

"Amen," screeches the twig. "Amen," mumbles an old man, no longer able to fornicate. "Amen," echoes a fat woman, wondering what fornicated means.

"—evil women possessed by Satan's lust," roars the Mouth, his eyes threatening to pop out of his head.

"I still do!" roars back a wino who obviously knows what fornicated means. He's sitting with half a dozen buddies under a big pine tree some ten feet away from Preacher Mouth's group of sinners, all drinking themselves stupid out of a giant-sized Coke bottle filled with cheap red wine. They're having a ball drinking that rotgut like it's going out of style and cutting up the Preacher whenever he shuts up to get his breath. Maybe they're having too good a time, for one of them, who hasn't stopped laughing for at least five minutes, suddenly falls to his side and flakes out. The others all cheer. One less mouth at the bottle. I take a good look at him; his face is as filthy and gray as the rags he's wearing, and except for the spit on his beard, you'd never know where his mouth was. Better things than being a bum, I suppose.

"I smoked cigarettes till my soul was black with nicotine!"

I light a fag and watch a couple of old guys playing chess. They're both bent over the board, and looking at them you'd never guess they're surrounded by howling kids, roaring preachers and almost on top of them, a group of Indians yelling out songs at another Indian who holds a guitar in his hands. He has a funny look on his face, and when I get closer, I see it's because he's one-eyed. A real cool, one-eyed Indian. He waits until they all tell him what they want him to play, and then he plays something none of them has asked for. Every so often he lets out a loud "yippee" and the whole tribe echoes him.

"Yippee! Yippee!"

A real fat chick, so white it's only by her eyes you can tell she's Indian, starts to dance to One-eye's song, a fast Country and Western, but man, she's so fat that all she can do is shake her big boobs around until it looks like they're going to pop right out of her blouse. That really gets the tribe worked up.

"Go, baby, go!"

"Shake them knockers, honey!"

"Yippee! Yippee!"

But, goddammit, they don't fall out, and when the song ends she sits down on the grass, her face and shoulders gleaming with sweat, mouth wide open, breathing in fast, painful gasps, her breasts still bouncing around in her blouse. I feel like telling her not to worry, that even though she'll never make a go-go dancer, the TV could always use her if Flipper got sick. But I don't feel like getting toma-hawked by the rest of the tribe, so I keep my advice to myself.

On one of the benches near the fountain a drunk woman is yell-ing at a passing European family: "You bunch of wops, you think you own the country." A joe sitting beside her puts his hand on her shoulder, hoping to shut her up.

"Take your hands off me, you lousy creep. You guys only think of one thing all the time."

Poor joe, if I was him I'd have put my hand in her yap, knuckles and all. The Europeans (they can't be wops cause none live here in Cabbagetown), all dressed up in their Sunday best, don't even look in her direction. After all, they may not speak English too good, but they got their dignity.

"Lousy wops!"

She burps at them and turns towards the joe, who still has his hand on her shoulder. "Hey honey, you got any beer at your place? We can go over there and have a good time."

"We drunk it all last night, baby," he replies.

"No more beer?" She looks as if she's going to cry.

"Well then, take your frigging paw off me, I told you once already." She slaps at his hand and gets to her feet, swaying from side to side. "I see Jim over there. I bet he's got some beer."

Now it's the joe who looks like he's going to cry.

"Hey Jim!" she yells in a voice hoarse from years of drinking. You know what I mean, like a car without a muffler.

"Hey Jimmy!" she yells again, stumbles forward a few feet, and crashes on top of a sleeping hippie.

"You're not Jimmy," she mumbles at the surprised hippie, who's trying to get himself out from under her, but she passes out on top of him, and as far as the hippie's concerned, that's the end of his trip this afternoon.

I finally reach the fountain and drink that ice-cold water till I think I'm going to burst. Christ, it feels good, pouring down my throat and splashing over my face and arms. You can really get thirsty watching people.

And talking about watching people, here's a good scene: some kids are playing tag over by the hothouse. Or I guess it's tag because there's a boy around seven or eight chasing five or six girls the same age. The idea isn't just to touch the girls, but to trip them and make them fall. They're having a great time, and so's the old guy watching them from behind some bushes. He's dressed in a suit that the Salvation Army wouldn't take if you begged them, and his hands are in his pockets. Naturally, every time one of the little girls falls to the ground, her skirt flies up above her waist and you can see her panties for a few seconds before she gets up again—in fact a couple of them haven't even got panties. But a few seconds is all he needs. His hands start moving in his pockets and his eyes light up like he was seeing Jayne Mansfield in her birthday suit. Then, when the kid gets up, he stops and waits for the next one to fall.

I'm just about to sit down and watch how long it will take him to finish, when I notice a real cute chick walk by. She has long red hair that falls over her shoulders, nice long legs and two little breasts that jiggle as she walks. I haven't seen her face yet, but who cares, they all look the same in the dark. I follow her to see where she's going and the sight of her little butt is just about driving me out of my mind, when she stops for a moment, looks around, and heads straight for the ice cream truck. What luck! Not only will this give me a chance to start hustling her, but I'll finally be able to get my Eskimo Pie, for most of the kids have left by now.

There was nothing to it. All I did was ask her if she wanted an ice cream and she smiled and said yes. Just like that.

I can't get over my luck. I buy two Eskimo Pies and we walk around the park and talk about stupid things like the weather, the heat, Sundays and Eskimo Pies.

She has a cute face—freckles, a tiny button nose, a mouth I'm dying to kiss, and large round brown eyes that look sad, as if they've already seen a lot of life.

I can tell she isn't from Cabbagetown just by the way she laughs at Mouth, who's blasting off about false prophets because some Salvation Army types have come to the same corner of the park with drums and trumpets and all, and everybody is going over to them. I enjoy her laugh. Gay, happy. Not like the broads around here, who've forgotten how to laugh by the time they are three years old.

Her name is Theresa ("call me Terry") and she just arrived in Toronto two days ago from some town up north, and no she's not working and yes she's looking for a job because she doesn't have much money and at the moment she's living in some two-bit hotel and no she doesn't have any friends here.

I ask her if she'd like a waitress job cause I'm remembering that a restaurant up the street had a sign up yesterday asking for a wait-ress—EXPERIENCE NOT NECESSARY—and she says, of course, no she wouldn't mind, so I take her there.

The Madison Avenue the place is called, and you have to laugh about that because it's a filthy greasy spoon run by a Chinaman we call Blow Job because that's the closest we can get to pronouncing his name right.

Anyway, we walk in and order a couple of hamburgers and Cokes and when Blow Job serves them, I ask him, "Still looking for a waitress?" "Sure I still lookie for waitless," he replies, and then I introduce him to Terry and before you know it she's been hired at

$1.25 an hour plus tips plus meals, six days a week, from nine to six, starting tomorrow.

Terry's so happy she puts her arms around me and gives me a big kiss and says thank you Michael about ten thousand times, and me, I'm feeling embarrassed about this show of affection, but at the same time proud that I should be helping her out. Deep down, you know, I got a big heart.

Naturally, she comes over to my place after, and though it's not much—an old wooden bed, two wooden chairs, a wooden table and a hot plate, the whole mess encased by four gray plaster walls—she says it's lovely and she looks as if she means it. Hell, where was she brought up, in a cave?

She's still raving about working for Blow Job tomorrow, so for a joke, I tell her: "Are you any good at snatching babies?"

"What do you mean, Michael?" She has a startled look on her face. "Well, what do you think he puts in those hamburgs, beef maybe?" I reply with a straight face. Her eyes start to mist and I think that maybe that kind of a joke doesn't appeal to her—like I said, she's not a Cabbagetown girl—so I go over to her and give her a little kiss on the cheek. "I was just joking, honey." She smiles at me and her eyes start shining again, so I give her another kiss, this time on those full lips of hers, naturally pink without a touch of lipstick on them.

As I'd been planning all afternoon, she spends the night with me. I don't have to work at it either. She doesn't really want to go, as if leaving would kill her or something. She holds on to me very tight and when it's all over she turns on her side and cries. I was going to say something nice to make her stop, but it's getting late and I'm tired.

July 5

She gets up this morning at eight o'clock, makes coffee and serves it to me in bed. Man, like that's living, having coffee in bed on a Monday morning. With a few kisses thrown in. Not many people have that happen to them, I bet.

Terry's all excited about her new job and she fixes her hair up in a pony tail, which seems a real shame, but she says that it's the only way to stop hairs falling in the food. Pretty logical, I guess. I sure as hell wouldn't want a long red hair swimming around in my soup.

Around quarter to nine she leaves and since I don't have to be at work till eleven-thirty, I lie in bed and think about last night. Terry's definitely not like the sluts around here. She has a thin, almost childish body (although it's very well formed, with the right amount of flesh in the right places), which, you can tell after last night, hasn't been pawed by every truck driver and sewer cleaner in town. Why, she almost acted like it was the first time, she was so nervous.

And her mind is clean too. She doesn't swear and she seems to be always telling the truth—you could tell if she was lying just by the look in her eyes. I asked her last night if she wanted to move in here with me. For a long time she lay there without saying anything, and just when I was ready to give up the whole idea as a lost cause, she whispered, "Yes, very much."

And that was that. After work tonight she'll pick up her things, and by the time I get home—my hours are twelve to eight—there I am with a gorgeous redhead in my room. Wait'll George hears about this.

At ten I get up and go upstairs to tell Mrs. Himmel that my cousin just arrived in town and is going to stay with me until she finds a place to live. She's very nice about it.

"That'll be ten dollars a week, then. And she better be over sixteen. I don't want no trouble with the cops." Terry's eighteen, but I tell old Himmelhag that she's twenty just to really shut her up. Then she slams the door in my face and I can hear her lover asking who it was and her replying "Just the jerk downstairs asking if he can bring a girl to live with him."

Nobody calls me a jerk! By Jesus, I'm so mad that I'm about ready to go into her room and knock her teeth so far down her throat, she'll have to stick a toothbrush up her ass to clean them, but I cool it by thinking about Terry and how nice it'll be to have someone to wash my clothes, keep the room clean, and make love to when I feel like it. On top of that, if I get into trouble I'd probably lose my job and I'd hate like hell for that to happen.

It's a great job, and a lot of guys around here wish they had it. You see, I'm a bartender at the Lord Simcoe Ladies' Club, a real highclass place, where all of Toronto's rich bitches hang out, and not only do I get sixty bucks a week and meals, but most important, I'm treated with respect. They call me Michael (like Terry), not Mike, and they say "please" and "thank you" when I serve them their drinks. The people who work there are pretty good too, especially Mrs. Waddling, the manager.

Waddling's the best name she could have been given, too. She's short, and fat. But real fat. A great big butt the size of a steam roller and two gigantic mammals that would fall to the ground if she ever took her brassiere off. Naturally she waddles—like a duck. But like I say, she's good to me. I think that secretly she looks on me like a son. She's a widow you know. Never had any kids either. I've got my theory about that. I think her husband just collapsed and died of shock on their wedding night when she took her clothes off and he got a good look at what he'd married. And, of course, she never remarried for fear that the same thing might happen again, and the cops would get suspicious that she was killing these guys or something.

The day goes by pretty good. There's a good meal of chicken and vegetables, instead of the usual garbage we eat like macaroni and fish, and it isn't very busy, so I have time to read some of the magazines that are left in the lounge for the ladies. After all, I've got to keep up on the news and things or else people are going to think that I'm an ignorant slob like Maggie, one of the waitresses, who can only talk about how many times Richard Burton screws Elizabeth Taylor in a day, or if it's true Prince Charles is a faggot. She really puts me off, old Maggie, cause she's always mentioning these things at mealtimes, which is bad enough, but if the food isn't too good to start off with, it's enough to make you puke.

At four Mrs. Waddling waddles off home, and Miss Virgin replaces her for the evening shift. Her name is really Miss Patterson, but I call her Miss Virgin because if you ever saw a woman who looks like she's never felt a good six inches between her legs, she's the one.

Pigeon-toed, knock-kneed, skinny, flat-chested, bucktoothed, slightly cross-eyed, pimply, dyed blonde-haired, bitchy, aggressive Miss Virgin. She'll sit on a chair across from you when she's talking and make sure that her skirt is raised high enough to show her bony legs, lean back so that you can be sure that she does have something besides Kleenex stuffed in her sweater, and tell you what a lovely Sunday she had visiting her parents.

When she figures you're overcome with passion at the sight of her fantastic body, she'll get up and tell you that the Club doesn't pay people to sit around and talk. She waits till you've gone past her and had one last look, then turns on her heel and strides into her office. Hell, you can almost hear her bones rattling when she walks. I remember seeing a movie once on the German concentration camps, and even the inmates there looked better fed than her.

Supper consists of this morning's chicken and vegetables heated up, so I gulp the stuff down fast and go upstairs to the lounge to set up the bar for the evening. Only seven couples come and they stick pretty well to Martinis and Manhattans—no mixed drinks like daiquiris and whiskey sours to bugger around with—so I have plenty of time to finish an article I was reading in this month's issue of *Réalités,* a fancy culture mag, on a race of people called the Basques, who live mostly in Southern France but yet haven't got a drop of French blood in them. In fact they have their own language and books and music and everything, and most don't speak French. Not that I blame them. I can still remember driving myself nuts at school trying to learn French.

I'm just starting another article on Expo when Miss Virgin rattles up to the lounge and tells me I can go home early, since there's nobody else expected for supper tonight. Big deal, it's quarter to eight anyway. I say, "Thank you Miss Patterson," and I'm rewarded for my good manners by her smiling at me with those teeth that would make Bugs Bunny jealous. God, between Maggie in the morning and her in the afternoon, I don't know how I manage to keep any of my meals down!

Twenty minutes on the streetcar and I'm home. I rush up the porch without saying anything to Mrs. Himmel and her lover, who are sitting with a twelve-pack between them out of which only six beers are missing—they must have just started five minutes ago—and charge into my room faster than a nun being chased by a horde of rapists. Sure enough, she's there putting away the last of her things. I notice she's only got one small suitcase with her and I'm just about to ask her why it's taken her so long to unpack when I look around the room and my eyes almost fall out of my head. Why, the place is so clean I'd never have recognized it as mine if they'd led me in here blindfolded. She's washed the floor and the walls, Javexed the table and chairs, left the stove bright as the day it was bought, washed the window, which was so dirty I hadn't been able to see anything out of it for the last six months, and even put new sheets on the bed.

This is one of the few times in my life when I am actually speechless. All I can do is stand there like a bump on a log and stare. I guess I look pretty funny, for she starts laughing, then she comes over to me and kisses me.

"How do you like your new room, Mr. Michael?" Her voice seems to be bubbling with excitement.

I still don't know what to say, so I tell her it looks cleaner than this morning, and pinch her bum. That seems to please her, for she kisses me again, whispers "I love you," and goes back to finish her unpacking.

I love you?

I hope she's not going to take all this moving-in-with-me bit too seriously. Hell, after all, I can get a dozen broads to come and live with me if I want to. And without any "I love you," or "please don't ever leave me," or "let's get married" jazz ever coming out of them. I'll have to have a serious talk with her about this before it gets out of hand. But she looks so happy right now, I wouldn't want to spoil it for her. We can always talk some other time.

She's dressed in a pair of tight green pants and a yellow blouse, and quite frankly, she's just as attractive in them as she was yesterday in the blue dress she was wearing.

When she's finally finished, she makes a good cup of coffee and sits beside me on the bed. She asks me if I want to know how her day was today and I say sure. She'd worked hard as hell, but at the end of the day there was $2 in tips in her pocket and Blow Job had told her she'd done a good day's work, so she knew she'd do all right there. Then, work over, she'd rushed to the hotel, paid the bill, packed her things, and come over here as fast as she could (I'd given her a spare key to the room this morning) in order to get the place cleaned up before I got back. Myself, I can't see anyone getting a kick cleaning a filthy hole like mine, but she's obviously enjoyed the whole bit. So much the better for me, I think, at least this way the cockroaches might get fed up and go somewhere else.

She must be reading my thoughts.

"And tomorrow, or the day after, I'm going to get something to kill all those horrible cockroaches with. Oh, Michael, we're going to be so happy here!" She buries her head in my shoulder and holds me very tight. It's too hot to be sitting like this fully dressed, and I'm about to pull her off me when I notice she's shivering. I lift up her face to see if she's pulling off another bawling scene, but before I can get a good look, her mouth is tight against mine in a kiss so strong, so violent that I can feel the tooth marks on my lips for a long time after.

She isn't as nervous tonight either.

July 6

She makes me coffee again at eight this morning, which is still a nice idea, but I don't want her to make a habit out of this, because, after all, why should I wake up at eight if I don't have to leave for work until eleven? That means I'm losing two hours of good healthy sleep, which, after balling with her half the night, I need more than ever.

I decide to tell her gently.

"Terry, baby, don't wake me up no more for coffee at eight in the morning. I need my sleep, you know."

Her eyes get that hurt look in them, like my dog after I'd hit him when he'd done something wrong. So just to make her feel better, I add, "Except for the weekends, honey. You can make me all the coffee you want then."

She smiles and her eyes light up, and I'm thinking that even though I work Saturdays too, it's worth the effort to wake up early once a week so that she can make me coffee if it makes her so happy. Yeah man, just like my old dog. Hit him and he'd look as if he was going to lie down and die, then scratch his ears right after and he'd stand up and start wagging his tail so fast you'd swear it would fly right off. He had the same eyes as Terry too; dark and moist and full of love.

After she leaves, I look out the window—I still can't get over being able to see out of it—and think what a nice idea it would be to walk to work. It's a beautiful sunny day and the sun isn't strong enough yet to make it too hot for walking. In fact, I'll make a bit of a detour and go along Bloor Street.

I always get a kick out of Bloor Street. The expensive dress shops, the bookstores, the good movie houses and the first-class night clubs and restaurants. But especially the people. There's everything on this street. Businessmen and artists, well-dressed queers, hippies and teeny-boppers, old ladies in furs and chauffeur-driven Caddies—and girls; big girls, small girls, fat girls and thin girls, beautiful girls and ugly girls; but all with one thing in common—miniskirts. Little bits of cloth that barely cover their lovely behinds.

Man, like they all wear miniskirts and all around you you're surrounded by the sight of hundreds of legs flashing by. All kinds of legs. It's a leg-watcher's paradise and after a while you can only take so much of all this untouched beauty, and if you don't control yourself, the next thing you know you're ready to slip your hand between a lovely pair of legs. Don't get me wrong, I'm no sex fiend or anything like that, but to be frank, I'd sure love to pat one of those cute little fannies one day. But then again, I guess most guys would, too—and probably the chicks would get quite a thrill out of it. After all, what are they showing all that tail for, if it isn't for that?

I'll bring Terry here one day and show her the shops, she'll enjoy seeing how the rich live and, who knows, if she's got some money, we might just get her a dress at one of these real top stores. A real short miniskirt and a low cut sweater so that all the guys will go hairy when they see her, and me laughing cause I'm the only one who gets to touch her.

Work's a drag—stew for lunch and supper and hardly no drinks to serve, which at least gives me time to read the article on Expo. It'd sure be nice to go and see it, but it's too far and would probably cost me half a year's salary just to spend a week there. And I work too hard for my money to blow it just like that.

When I get home tonight there's Terry ironing my pants. The dumb kid, the iron must have cost her at least ten bucks. It's one of those steam things, you know. Not that I really care. What she buys is her business. She made three bucks in tips today, which isn't bad, but she was nervous all afternoon because a couple of guys had said something to her that shook her up so much she'd had to go to the toilet until she'd stopped shaking and was ready to go back to work.

"How can men think of such horrible things?" she asks as she lays in the crook of my arm and I stroke her hard little boobs with my free hand.

I don't think what they'd told her was so bad, hell, I've had quite a few chicks do it to me, but I feel I have to say something.

"That's because they like you."

"Oh, Michael," she snuggles in closer to me, "you'd never ask me to do anything like that would you?"

"Of course not, baby, I respect you."

I know that is the answer she is waiting for because she pulls my face close to hers and whispers that she knows that I'm not like all the rest and that she's never met a fellow as gentle as me, and so on so forth.

Me, I just lie there, feeling her up and wondering what it would be like to have her do what those guys had asked her.

July 7

Just before we get into bed, I ask her if she's using anything to stop her from getting pregnant. She blushes and just gets into bed and doesn't say anything, so I take it that she is. Dammit, she better because I'm sure as hell not. There's nothing worse than wrapping a rubber around your pecker. It cramps your style. It's like taking a bath with socks on. And besides if a dame hasn't got enough sense to put something in her at the time, then she deserves whatever's going to come out nine months later.

July 8

I tell her this morning that if those guys come back and bother her again, to go and tell Blow Job, and he'll fix them. We call him Blow Job, but never to his face, because though he might be small and skinny, that Chinaman's tough as they come. I remember a drunk coming in one night, ordering a coffee and throwing it to the floor, saying it tasted like dishwater. Before the coffee was halfway out of the cup, Blow Job had leaped over the counter and given the guy a judo chop on the neck that laid him out flat. And the whole affair took less than two seconds. Fast as a snake, old Blow Job, and just about as mean. Terry'll have nothing to worry about in his place.

It's over ninety degrees and the ladies are drinking daiquiris so fast, they must think it comes out of a tap. But I don't really mind because anything's better than sitting around doing nothing, especially since I've read all the magazines.

Maggie's working the late shift, so for supper we have burnt macaroni and Marilyn Monroe's sex habits—"She liked doing it dog style with DiMaggio"—Miss Virgin turns fire truck red and a fresh pimple breaks out on her face. So that's why she's got so many pimples! I laugh thinking about that and Maggie, thinking I'm laughing because of what she'd said, goes even deeper into MM's ways of getting the thrills. I leave without eating the pie and ice cream dessert. Maggie's married too, and I'm really curious to see just exactly who or what he is. My guess is he's deaf.

Terry's bought a can of bug killer and we spend the evening wiping out cockroaches by the bucketful. After an hour there's so many on the floor I'm worried we'll need a shovel to move all the bodies out of here. It'll be nice being able to eat a sandwich without worrying that if you take your eyes off it for a second, it'll be snatched up by those little brown bastards.

July 9

Today's one of those days when I wish I'd never woke up. Everything, but everything, goes wrong. Like I'm on my way to catch the streetcar and I'm passing Allan Gardens just as a pair of cops are starting to drag away a sleeping bum. Naturally the guy protests, and before you can count to ten the nightsticks are flying and the poor bum's lying on the ground trying to keep his head together with his hands. There's blood all over the place; and what are the cops doing? They're laughing, the bastards! Hell, they probably haven't enjoyed themselves so much since the last time they gang-banged some whore they picked up for vagrancy.

I'm so pissed off at the sight of those creeps and what they done to that harmless bum, that I'm about ready to lose my cool and go over there and give them a good thumping. But then what's the use, all I'd get for my troubles is some of the same that they've just handed out to the guy and maybe thirty days in the poky, too. So I keep on walking, but inside I'm burning. Those cops, they're all the same; mean, narrow-eyed, two-bit hoods in uniform, who spend all the time they can beating up on people who can't complain cause the courts won't believe them anyhow. It makes them feel good. Big men. Tough guys. They even get to carry a rod. Real big men. It's a wonder those flat-footed buzzards don't get shot at more often than they do.

Anyway, because of what I've just seen I'm in a real dark mood and on top of that I miss the streetcar and I'm late for work. Not much, only ten minutes, but Mrs. Waddling gives me a look like I've been spiking the drinks with rat poison or something. For lunch we get cod which looks like a slab of frozen sawdust, and I got indigestion all afternoon. Supper time, we're eating this morning's leftover cod, which has been fried, so now it looks like a slab of fried frozen sawdust and tastes just as bad too.

God, am I put off after supper! So put off that I spill half a Manhattan on a lady's dress. She stands up and lets out a holler like I goosed her or something, and that flusters me so much that I spill the rest of the drink on her. Whoop. Holler. Screech. If it wasn't for the fact that she hasn't paid for the drink yet, I'd strangle her, the old bag. Miss Virgin comes rushing up and starts wiping her dress so hard you'd think she's trying to polish it, flashing me dirty looks all the time. Me, I go back behind the bar and get ready to have a nervous breakdown. Oh boy, have I got the blues!

At last it's eight o'clock and I rush out of the place doing sixty a minute, full blast into a rainstorm, and by the time I reach the streetcar stop I'm soaked right through, and of course, the streetcar's nowhere to be seen. Ten minutes later, it arrives. The car operator gives me a look as if to say that drowned rats aren't allowed on streetcars, then says, "Quite a storm, eh."

There he is, dry as a whistle, safe and sound in his streetcar, and he's telling me it's quite a storm! Now I know why people kill, I'm thinking as my feet squish down the aisle. No seats free.

A hell of a day. My nerves are shot and I'm still thinking of murdering people, but Terry has taken my wet clothes off and dried me with a towel. She practically pushes me into bed and fixes me a hot coffee laced with a couple of aspirins in case I've caught a cold. Then she hangs the clothes up to dry and gets the iron out.

The radio's playing some nice soft Rhythm and Blues and I'm smoking my first peaceful cigarette of the day. It's just great to be living with a chick like Terry, there's no two ways about it. She doesn't mouth off and she works hard, and she's good-looking too. Who knows? I might keep her around permanently.

July 10

Saturday at last, and everything's just fine; Terry makes me a coffee and serves it to me with a doughnut—I don't usually eat anything in the morning—pretending all the time she's a waitress and I'm one of the customers at Blow Job's. She's got her uniform on with her name sewn over her right tit, and I ask her, "Excuse me Miss, but what do you call the other one?" We both laugh over that and she goes off to work after giving me a big kiss. No doubt about it, its a groovy way to wake up in the morning.

Outside it's sunny and there's not a cloud in the sky (a sky so blue you'd swear you're looking at one of those photos of a Caribbean sea). There's a couple of kids running around in the Gardens, and the streetcar arrives on time. A great day. Work's a breeze cause there's few people, it's Mrs. Waddling's day off so there's nobody to bug me, and there's some new magazines in the lounge. In fact it's Miss Virgin's and Maggie's day off too, so, except for the food—sausages, boiled in the morning and fried in the evening—it's a very relaxing day and at eight I head for home in a pretty good mood.

We're going out tonight, Terry and me, with my best friend in all of Cabbagetown, George. He's twenty-five, a couple of years older than me, and lives in a room on the same street as mine, so after I've had a bath and got changed, we walk up to his pad, which is only five minutes away.

George is a sort of hippie. He wears hair down to his shoulders, smokes Mary Jane and drops acid whenever he's got the bread, which isn't often, since the guy only works long enough to be able to get fired and collect pogey. But don't let him catch you calling him hippie cause he doesn't like that. He belongs to some political group and his job is, as he puts it, "to make the exploited masses of Cabbagetown aware of the possibilities of changing their status as the Negroes of Toronto through revolutionary methods and the enlightened teachings of Chairman Mao Tse-Tung." Now isn't that a gas? Can you just imagine all the bums, hippies, whores, queers and winos around her picking up guns and taking over in City Hall? That's too much, man.

But I really like George in spite of his Mary Jane dreams. We've known each other for a long time and he's always treated me fair and square, helping me out when I've needed it, and even letting me stay at his place when I was thrown out of a room once for getting drunk and spitting in the landlord's face. On top of that I learn a lot of things through old George. He's very intelligent and he lets me read the books he's got and when I don't understand something he explains it to me. I've always liked reading, and I don't mean those pocket books showing two enormous boobs on the cover and saying nothing inside either. I mean history books and good adventure books, and thanks to George, political books. As long as they're not too heavy. In some ways, it's thanks to him I've still got something on the ball when it comes to gray matter between the ears.

As you walk into his room—which is even dirtier than mine was—the first thing you see is a big poster of Che Guevara (I used to think it was a Super Hippie before George told me that it's one of the guys who's running the show in Cuba) taped to the wall over his bed, like the painting of Jesus I had over my bed when I was a kid. Facing it on the other wall is another poster of Mao holding a little red book in his hands and smiling like a daddy at us. On the third wall there's a map of the world with red lines drawn over some countries ("showing the irreversible progress of world revolution") and on the last wall a giant-sized photo-poster of Sophia Loren coming out of the water with her clothes on, her big bouncy breasts showing through her wet dress. The place is littered with papers and books and there's an old typewriter on the table.

I introduce Terry to him and he kisses her hand like you see in the movies. Terry blushes and George is happy, cause if there's one thing George likes doing it's flattering the girls, mainly because that way he's always got a steady supply of tail on hand.

Terry's wearing the same blue dress she had on when I met her and with her hair down she looks like a princess. By the look in George's eyes you can tell he'd love to spread her legs out on his bed, but I don't mind because that's one thing I don't have to worry about with George. Hell, he'd sooner cut his balls off than take a broad away from me.

He excuses himself for a minute to go to the can and I turn to Terry, "Well, what do you think of him?"

"He's a nice guy, Michael, but that hair, it's as long as mine!"

I guess she's never seen long hair like that in the town she comes from.

We go out into the street and as we approach the bar Terry whispers in my ear, "Are you sure they won't ask me my age?" George is looking at us and I tell him what she said. He laughs and tells her not to worry, anybody fourteen and over gets into the Harmony Hotel, which is where we're going. "Especially pretty girls," he adds, and she looks up at me and smiles in a way that shows she's not worried any more.

The Harmony Hotel, a two-story wooden building that should have been burned to the ground years ago. There's a sign over the entrance, "Enjoy Country and Western Music as Played by Your Favourite Entertainers in the Harmony Room," in big red letters. You step in through a dim hallway and walk down concrete stairs into a long room that makes Terry stop and stare—her eyes opened wide in fright—for a full thirty seconds. Not that I blame her. Here's the scene. Some thirty wooden tables scattered all over the place and filled with loud beer drinkers. A small wooden platform for the "entertainers," who are nowhere to be seen. At one of the tables near the end a woman lets out a scream which turns into a high-pitched laugh. Two Indians, their faces black with a month's load of dirt, are sitting beside her and one of them has just slapped her in the face while the other has put her right hand between his legs and is moving it back and forth. Beside them a guy lies over the table, his face in a puddle of beer while his wife talks to someone across from them. Two white-haired women are arguing over which of their husbands could fuck the best, and their voices carry over the general roar of the place.

"Joe had one eight inches long."

"So what, no one could keep it going as long as Freddie. I'd come six times and he'd just be getting into the mood." They're sitting there alone.

A drunk, unshaven, dirty blue overalls, staggers towards the washroom bumping into tables. Somebody pushes him and he falls sideways, knocking a guy's beer into his lap. The guy, who looks strong as a bear, stands up and gives the drunk a punch in the chest that sends him reeling right back to where he started from. He sits down, forgetting he had to piss.

Near us a young girl who looks about Terry's age is sitting at a table with another girl and two guys. She's dressed in a shabby dress that's so wrinkled it looks like my grandmother's face, and she's dead drunk. Sitting on the edge of the chair with her legs on either side of it and her skirt up past her stockings. Just sitting there with a dumb look on her face. The two guys are talking to her girl friend and the conversation goes like this.

"Why don't you want to come with us after, honey?"

"I told you, cause I'm on the rags."

"So, your mouth still works don't it?"

"Hey, whattaya think I am anyway?"

"Your friend here does it."

"I don't give a shit what *she* does."

She's got blonde hair with black roots about an inch long and narrow eyes. I say to George, "Bullshit, she sucks like a vacuum cleaner." Terry doesn't hear that, and it's just as well because she looks like she's going to faint just from looking at what's going on.

I take her by the arm and we head towards the nearest table, about halfway down the room and close to the wooden platform.

In a minute the waiter comes up, a trayload of beers in his left arm. It's Big Jim, a six-foot mountain of blubber, who's so bowlegged he must have been tied to a horse all his life. He slops three beers on the table, splashing all of us in the process, and waits for us to pay him.

Terry's looking around the room with that scared-child look still on her face. George is reading the notices posted on the walls:

BEER 15¢ PLUS 2¢ HOSPITAL TAX

NO GAMBLING

NO SINGING

**ALL BILLS OVER $2 MUST BE
CHANGED AT THE COUNTER**

NO SPITTING

**TO ORDER A DRINK YOU MUST
BE 21 YEARS OF AGE
AND PROVE IT**

so, naturally, it's me who pays. I don't bitch about it, though, cause I know the Unemployment doesn't give George too much and I can't ask Terry to pay the whole shot, at least not the first round.

Suddenly there's a great drunken roar and we all turn around to see our "favourite entertainers" come marching up to the platform. There's two of them: a skinny sixfooter with a cowboy hat and a scar running up the left side of his face, and the one-eyed Indian who was at the park last Sunday. They both carry guitars, only Scarface's is an electric one and he takes ten minutes plugging his noisemaker to an amplifier and testing it for sound.

For the next half-hour it's bedlam as Scarface and One-eye belt out Country and Western songs with voices flatter than a cop's feet. Every now and then One-eye comes out with one of his famous yippees! and the whole place yippees! back at him. Sweat pours down their faces and their fingers run up and down the guitar strings like they were whacking it off. They stop for a minute.

"More, more!" everyone yells, and they swing into a fast number that starts fingers snapping and feet stomping. The singing and the yelling blend into one deafening sound and an Indian chick with long black hair and a short green dress jumps up onto the platform and starts shaking her body in a parody of a go-go dancer, her eyes shining as if she's having an orgasm, her legs kicking higher and higher till you can tell what colour pants she's wearing. Everybody's clapping their hands to the beat and screaming "Faster!" hoping to see more of her. She whirls and kicks and jumps up and down until her entire body—breasts, belly, behind—is one uncontrollable rubber ball, bouncing in every direction.

Unable to contain herself any longer, another girl, fatter than the one who's dancing, jumps up beside her and starts pushing her sex back and forth like she's getting laid. The crowd goes wild. Some of the men stand up looking like they're going to screw her right there and then, and the women sitting with them are all hopping up and down on the chairs hoping the sight of their boobs bouncing around in their dresses will make the men sit down again. The sound in the room is rising to such a height that the walls seem to start shaking. Yells. Screams. Groans.

Then, just as suddenly as it started, it stops. The singers leave the platform and the two would-be dancers go back to their tables, wild-eyed and sweaty. Everybody quietens down and goes back to the serious business of drinking beer.

All through that performance, Terry's been holding my hand so tight that it feels like every bone in it has been broken. I put my arm around her and give her a little kiss on the cheek just to let her know that everything's all right. She looks pale and her eyes are even brighter than usual.

George, who's been sitting through that whole bit with his eyes riveted on a cute piece sitting almost directly across from us, turns to Terry and asks her, "Well, what do you think of Cabbagetown entertainment?" She gives a sickly little smile which sums up pretty well what she thinks of it, and, just in case George is thinking of giving her a speech on the "evils of a society that will allow people to revert to the level of animals," I cut in with one of my witty remarks: "Don't bother trying to hustle that chick you've been eyeing all evening. She's got VD." Now that's not true at all. Hell, I don't even know her, but it's good for a laugh cause Georgy boy was really looking her up and down for a while. I continue, "Besides, you still got Janet, haven't you?" George looks at us with those brown eyes of his that have got more than one chick into his pad just so they could have a closer look at them, and says, "Yeah, Janet, I had to throw her out last week."

"Why?" I ask. Terry's wondering too because some colour has come back to her face.

"She was always singing."

"Well, what's wrong with that?"

"Nothing. Except she was doing it when we were making love." I guess Terry and me are both looking at him with a weird look on our faces, so he goes on. "Every time we started to ball she'd come on humming and she'd slowly work it up to a song that she'd sing louder and louder until by the time we had a climax, the whole house could hear her."

Terry and I are laughing our heads off, and George is going on with his sad tale, "What else could I do? She's a great kid and all that, but good God, a broad who sings when she's getting laid! And with the body she had, too!"

We order three more beers and I end up paying again cause George suddenly has to get up to take a piss and Terry's still laughing. Christ, next time someone else pays or I drink alone! What am I, Santa Claus or something?

"Oh Michael, wouldn't it be terrible if I sang like that?" "You're not kidding babe," I answer. "I'd have to stick a cork in your mouth every time, and that doesn't make for good kissing."

She laughs again, and I'm thinking that it's good to hear her laugh in here, especially since she was so scared when we come in. I bet she never seen anything like this in her life before she met me. She probably comes from a family of farmers that took her to church every Sunday and made sure she was home by twelve every time she went with a guy. Probably whipped her if she didn't. She got so tired of being treated like a kid that she ran away from home one day and came to big, swinging Toronto to get some freedom. Lucky she met me too, or something might have happened to her. She's so dumb when it comes to knowing your way around here.

I'll have to ask her one day exactly why she came, but bet an elephant's prick that I'm not far off.

Just as George is sitting down there's a loud crash at the other end of the room, and we all turn around in time to see the Indian girl with the long hair fall to the floor. The woman who was dancing with her on the platform is standing up in front of her and as Long-hair hits the ground she grabs one of her legs and tries to break it over the edge of a table. Long-hair is yelling and twisting around on the floor and everybody has stood up to get a real good look at her pussy. The other woman keeps trying to bust her leg, screaming, "You fucking whore, you tried to take my man off me. You dirty, fucking whore!" Her man, meanwhile, has got down on his haunches and he's trying to put his hand in Long-hair's pants, but she's twisting around so hard, he's forced to yell at his girl, "Keep her still, dammit!"

Terry's grabbed my left arm in both of hers and I can feel her trembling. "Oh God, where's the waiter? where's the waiter?" she's half-screeching in my ear. Me, I couldn't care less cause I'm enjoying myself watching the show. I'm especially waiting to see if he'll get his hand up her pussy, but just so Terry won't faint or something, I look around for Big Jim and finally spot him near the crowd. He's watching just as hard as everybody else and I know he won't break up the fight unless that babe's in real danger of getting her leg busted. And that's doubtful because they're all so stoned they can hardly stand up, let alone fight.

"There he is over there," I point towards him.

"Well why doesn't he stop them before they kill each other?" She's almost crying, the poor kid.

George is gone. I look around and spot him next to the chick that I'd been joking about before. She's alone, which doesn't surprise me, since every guy has gone over to see the fight, and I can tell by the look in her face that George is doing all right. Funny thing, but the chicks seem to dig his long hair. He's tall and strong and reminds you sometimes of a pirate. And those eyes of his. Man they dig that.

The fight's starting to break up now and everybody's going back to their seats. George's gone by now, and the chick too, so we won't be seeing any more of him tonight. Just hope *she* doesn't sing, too.

As the evening wears on, we drink three or four more brews apiece (I even get Terry to pay for one of the rounds), and before you know it, it's closing time. Big Jim bellowing up and down the room: "Drink up, everybody! Last round! Last round!" And everybody bellowing back: "Three more over here! Four over here! Move your ass!" Christ, like prohibition was coming tomorrow.

I say, "Terry, let's go home," and you know what she does? She hiccups! That's when I realize that she's drunk. But real drunk. When we go through the hallway, I have to help her along, and outside she staggers into the alley beside the building, leans against the wall and vomits. I'm so mad that I'm just about ready to leave her there and go home. Jesus H. Christ, she can't even drink!

But there's some sort of a fight taking place in front of the hotel, so I stick around and watch. Nothing serious, really, just a couple of guys ganging up on an Indian. The Indian's so tanked all he can do is stand there with a dumb smile while the guys are punching his face in. It looks like he'll never fall until one of them steps back and gives him a boot in the crotch that drops him like a stone. The second guy is just about to finish off the job by kicking in the poor bugger's teeth when someone yells out "Cops!" and all he manages is a kick at the side of the Indian's head as he runs past.

We all look around ready to beat it at the first sign of the fuzz, but whoever yelled cop must have done that to scare the guys off, cause there's no one around except us. I turn back into the alley to pick up Terry, who's stopped throwing up by this time and is trying to clean up the mess on her dress with a little lace handkerchief. Her eyes are wet with tears, and with the vomit splattered all over her, even on her face, she looks a sorry sight. I feel sorry for her for a minute and tell her, "Don't worry, kid, I seen chicks worse off than you." Then I grab her by the hand, keeping some distance from her so as not to get my clothes mussed up, and drag her home.

All the way she's crying and mumbling, "I'm sorry, I never drunk so much before in my life. The last time was at Christmas and that was only two glasses of wine. I'm sorry, Michael."

Just to shut her up I tell her it's okay, she hasn't any reason to worry. I love her even when she's drunk.

She tries to kiss me when I tell her that I love her but like I said before, I'm not going to get my clothes stained with all her puke. I push her away and she starts bawling again just as a bum comes up to us and says, "You got a minute to spare?" He's short, he's old, and he's dirty. He smells so bad, I'll bet he's never taken a bath since his mother washed his ass for him.

"A minute I can spare, but not a dime," I answer and cross the street to head through the Gardens which saves us five minutes' walking time. It's dark as we walk through; the trees hide the moonlight, and it looks like there's nobody there, but as we approach the fountain and the bushes behind it I make out a shadowy figure standing between the bushes and the hothouse. At first I think it might be a mugger, but as we get closer I see it's just a queer standing there waiting to pick someone up, or to be picked up. The bush rustles where he's standing and some moonlight squeezes through the trees. Just enough light to show that the queer's not alone. There's another on his knees in front of him, his face buried between the first one's legs.

I remember when I was young and a queer would come up to me and ask me if I'd like to play games with him. I always wondered what he meant, since he was so much older than me. As I grew older I found out. But girls do it just as good as men, and they're softer—no unshaven face or calloused hands—so I never got to play games. Lots of my friends did though. They'd go out to the park if they had nothing to do that night and line up in front of some faggot sitting on a bench and tell him to come behind the bushes with them or they'd cut his prick off. Naturally, the guy'd go with them, but it can't have been much fun for him since sometimes there was as many as fifteen of them all lined up in front of him.

One night they'd almost talked me into going with them (I'd had a mickey of whiskey) when Spike, the toughest fellow in the bunch, comes walking down the street swearing like a truck driver. He's fit to kill cause one of the fags they'd had a couple of weeks ago has given him a dose of VD. That got everybody running off to the hospital for a checkup and me cured of the curiosity to try one of these guys out.

But there's nights like tonight when you're trying to drag a drunken broad home, she's puked all over herself and she's bawling loud enough to wake the dead, and you wonder if maybe it's worth all that trouble just to have her in your bed. When you feel like it, why not come over here and in five minutes it's all over? No muss, no fuss, no bother, no I love you. One problem though, if someone you know sees you here one night with your pants around your ankles, you've had it. In twenty-four hours all Cabbagetown will be talking about how you've turned queer. And what if someone with a chip on his shoulder phones the Club to tell them about me? No man, it's just not worth it. You can't do at twenty-three what you did at thirteen.

We hit the bed and in ten seconds Terry's asleep and her dress is stinking up the room. Some Saturday night. I haven't enjoyed myself so much since the day we got nabbed swiping a pack of smokes from the corner smoke shop. A real ball.

July 11

National Hangover Day, that's what they should call Sundays. The whole goddam world is suffering today. Look at me. I thought I hadn't drunk that much last night, but when I wake up this morning my head feels like a tank run over it, and Terry's so far gone that she doesn't even wake up when I turn the radio on. "It's going to be a scorcher today folks." So what else is new? I go outside and there's Mrs. Himmel sitting on the porch with her lover and a twelve-pack between them. The only difference from last Sunday is that it's a new guy. A face that looks like somebody's backside and cowboy boots. In this heat he wears cowboy boots! She sure picked a prize this time. He probably rides her like she's a horse too. They open a couple of bottles and the sight of the foam gushing out white and bubbly starts me gagging and I go back down to the room.

After I've made a coffee and smoked a couple of butts I get to feeling hungry, so I give Terry a kick on her bum, which is sticking out over the bed, and tell her to wake up. She sits up holding her hands to her head and looks around the room for a few minutes.

"What's the matter? Don't you know where the hell you are?" She answers by groaning and falling back on the bed. At this rate I won't be eating till I get to work tomorrow, so I give her another kick, and look around for something to make a sandwich out of, some bread and cheese she brought home last night from work. Better than nothing, I guess, so I gulp it down and drink a glass of warm water. It's getting hot in here and Terry's starting to snore. She looks miserable flopped out on the bed with her stockings and pants still on and flakes of vomit around her lips. Pale-faced, her hair twisted around her head like a towel and her mouth open so wide you can see her tonsils. I'm feeling so disgusted by the sight of her that I go outside again.

I'm feeling like a cold Coke, so I head for Blow Job's. At the same time I'll ask him how Terry's doing. But Blow Job isn't there. It's his day off, I guess, and Bum Bum, his cousin, has taken over for the day. I order a Coke and ask anyway. And he answers with something like, "Telly velly good wolkel." Christ, he's even harder to understand than Blow Job, so I get up and step out onto the sidewalk. The sun's really blazing now, but there's a fairly strong breeze coming up from the lake. Enough of a breeze so that you don't feel like a lobster in a bucket of boiling water. What to do? What to do? Terry's probably still sleeping it off, and I don't feel like seeing her anyway. No use standing here, that's for sure. I start off for the Gardens. Maybe I'll see George there. I'm dying to hear how he made out last night.

The ice cream truck's there, and so are the kids—like nobody's moved from that spot all week. I just had that Coke and I don't feel like an Eskimo Pie right now, so I move in towards the centre of the park.

Mouth is at his usual spot, and the only difference from last week is that his wife is holding a new sign which reads:

SODOMITES!
BOW DOWN
YOUR HEADS
IN
SHAME!!

Pretty impressive, yessiree. Wonder how many people here know what sodomite means. Probably not even the ones who do it.

George is nowhere around and I'm just about to head for home when I hear a big ruckus to the left of me. It's another preacher and he's got a whole mob of sodomites and things all worked up and yelling away at him.

I approach them and push my way through to get a look at the latest saviour to hit Allan Gardens. He's a chubby little guy with thick spectacles and red veins sticking out on his face. In his left hand he's holding an open Bible that's so worn it's only holding together by the grace of God (*Ha-ha*) and in his other hand he's got an ordinary old piece of broomstick. His voice is real squeaky, like Mickey Mouse, or Miss Virgin when she gets mad, but his sales pitch is something else. A real con man. He holds the stick high in his right hand and squeaks at the rabble: "You're all sinners. Your souls are black, and God'll have nothing to do with you. You've been cast away from His holy presence," and as he says that he throws the stick as far as he can. "But," and at the word *but* a mangy, flea-bitten mutt that's been lying at his feet in the shade of the guy's belly, gets up, bites at a sore on his side, and runs for the stick as fast as he can, "God is *com-passion-ate,* and all he wants is that you repent and right away he'll take you back and forgive you your wrongdoing." The mutt rushes back with the stick between his jaws and drops it before the preacher, who picks it up and holds it high again so that we can all see the dog's saliva on it.

"Yes, fellow sinners, ask Him to forgive you your sins, and like this stick I've thrown away and got back again, God will do the same. Just remember, no matter how many times you've sinned and cussed," he throws the stick away again, "God will *always* accept you without complaining if you're truly, truly sorry"—dog comes back with the stick—"for all that you've done. Nothing, *nothing*, is so terrible that He won't say 'That's okay bud, as long as you're sorry and promise not to do it no more.'"

Of course, this bunch of hungover sinners is really digging the show cause it's one thing to be told about sinning and forgiving, but to see how it works right in front of your very eyes!

He stops for a minute to give the mutt a rest and smiles at an old woman who's so overcome with the whole thing, she's broken out crying. "See, you wretched sinners, how all-forgiving God is," and he points at the old woman. Someone beside her starts bawling too, and the preacher gets so excited that he throws the stick away, squeaking as loud as he can at the same time: *"God always forgives!"*

But the dog hasn't moved. He's chasing a flea up and down his back with his mouth and didn't see the stick go flying. The whole crowd goes silent, even the criers. The preacher's face starts to turn fire-engine red. "I said, *God always forgives!*" he squeaks. So high-pitched it could break windows. The dog's still chasing the flea. Someone laughs and the criers wipe their noses with their hands. Two or three people start to leave. Preacher blows his top. He gives the mutt a boot that sends him flying about ten feet in the air, and screeches at him to get that goddam stick before he busts him good. Mutt rushes around all over the place trying to find the stick and preacher screeches, squeals and whoops, "Over there you goddam dog, *over there!*" Everybody breaks up laughing and hollering so much that mutt gets more confused than ever and runs over the stick twice without seeing it. Finally preacher gets the stick himself and walks over to mutt with murder in his mind. Mutt, who isn't as stupid as all that, takes off as fast as his bony legs will carry him, and the last we see of preacher is his fat ass as he chases after him.

I been laughing so hard I got tears in my eyes and a pain in my side. I'm just about to sit down under a tree when I see George walking away from the fountain. I yell at him and he waves his hand and sits down beside me. He's looking kind of tired, so I ask him how it went with that chick.

"Not bad at all," he replies, picking at a blade of grass which he puts in his mouth. "Spent half the night screwing her, but I was the only one that got tired. She lay there on the bed like a frozen turd and let me do all the work. It was getting so damn boring that about three in the morning I told her I've had more fun sticking my prick in a hole in the ground, and booted her out of the room."

Lousy luck George has with the girls.

"But what really drove me up a rope was when she'd say, 'Shit, baby, was that ever good. Oh, shit baby!' right after we'd finished. Real romantic."

There's one big difference between George and me. I couldn't care less what she said afterwards as long as I got what I wanted. Not George though. He says that love should be more than just making the bedsprings squeak, and until he's found the perfect love partner, he won't settle down with any one girl. Gotta say one thing for him, though, he sure tries hard. He's got a different one at his place every week. Like Mrs. Himmel.

What turns a lot of the chicks off George is the fact that after he's laid them, he'll give them a political speech. Try and make revolutionaries out of them. Hell, the broads around here never read anything more serious than *True Romance*, so you can imagine how that goes over with them. One even thought that he was swearing at her and punched him right in the eye. But, like I say, George is a romantic. He keeps trying.

The breeze has stopped and you can really feel the heat. Over by the public john there's a chick dressed in her great-grandmother's hand-me-downs, with stringy dirt-brown hair, trying to hustle some of the creeps that are always hanging around there. Her name's Marie because she's half French, and she's got the mind of a ten-year-old even though she's seventeen. The noise around the neighbourhood is that her old man raped her when her mother run off with a truck driver. She was only fourteen and since then she's had two kids off him. In order to feed them he started her off hustling; first with the guys that live on his street, then, seeing how much money she was bringing in, sending her off to the park where there's always a bunch of weirdos dying to bust young kids like her. She's had everything done to her, but because of her kid's brain she still likes skipping and playing with the nine and ten-year-olds. I feel kind of sorry for her sometimes, especially when I know that her old man hasn't worked a day since he got her on this kick.

George and me both watch the guy walk off with her, and I wonder what his specialty is.

"It makes you sick when you see what goes on around here. And what do those fat-assed politicians at City Hall do?"

No use me saying, cause George has already got the answer. "Nothing!"

I can tell he's getting mad. His voice is getting louder. "Nothing," he repeats. "They sit on their fat asses in their brand new city hall that looks like a piss pot for the Jolly Green Giant, and talk about Yorkville turning into a centre for the corruption of our young people and ignore districts like Cabbagetown where every boy is a hood by the time he's six and the only girls still virgin are the ones eighteen months or under.

"Like yesterday in the paper. There's that mongoloid Lamport bitching that Yorkville should be closed up because the hippies there don't take a bath, and here there's kids that don't even know what the word means. Their parents stink, the school they go to stinks—when they go—the houses they live in stink. Everything stinks! This is Toronto's garbage dump where society can throw away the people it's got no use for. Just throw them in here and let them wallow around like pigs for their existence. And make sure they stay here too. We don't want to see them in the nice part of town. Bring cops in and if they mouth off too much about their condition, bust them on their lice-ridden heads. Let their girls become whores while our daughters are learning how to be proper young ladies. Who knows? One day their daddy will have a night out with the boys and they just might want to end up the evening with a broad, the younger the better. Let the kids quit school at grade eight. That way there's lots of cheap labour. Let the whole putrid lot of them get drunk in some stinking bar and lose whatever remains of their human dignity. We don't give a shit. We don't have to see it. There's lots of jails here if they get out of hand. Cabbagetown? Never heard of it.

"What a fucked-up society this is!"

"So why don't you run for mayor and do something about it?" I cut in. I'm getting a headache from the heat and all the noise is getting on my nerves.

"Run for mayor!" he shouts at me, practically busting my eardrum, "and end up like Dennison? A puppet and stooge useless bunch of them, should be strung up right there in City Hall and their bodies left to bloat in the sun until they smell as bad as the people here!"

"Hey cool it baby," I cut in again cause he looks like he's going to start rolling on the ground in a fit. "There's a cop coming this way." I point with my thumb towards the fountain and George quietens down. I'd noticed the cop a few minutes ago coming in off the street. He's walking up the tar path that cuts the park in half from north to south and branches off at the fountain east and west. He looks to either side of him, his eyes cold and blank like cops everywhere, hoping to bust somebody so at the cop shop they'll see what a hardworking slob he is. The people either ignore him or gaze at him with a mixture of fear and hatred. Most of them have been busted more than once by the cops and they know what happens when you're pulled in. And who's going to believe you when you complain that they beat you up and you come home with lumps and bruises all over your body, hurt so bad you spend two days in bed too sick to even go out for some fresh air. George is right in that sense: we're just garbage as far as they're concerned. Just something to play around with when they're bored, like a cat does with a mouse. But hell man, they're the Law, and if you got a good job like mine, you stay out of their way.

The cop walks by, giving us the look-over, which George returns, his eyes blazing. He almost stops, then figures we're not worth the trouble and continues up the path.

"By the way, I'll be over Wednesday evening with a couple of books I want you to read. You be there?"

"Sure," I answer, as he starts to get up.

"Okay, be seeing you then. I got a meeting tonight and I want to eat first."

He takes off in the same direction as the cop, and I can tell by the rumbling in my gut that it's time I left too.

The Sally Anns have just arrived with their noisemakers and everybody's going over to see them. Boom boom, rat-a-tat-tat. They make more racket than two prosties fighting over a customer. My head's aching more than ever.

I whip up the porch, trying not to step on Himmel and the cowboy, who've fallen asleep right on top of the twelve-pack, and get a real bang when I open the door of my room. Supper's on the table and Terry's humming away, with a dark green dress on that I haven't seen before and her bright red hair combed and parted in the middle and shining like a waterfall of copper. She looks so good that I stand there for a minute not believing it's the same kid that was here this morning.

She comes up to me and puts her arms around my shoulders, planting a big wet kiss on my lips. And another, longer and not so wet.

"Michael," she gasps out after a while, "I thought you were so mad at me that you'd left for good. That you'd never come back. Oh, I was so worried," she kisses me again.

"Hell, Kitten, I've forgotten about that already." Me leave for good? This is my room. If anybody leaves here, it'll be her.

"I'm so sorry about last night." She kisses me again. "I'll never do that again." Kiss. "I don't want to do anything to make you ashamed of me." Kiss. "I want you to be proud of me," kiss, hug, "so that everybody will be jealous that you have a girl that loves you so much," kiss, kiss, "and works hard, and cleans your clothes, and, and lives only for you. Oh, Michael, Michael." She crushes herself against me so hard that I'm having trouble breathing.

"What's for supper, baby?" I ask her, just to break up this lovey-dovey stuff, although deep down I'm really touched by all this show of love. In her own way she's tremendous, this kid, and I think I'm starting to realize what love is, maybe for the first time in my life. Could be that George is right. That it's more than a quickie in the back seat of the car or in the alley behind the church. I'm actually thinking what it would be like to get married and settle down and have kids and all that jazz, and then my stomach rumbles again and I get back to the serious things in life.

Ham, eggs and cheese. I eat till the food's coming out my ears and let out a good burp to show how full I am. She giggles and asks me if I'm still hungry. That's one thing I don't like about her—she acts like she's never lived with a man before, she's so innocent. I mean, every chick knows that when a guy burps it can only mean that he's had enough. Of course, maybe she hasn't lived with a guy before.

Tomorrow, I'm going to ask her about her life before she came to Toronto.

She's happy as a pig in shit and we spend a couple of hours fooling around on the bed. All laughs, giggles and sex. Upstairs, Mrs. Himmel and the cowboy are crashing and thumping and yelling.

"Sounds like Cowboy's riding her again." She giggles and I laugh cause we've made up a little joke about Himmel's horse riding and every time there's a noise upstairs, we're reminded of it.

"Michael, do you know it was a week ago today we met?"

"So it was," I answer, and not knowing what to add, I tickle her left breast and we have another go at it.

A week, a month. What's the difference?

July 12

I'm tired as hell. Exhausted from last night. Worn out. Dead. But just think of all those joes that work in offices. They live in some stupid suburb ten miles out of the city. They have to get up at six in the morning, drink an instant breakfast, kiss wives whose faces are covered in beauty cream so you can't even see them, run like hell so they don't miss the bus, and spend an hour on it with about ten thousand other joes all crammed in like so many sardines in a can, fight their way into a subway car, get their feet stepped on about twenty times, and all that so that they can arrive thirty seconds late for work and have the boss give them a dirty look and write their name down on a piece of paper.

So I guess I shouldn't complain when I get up at ten.

Thinking about those poor suckers makes me feel better, and I'm singing a dirty song when I arrive at the Club.

Nothing happens there all day, unless you want to count Miss Virgin—coming in with her hair done up in a beehive style, which makes her even more ugly—something I thought was impossible.

Terry's got the blues when I get home. It seems that Marty, the biggest pimp in the district, was trying to talk her into working for him. At first she didn't know what he meant, but when he explained exactly what he had in mind ("All you gotta do is entertain certain friends of mine"), she rushed into the kitchen and told Blow Job who came out and gave Marty thirty seconds to get the hell out of his restaurant. And he left too. Like I said before, he's a tough Chinaman, and if he can't fix you he'll get buddies of his that can. They don't fool around either. Tough Chinamen with axes and guns.

At first she doesn't want to talk about herself, saying there isn't anything that would interest me, but I keep pressing her and finally she comes out with the whole story.

She's an only child, and her parents are pretty strict people, just like I thought the other day. They lived in a farm in some hick town up North—dammit, I keep forgetting the name of it—and she went all the way through grade school there, and two years of high school too, but money was running low and she had to leave. She never did anything. No parties. No dances. Nothing. She was sixteen when she was allowed out on her first date, and even then she had to be back in the house by ten. Once she was half an hour late and her old man took a belt to her and beat her so hard she couldn't sit down for a month. Didn't let her have supper for a week either. And she's sixteen, the kid! Anyway, to cut a long story short, since I already guessed all this, she kept sneaking off to see the guy who she'd come home late with that night until her folks found out about it. They beat her again, called her a whore, took her to a doctor's to see if he's knocked her up, and then kicked her out of the house. "The street's the place for you, not this house," they told her.

I ask her why she agreed to live with me so soon after having met me and she replies, because I've been nice to her and helped her find a job, and she could tell that I was a gentle person, and she was scared of living alone in Toronto, since she's never been in a big city in her life before.

I just sit there thinking for a while about what she's said and I come to the conclusion that the reasons she's given are valid. I *had* been nice to her—I'd bought her an Eskimo Pie—and I had found her that slob job at the restaurant, although she'd thought it was great, which is what counts. And especially I've been gentle to her. I haven't hit her or called her names, hell, I haven't even made her do the sex things that a guy expects from a broad and that any ten-year-old girl is an expert at around here. We just do the plain old bit, and even that, at first, was hard enough with her, she'd freeze up so much the first few times.

Yeah. I can see why she's staying with me all right. A lot of chicks would give their right arms to have a nice guy like me.

Yet, somehow there's somethings that bugs me about her sob story. Like somewhere it doesn't click. Sure, I believe it and all that, but in the back of my head there's a little voice telling me that she hasn't told me the whole story. That it's a lot deeper than that.

Nothing to get in a heat about though. Doesn't everyone have a little secret he keeps to himself?

Still, I better try and find out one day. Just in case.

July 13

Have you ever stopped to think sometimes whatever became of someone you knew, say, ten years ago? Like me this morning, I'm wondering whatever the hell happened to Sonny. Sonny, the most popular kid in our school, and the only guy in the world that's ever really scared me.

A nice kid who sang like Elvis Presley (the boss singer at the time), danced like Chubby Checker, hustled the chicks like Casanova, and would stick a rusty nail in your eye when you were looking the other way. We were around fourteen then and in grade nine, and the big thing in our lives—apart from hustling—was football. After school we'd all run into the locker room beside the gym and put on our football uniforms as fast as we could for a couple of hours of hard, fast football. Sometimes it'd get pretty rough too, and as often as not there'd be somebody with a bloody nose or a fat eye by the end of the game. Nobody cared, though. It was all part of the game. Except Sonny. One day Pretty Paul (and he *was* good looking, too) knocked Sonny over in a hard rush up the side, his knee catching him in the face. Nothing serious, just a couple of loose teeth, and Sonny was the first to laugh about it.

A week went by and the games continued every afternoon, Sonny always joining in. Then it happened. We were in the locker room and Pretty Paul was bending over tying up his football shoes when Sonny, who was fully dressed in his uniform, shoes and all, walked up to him and kicked him in the face. I don't think there's anything worse than being booted with a football shoe. They're pretty heavy and there's steel cleats on the soles. We all heard the thud of shoe meeting face and turned around just as Pretty Paul was starting to get up. At first we didn't know what had happened, but there's PP standing there with his front teeth sticking right through his upper lip and his nose the size of a football. Blood all over his face, his nose already turning blue. He walks towards the door, like Frankenstein, stiff, looking straight ahead, his face something out of a nightmare, and pitches to the ground just as he's reaching for the door. We still didn't know what the score was, but there's Sonny against a corner of the locker room looking at us with the most dangerous look I've ever, ever seen in a pair of eyes. It was pure murder. Like facing an executioner. A look I don't think I'll ever forget. We couldn't stand it after a few seconds and had to lower our heads. It was almost murder too. Pretty Paul's nose was busted in three places, all his front teeth had to be pulled (what was left of them), he had a three-inch gash in his lip and he spent a month in the hospital with a brain concussion.

The judge asked Sonny why he did it and Sonny just laughed— didn't say one goddam word! The same laugh as when Pretty Paul had knocked him during the game. He got eighteen months at Burwash and I heard from a buddy of mine who'd done time there that Sonny was real popular with all the fellows and even with the screws. Then one day he did it again. There's a bunch of them cutting down some pines in a nearby woods when Sonny walks over to some guy who'd beat him in a lousy game of checkers, and smashes him right in the mouth with the blunt end of an axe. According to my buddy, who'd seen the whole thing, Sonny hit him with such force that the guy almost did a complete somersault, teeth, lips and blood flying in the air like confetti at a wedding.

This time he talked.

"The bastard was out to get me, and I got him first. I got him real good too. If you're going to get a guy, *make sure you get him good*, cause if you don't, he'll be after you in a couple of days."

They took him out of there and sent him to the nut house at Penetang and as far as I know, he's still there. But then again, maybe he's out. One day I'll meet him on the street. He'll ask me how I'm doing and then he'll laugh and say "See you around." And that's the day I'll leave Cabbagetown.

July 14

Mrs. Waddling comes up and tells me what a great job I'd done yesterday and how happy the hostess was. It was a cocktail party for thirty in a private room of the Club and I'd worked like a nigger in a cotton field for two hours serving them drinks. Naturally Mrs. Waddling's praise comes as no surprise—I deserved it. Too bad they wouldn't give me a big tip instead of just telling me what I've already taken for granted, but at least that proves how much I'm appreciated here.

I'm in a good mood all afternoon and for once I actually find myself enjoying supper in spite of Maggie ("Jayne Mansfield always whipped her men before going to bed with them") and Miss Virgin goes so far as to say good evening to me.

Happy, happy, happy. That's my middle name as I open the door of my room and find Terry sitting on the bed talking to George and a tough-looking Indian kid who's about nineteen years old.

George is wearing a red scarf around his neck which means he was at a political meeting tonight.

"Mike the Mugger!" George yells at me as I close the door and go over to the bed to sit down. "How's the worst bartender in Toronto?

The only one who'll ask a customer if he wants his hot toddy on the rocks?"

We all laugh over that and I'm glad that everybody's in as good a mood as me. Whoops. Nearly everybody, that is. The Indian's face hasn't changed expression. He just scowls. Where the hell did George dig him up?

"Mike, I want you to meet the second Louis Riel."

I nod at Louis Riel and wait for George to tell me his name cause even I know that Riel was a half-breed who was hung eighty years ago for leading a rebellion against the government, but he walks over to the table and hands me a couple of books. One is called *The Theory of Terrorism* and the other, *150 Questions for a Guerilla.*

"Read them very carefully, Mike, for this evening John (so that's his name) and I and a few other activists have decided that the time is ripe for a frontal assault on the Establishment. Our methods will not be those of Che Guevara, who advocates rural insurgency, but primarily those of the NLF in Algeria. In other words, urban warfare."

What the hell's he talking about?

"Urban warfare, or, if you prefer, terrorism. Terrorism—selective or blind. The only way to arouse the masses to take the lever of government in their own hands and successfully bring about a socialist revolution in this country.

"We are going to begin in Cabbagetown, since it is the most under-privileged area in Toronto, and its inhabitants the most exploited and humiliated. John, here, will work with the Indians, who form the largest racial group in the area, and my sphere of responsibility will lie with the young people. To make them aware of the reasons why they will never be able to escape from their vicious circle of jail–street–jail as long as the present economic-political system exists."

"George," I finally manage to get a word in, "what the hell are you talking about?"

"Simply this baby"—it's amazing how quickly George can slip from university-type words to street slang. "We're going to start with a petition for more schools, better jobs, decent housing. It'll be signed by the Revolutionary Action Party. RAP for short. Like Rap Brown you know."

I didn't know.

"Naturally, they're not going to do a goddam thing, so we're going to show them that we mean what we say. And the word is bombs, baby, bombs. We'll start off slowly with selective terrorism. By that I mean we'll zap the politicos in City Hall first. At their homes, in their offices, wherever we can hit them the easiest. Lamport will get it first, and if that doesn't accomplish anything, we'll blow up a few others. Then the Mayor himself. We'll put a bomb right under his desk.

"Of course, by that time, police repression will be particularly strong, but we hope by then to have the masses of Cabbagetown sufficiently aroused to take in their own hands the defence of their homes against the Establishment cops. We'll teach them how to make Molotov Cocktails and booby traps. John will be leading a commando of revolutionary Indians, who, with the experience they'll have gained in urban warfare, will be able to return to their reservations and teach their brothers the proper road towards full equality and participation in tomorrow's new society."

George is sweating, Terry's got that scared look in her eyes, and Stoneface has leaned over in his chair, his hands joined together as if he already had a bomb in them. I'm feeling the tension, too, cause I'm starting to pick my nose and I only do that when I'm excited about something.

"If by September the rich bastards haven't learned their lesson yet, we'll stage an uprising to coincide with the assassination of the Premier of Ontario. That'll be at the opening of the Ontario Parliament when Robarts comes to give the first speech. He'll be shot as he's going in the door, and as the whole police force of this miserable city will rush up to the Parliament Buildings, Cabbagetown will be left relatively unguarded. John's commandos and my own special youth section will hand out arms to the people and at Allan Gardens we'll proclaim the Free Cabbagetown Republic.

"If we're defeated, we'll hide our weapons and go back to being plain old slum dwellers, and within a month we'll pass on to the next stage of our revolutionary struggle—blind terrorism! We'll bomb indiscriminately. In the subways at rush hour. In the movie houses. In the department stores on Saturday afternoons. Everywhere there are crowds of people. Think of the CNE when the Fair's on! We'll completely paralyze the life of the city. People will be so scared they won't leave their houses.

"When winter comes we'll firebomb the houses in Cabbagetown and the city government will be faced with hundreds of angry people yelling for housing. They'll be forced to act, but our men will be there with the demonstrators and we'll turn the demands towards our slogan, 'A Free and Equal Toronto.' A riot will break out and we'll storm City Hall and successfully defend it against the police and army. By then, of course, our example will have spread to other Canadian cities and there will be simultaneous uprisings throughout the country. Ottawa will be enveloped in a series of riots that will topple the government, and just to make sure, I'll send our best marksman to kill Pearson. Without a leader, the bourgeoisie and their lackeys will run around like a chicken with its head cut off. The army will be powerless against the wrath of the people. By Easter, Mike baby, we'll be in!"

"You're nuts," I gulp out. My mouth's drier than a snake's tail.

"You don't think it's possible? Look at Newark. And Detroit. The blacks are doing it in the States. Look at Vietnam. With all their bullets and bombs and bullshit the Yankees can't do a thing against those people. We'll do the same here. Once the people realize exactly why they have to live like pigs while everybody else is living in fine houses and driving cars, they'll grab for the nearest gun. Just wait till we get a few guys together and train them! Just wait till those bombs start going off in City Hall!

"Anyway Mike, read those books and let me know if you're ready to become a part of the revolutionary vanguard in the people's armed struggle."

"What!" I sputter, not believing my ears. "You want me to go along with you in this shit dream of yours? Did you smoke a joint before you came here tonight? Like I said, you're nuts, George boy."

"Well, think about it," George is getting up to leave, followed by the Indian, "and let me know your decision when you've read the books. Let's say the first of next week."

"I just finished telling you, you're nuts. Hell man, I'm not going to hang for blowing somebody's butt all over the city. Leave me out of this." But George hasn't caught a word, and my only answer is the slam of the door as they leave.

"Gorgeous George, the rabble rebel," I say in a joking tone to Terry, who's still sitting on the bed, but deep down I'm worried about all this. What if he actually decides to start putting bombs all over the city?

"Do you think he meant all that?" Terry asks with a nervous edge to her voice. "Do you think he really meant it?"

"Na. Hell no, kid. George is all mouth. Shit, he doesn't work or nothing, so he's gotta have something to think about all day long. Otherwise he'd end up on skid row like every other bum."

That's all bullshit cause I know George, and if there's one thing he's serious about in life, it's starting a revolution. He thinks, breathes, eats, sleeps, pisses and craps revolution. That's part of him, like his liver or his Adam's apple. But actually killing people? Man, that's something else. I mean, as far as I'm concerned he can put the torch to the whole city if he wants, as long as he doesn't get me mixed up in it. But I know goddam well that he's going to try his hardest to get me to join his "commandos." And that's what's burning me up right now.

"Michael, whatever you do, don't get mixed up with what he's doing. You'd go to jail and we wouldn't have a home any more." Terry's got that sad dog look in her eyes. Funny how beautiful she looks when she's sad. "I'd be all alone again."

I go over to her and stroke her hair ("good boy, Rover"), saying at the same time, "Don't worry Terry baby. You think I'd do something stupid like what they're planning and risk getting thrown in jail and leaving you all to yourself in this big city?"

She gobbles it up like it was a banana split, putting her hand over mine and pressing her face against my chest. "Hell, you're the best girl I ever had, and the truest too. You're worth a million bucks."

I plant a big kiss on her forehead, and suddenly she's stopped looking sad. She smiles and puts my hand on her breast and just lies there against me without saying a word.

For some odd reason, I know she's not feeling sexy, so I just lie there without saying or doing anything either. And you know something? It feels great. Like two best friends, or a brother and a sister.

I gotta laugh at myself. Who'd ever guess I could lie beside a broad and not think of laying her!

For about fifteen minutes we stay like that, then Terry says "Perhaps when we've got a bit of money saved up, we can move into another place. Wouldn't it be nice to have a great big apartment all to ourselves, with a proper kitchen and bath, and a big double bed?"

I'm still in this mushy mood, so I play along with her little game.

"Yeah, it'd be great. And a fridge full of beers."

We talk for a while longer about the super apartment we're never going to get, and then I get up to piss.

Terry just lies there, her eyes wide open in a faraway look, like an acidhead when he's on an LSD trip.

While I'm pissing, I'm wondering just what exactly goes through her mind sometimes. She's a thinking broad, and that alone sets her apart from any other broad I've ever known. Not that I mind a broad who can think. As long as it doesn't get in the way of my having fun with her.

July 15

After lunch everybody's been called in to the dining room of the Club by the president of the Club herself. They're all there— Mrs. Waddling, Miss Virgin, Maggie, the handyman, the waitresses, the dishwashers: everybody. And they're all sitting there like they were waiting their turn to walk into the gas chamber, they're so nervous. But it's nothing, man, just the quarterly distribution of gratuities, which only comes to about twenty bucks anyway. I been here a year and I still haven't figured out why they just don't give it to us without all this screwing around. But who cares? It means one hour we don't have to work.

When we've all sat down, the president, who looks about a hundred and eighty years old—call her Mrs. Hag and colour her white— stands up.

"I'm so glad to see you all here today" (I bet) "and very excited because I have some very important news for everyone working here" (we're all going to get fired). "The board of directors" (colour them white too) "has decided that, starting this summer" (summer's half over already), "all those who have worked at this club for ten years or more will receive *three* weeks of paid holidays!"

She clasps her bony hands together and gives a death smile.

"Now isn't that happy news?" she asks.

Real happy. The only ones who are eligible are the handyman and Mrs. Waddling.

"And on top of that, there's something else" (more happy news like that and the whole place is going to start crying). "The board of directors has also decided that three days compassionate leave will be granted to any member of the staff who has a close member of the family die" (oh boy, it's a real orgy of happiness today). "And by close member, we mean right up to second cousin."

Naturally, we all clap when she sits down, and the same thought is going through everybody's mind: "Where's the money?" Mrs. Waddling, who's probably wondering if she should spend her three weeks in Hamilton or Barrie, or some other exotic place, gets up on her webbed feet and thanks Mrs. Hag in our name. Yeah, thanks a whole pant load. I've sure benefited.

But you know what really grabs me? It's Hag's way of talking. Like she was giving us a candy for being good little kids and not pissing our pants all day long. Hell, man, except for me and Miss Virgin, the youngest staff member here is about sixty years old. And when you think about it, what the hell has she offered us? When you get down to it—fuck all. And I thought I was cynical!

Oh well, the twenty bucks sure comes in handy.

I think I'll buy Terry a rose on the way home tonight. And a case of beer for me.

July 16

I'm pooped. We had a wedding party at the Club today. There were a hundred and eighty people there, and me all alone serving them champagne. Christ, there was a moment there when I was opening champagne bottles so fast, it sounded like a machine gun was going off in the room. Pop-pop-pop-pop-pop-pop. Goddam weddings.

I hate them. You work like a sonofabitch and all you get for your efforts is cigarette butts in the glasses and confetti all over the carpet.

You shoulda seen the creeps who were getting married, though. He looked like Alvin the Chipmunk—great big buck-teeth good for cutting wood and a potbelly—a first-class catch. But then again, she looked no better, with freckles and pimples all over her face and absolutely no tit at all. And I thought there was only one Miss Virgin.

The bride's mother cried when they cut the cake. The photographer took pictures right and left. Every jerk and his uncle made a speech, and in showers of confetti and "Good Luck" the newlyweds rushed off in a hired limousine to wherever it is they were heading for, to have their first go at each other.

It seems every time I walk into my room now there's been a change in it. Tonight it's blue curtains on the window.

"Don't they look nice Michael?" She's just dying for an answer, so I tell her, "Just beautiful, honey, simply divine." That grabs her by the short and curlies.

"I chose sky blue because it matches the colour of your eyes on a sunny day."

"You mean when I'm not hungover." No doubt about it, I'm a born comedian.

She ignores this joke of the year and goes on to tell me that I've got real funny eyes because they change colour according to the weather. On cloudy days they're dark blue, on sunny days they're light blue, and at night they're a sort of bright blue-green and shiny.

"You have the most beautiful eyes I've seen on a man. They're— they're—" she stops for a second, thinking of the right word, "they almost hypnotize you. They're warm. They're cold. They're—"

Now I like a bit of praise where it's due, like anybody else, but this is going too far, especially for eyes. If she wants to build me up, let her tell me what a good lover I am or something.

I grab her arms and throw her on the bed, kissing her at the same time, which is still the best way I know to shut a broad up. Apart from sticking you-know-what in her mouth. I kiss her face and neck and shoulders and pull up her sweater. She's breathing heavy by now and when my lips reach her little pink nipples she starts to pant like a dog in heat.

A few more kisses here and there and she's ready. Her body's soft and I get a kick out of feeling and kissing it, and she likes it too. Man, when my tongue starts working its way around her tummy she bounces all over the bed like a loose piston in a car.

Naturally, I finish before she does (how come it always takes a chick so goddam long?) and as I'm pumping away trying to get her to come off I'm thinking how most of the other broads I've known have told me the same thing about my eyes. As far as I'm concerned they're blue and that's that. But they see all kinds of things in them. Like the hypnotic bit. I sure wish they were. Just think, whenever I want a fast piece of tail without all the bother of working a whole evening on a broad, getting her stoned and telling her how much I love her and everything before she finally gives me what she's given about a thousand other guys, all I'd have to do is stare until she falls into a trance, screw her, and have her forget everything when she wakes up.

"Oh, Michael, that was wonderful," she gasps out, her body shaking like a leaf. "You're a dream lover."

I'm beginning to think that this kid really can read my mind. Funny how she's changed. The first nights together, she'd turn over on her side afterwards as if she was embarrassed, put on this Li'l Abner nightgown she always wears, and run off to the toilet to wash herself. And she wouldn't say a word till she was back in bed and I put my arms around her again and told her what a great chick she was.

Now look at her. All grunts and gasps and making love with the light on. Just goes to show how good I am.

It's getting kind of late so we stay in bed. Me with a beer and one of George's books and her just lying there with a strange smile on her face. She looks like she's a million miles away and I'm just about to ask if it's a good trip when I get to an interesting part of the book. She's probably just thanking her lucky stars that she met me, anyway.

One last thought: me—the biggest boozer and whorer around Cabbagetown—spending a Friday night at home reading a book. Something to think about all right.

July 17

Saturday again. God, how time goes fast.

Mrs. Thomson, a nice old lady who always comes alone to the Club, and I spend some time talking about today's lost youth, like the hippies.

She thinks it's their way of defying teachers and parents and that they'll grow out of it. I think that it's their way of showing their dissatisfaction with a society that has nothing to offer them except a mortgaged home and a financed car (I read that in a magazine). We spend about half an hour talking about this and in the end her opinion wins over mine. She's a member of the Club.

But this is one of the reasons I like working here. These people will talk to you as if you were somebody and for a guy like me it's a great feeling because here I can put my brains to good use. Sure I dropped out at grade nine, but I'm no fool. I've always liked reading and I was so good at history and English lit. and comp. that my teacher—we called him Sirs cause he was as fat as two men—said that I should become a teacher.

When I left school I kept up with my reading, and thanks to George I branched out to politics and books about today's societies, and things like that. So you see I'm not the ordinary Cabbagetown slob, all mouth and no brains.

And they know that here too.

Nope, I read a lot, and it pays off. Like respect, man, that's what counts with me.

Of course, I don't always know what all the words mean, and I guess I should buy a dictionary, but with George around it's that much easier just to ask him. He's got one year of university and he knows more words than I've drunk beers in my life, and that's saying an awful lot.

Feeling all full of culture like I am, I tell Terry that we're going to the movies tonight. She's so happy that she jumps up and down like a Ping-Pong ball. I guess she was worried that I was going to take her to the Harmony Hotel again.

The only good one around is *Bonnie and Clyde,* at least according to George. "It'll give you an idea of the poverty and misery during the Depression, and how some people rebelled against it."

Naturally there's a line-up about a mile long, and the humidity hasn't dropped a bit from the day. The sweat's pouring down my neck and I'm starting to see frosted glasses of ice-cold, foamy beers parade in front of my eyes when finally the line starts moving. Lucky Terry. Two minutes more and we'd have been sitting in a bar.

The movie's a gas. It's about this ex-con who meets a waitress and they rob banks and grocery stores till they're shot full of holes by the fuzz. And man, some lover the guy is. Like, the broad's a real dish. Something every guy dreams of having at least once in his life, and Creep Clyde can't even get a hard-on when he's in bed with her. Some hold-up artist too—he almost gets his head cut off sticking up a food store, and his first bank heist is a flop cause there's no money in the place.

Anyway, these two clowns team up with a kid who looks like he escaped from a zoo, and with Clyde's big brother and his woman. Big brother's a fink and his woman hasn't ever learned to talk—all she can do is scream, so you can imagine the fantastic jobs they pull off.

Lots of good fighting scenes, though. They shoot the cops; the cops shoot them back, and there's enough blood to take a bath in. The last scene's a dandy: the two of them are hit by at least ten thousand bullets and man, do they kick! Terry was all sad afterwards cause she felt sorry for them, so I explained to her that they got exactly what they deserved.

"Shit, a guy that can't lay a piece like that deserves to be shot."

"But, Michael, there was more to them than that."

I don't feel like arguing the finer points of the movie with her, so I drag her into the nearest bar and get kicked out because she's underage.

Oh Jesus, am I mad! I take her to the next one, telling myself that if they throw us out of this one, I'll bust the place up. Sure, we could just go to any Cabbagetown bar without being bothered, but

I think it would be good to show her some of the nice things in town. Besides, these places all got go-go girls.

We sit down with no trouble and order two beers. It's a swank place with dark lighting, leather chairs, and a Rock and Roll band blasting out a tune behind a curtain of psychedelic lights. There's mostly business types with their wives and girl friends sitting at the tables. I glance over to Terry and notice she looks embarrassed because the broads here are all real well dressed. Next payday I'll take her to Bloor Street and pick her out the best rag in the place. Her next payday.

The go-go girls come out in two-piece bikinis, white coloured and so thin you can see right through the material. They get up on the stage next to the band and start swinging their bodies to the rhythm of the music. Everyone's eyes are on them and as they jerk faster and faster, their breasts and asses almost popping out through the cloth, you can feel the tension build up in the place. The guys' eyes are popping. Their hands are sweating. Some of the chicks too. Tough butches with their hair cut short like a man's. The whole bar is dying to screw the dancers, and the chicks, knowing it, shake their bodies even faster, knowing nobody here will ever touch them.

The music gets louder, the girls give it all they've got, and the audience stares, their eyes filled with sex. When it's over and the girls have left, the guys who've got chicks sit closer to them, and the ones who are alone look around with frantic eyes. Hell, take their suits off and put them on wooden chairs, and you've got the crowd at the Harmony. When it comes to sex, they're no goddam different than we are. They just got more money, that's all.

Thinking about *Bonnie and Clyde* again; have to ask George why he thought there were what he calls revolutionary overtones in that film. After all, it's clear enough why people rob banks, isn't it? Who gives a shit if there's a depression going on or not? I didn't see those two jerks giving their money to the poor or anything.

And what's more, what did they get out of it? One good fuck at the end, and a faceful of cop bullets.

Terry's pretending she's Bonnie. With her hands, she's made a machine gun and she shouts, "Hands up, Clyde Barrow." Me, I reach for my rod with my left hand, pull her over on the bed with my right, and let her have it right between the legs. It's a good game, Bonnie and Clyde, especially on a Sunday morning.

I can hear church bells ringing somewhere in the distance.

The game over, we dress—or at least she does—and have something to eat. Why is it Sundays have to be so goddam hot? Upstairs, there's a thumpety-thump followed by loud voices, which means Mrs. Himmel is waking up. I'm wondering if she's got a new guy with her.

"Let's go for a walk, Michael. It's so lovely outside and it's the only day in the whole week I can get a bit of sun."

"Sure, baby." One way to see what Himmel's got.

As soon as we step outside I see those cowboy boots and I'm wondering what the hell is keeping the guy here.

We step over the twelve-pack and Terry gets the once-over from both Cowboy and Mrs. Himmel. She's wearing that brown dress that goes so well with her eyes, and it sways to and fro as she walks. Her hair shines in the sun, but it's her legs that are the best part of her (as far as looking goes). Long, not too fat, curvy, the legs of a dancer. The kind you like to have wrapped around you. Her little breasts bounce up and down inside her dress. Cowboy and Himmel look desperate. Him because he'll never get a lay like this in his life, and her because all his attention is wrapped up in Terry instead of her and the beer.

Me, I feel proud as a rooster.

"Good morning Mr. and Mrs. Himmel" (it's two in the afternoon), I say as I step over them. "Lovely day for drinking beer, isn't it."

Cowboy says, "Yep, shure doggone is," and Himmelhag looks like she's going to burst a blood vessel. Her face is so red that if you put water on it, it'd boil.

The first thing we notice as we walk into the Gardens is a pile of hippies sitting under the statue of Robert Burns. Yeah man. Robert

Burns in Allan Gardens. Isn't that a laugh? One of them's playing a guitar, another's making noises out of a flute, and the rest are singing and humming to whatever the hell the song is. Burns is looking down at them as if he's going to piss on the whole crew. That's only fair, I guess. I remember studying his poems at school and sometimes I'd get so mad figuring out what the words meant, I felt like pissing on him too.

The only thing wrong with hippies is that you can't tell if they're guys or broads unless you get real close, and I wouldn't advise that for everybody cause some of them stink real bad.

No trouble figuring out this one though. She's wearing what looks like a dirty bed sheet (sitting beside the guy with the flute) that's so worn out you can see right through it. Her boobs are tremendous. At least twin 45's and they don't sag either which means she's a real young one. I could sink my teeth into them cause that's one hangup I got. Big boobs. The bigger the better. And that's the one real beef I got about Terry. Hers are only normal size. But rather than bitch about it, I remember what we used to say when we were kids— "Whatever you can't hold in your hands is waste."

I can't stand it any longer. I grab Terry by the arm and pull her away. She knows I was looking at that chick with sex written on my eyes, but she don't say anything. She's good that way. Most broads, when they think they got you hooked, bitch like hell if you look at anything at all rather than them.

She puts her arm in mine and says that it's great to be walking together in the park where we met.

"I've known you for two whole weeks and this is the first time we've returned to the place where we met."

I'm about to tell her that if she hadn't got stoned last week, we could have come then, when there's a yell behind us followed by a loud groan.

We turn to where the noise comes from, thinking one of the hippies has dropped dead or something, but it's only a couple of Indians fighting. One of them is sitting on the ground holding onto his head and there's blood oozing out between his fingers, while the guy who thumped him turns to some other Indians standing in a row to watch the fight and mumbles in a drunk voice, "Next time I kill the mother-fucker." The guy on the ground keeps groaning. He bends his head between his knees and starts to vomit.

A few feet, away, Mouth is roaring something about brotherly love and how we should love our neighbours—his wife's got a placard reading:

HEAVEN OR HELL
WHAT'S
YOUR
CHOICE?

—and everybody's digging him so seriously that no one, but no one, goes over to see if the Indian's all right.

Terry, the mind reader, cuts in, "Michael, shouldn't we see if he needs help?"

"I'm not helping no Indian. You want me to get lice?" She's about to say something else, so I grab her arm again and head for the opposite side of the park. Christ, when is she going to learn to mind her own business? What the hell does she care if someone gets busted in the head? That's his tough luck. All she has to worry about is keeping me happy. After all, that's all that should count as far as she's concerned.

If she's going to help every joker in Cabbagetown that's bleeding at the head or lying in some alley with an empty bottle beside him, she'll be working so hard that in a week she'll be fagged out and ready for a month's stay at the hospital. It's about time she learned that these people like what they're doing and all that a do-gooder gets around here is a swift kick in the ass. And if she doesn't get it from them, she'll get it from me.

July 19

Tonight I'm feeling in one of my cultural moods, so I grab one of the books that George left me—*150 Questions for a Guerilla*. For a while it's a drag, but halfway through it gets interesting and I stay up till two in the morning reading it right to the end. It tells how to form a guerilla band, how to equip it, how to watch out for traitors, what tactics to use, how to train for guerilla warfare, how to escape, and so on.

But what really gets me interested is when I get to the part on terrorism and bombs. You wouldn't believe it! This crummy little book not only tells you where to place a bomb; it tells you how to make it. Like dig this:

Pocket Incendiary Bomb

A glass or cellulose tube is filled with 3/4 potassium chlorate ($KCIO_3$), 1/4 sugar mix. The fuse is a small tube of concentrated sulphuric acid, plugged with cork or paper and inserted in large tube. Plug up. Invert bomb to activate.

Place these incendiary bombs in movies, cars, files, mailboxes, next to inflammables. Once acid begins action, one leaves quickly.

Or this:

The best way to destroy a toilet is to flush down cotton and newspapers, mixed with nail and wires.

Or this:

Sabotage

Molotov Cocktail – A bottle is filled with 2/3 gas and 1/3 oil. A fuse is lighted and the bottle hurled at objective. On breaking, the contents will ignite. The enemy will be unable to extinguish it with water. The bottle with its lighted fuse, stoppered or not stoppered, *never explodes!* This point is stressed to insure the thrower that he is never in any danger.

Great. I'll remember that next time Himmel and her cowboy start screaming and yelling all over the place.

Anyway, the book gives you other pieces of information (to set a fire, a lighted cigarette is placed in a book of matches and left on combustible material) that are useful if you're a firebug or a revolutionary. I get my kicks out of this by seeing how easy it is to make a bomb and imagining what a ball I could have plugging up the toilet at the Club. I laugh thinking how those ladies would react when they saw their john flooding and their turds floating around on the floor. Bet they never seen their own shit in their lives, those rich bitches.

Hell, I get so excited that I jump on Terry and lay her. I blow my load before she's even fully awake, and by the time she realizes what's happening, I'm turning over to my side of the bed ready to get a few hours' sleep. I feel her raise herself up on her side and I know she's looking at me. Wonder what she's thinking? Probably that it's nice to know that I can love her even at two in the morning.

It *is* nice too. Beats having to whack yourself off, and it's more fun, too.

By the way, Miss Virgin had three big juicy new pimples on her face today. She must have had quite a weekend. I asked her and she said that all she'd done is go to the show. Somebody probably poked his finger up her skinny little butt while the movie was going on.

July 20

Here I am this morning, tired as hell, and Terry lets a cup crash to the floor while she's making her breakfast. Naturally the noise wakes me up, and I get so goddam mad at having my sleep busted up that I tell her next time she does that I'll shove the pieces down her throat.

For a few minutes she goes on getting ready for work without making a sound, then quietly at first, then louder, she starts crying. Boohoohoo—sniff sniff—boohoo—sniff—bawl. I sit up for the second time, farting mad and ready to let her have it. She just sits there on a chair, her head bowed and a handkerchief in her hands.

If I were like some of the other guys around here, she'd get a good swipe across the chops and that's the end of that—especially at eight in the morning—but I'm not like the other guys. I realize I'd been too hard on her.

"Hey, Terry baby, don't cry. You'll spoil your makeup."

She keeps on crying.

"Aw honey, I was just joking about shoving a cup down your throat." (There's only one left, anyway, and I need it for my coffee later on.)

"Come here, baby, and tell me what's the matter."

She comes over and cries on my chest. She cries so much I know that I'm going to end up with a wrinkled chest, but I put up with it without complaining. After a while she stops, blows her nose, and gives me a shy little smile.

"Don't feel bad about bawling, sugar. All broads bawl once in a while."

I know that makes her feel better cause she kisses me and tells me that she'll be quieter in the mornings.

Amazing what a few kind words at the right time can do. Maybe there'd be fewer divorces if people did what I just finished doing.

She goes on again about how sorry she is, and suddenly it comes to me why she was crying. She was scared I'd boot her out of the place! Poor mixed-up kid. As long as she does her work and doesn't bug me too much she's got nothing to worry about. Of course, I don't tell her that. Always good to keep some things to yourself. You never know when they can come in useful.

I'm walking to work today cause it's no use trying to go back to sleep, but God knows I'm tired enough. The sun's out and it's almost chilly from the lakeshore breeze, which is blowing in stronger than usual today.

I short-cut through the Gardens and I notice a faggot standing by the men's can. He looks at me as I walk by. His eyes narrow and lower to the crotch of my pants. Ten in the morning and this guy's thinking about sex! Man, oh man, nothing like overdoing it, is there?

Over to Church Street which is where the food and variety stores are located. I pass by a Brights Wines store and already there's a line-up to get in. About twenty winos standing there unshaven, tired, their filthy rags bug-ridden, waiting for the place to open. It should have opened at ten but the manager's late so these human garbage cans just stand there without moving, their faces wiped clean of any expression, holding in their grimy hands the money necessary to buy a bottle of the cheapest rotgut in the store.

When they get it they'll stumble over to the park and spend the day in a haze of booze and sun until night and hunger force them to leave either for the nearest garbage can or the nearest mission, where they can get a plate of hog food in exchange for a prayer. The lucky ones will sleep there too, the others will drift back to the park, search around in the trash cans for some newspapers, and find a park bench for a bed. Around midnight the cops will make their rounds and either bust them for the night or make them move somewhere else. And so on for them until morning and the magic hour of ten. (If they've managed to steal or beg enough money the day before.)

Thinking about these living dead makes me realize how lucky I am, and I arrive at work cheerful as a cat that's just caught a robin.

There's a new cup on the shelf when I get home tonight and Terry is happy as a robin that just got away from a cat. She's made $4 in tips and Blow Job is so happy with her work that he tells her he is going to give her a raise as soon as she's done six months there.

That's Blow Job for you. Hell, everybody gets a raise after six months working in one place. But he's gotta make it sound like he's cutting off his right arm or something. But what counts is that Terry's happy.

We hit the sack early tonight cause we're both pooped from last night and this morning.

July 21

Serve a party of seventy today and nearly go mad. About sixty-six of them order gin Collins. Hell you'd think that was the only drink ever invented. Naturally at supper Maggie has a new story about how some star (I can't remember the name) has a big German shepherd and that's the reason she never married. And guess what we're eating? Shepherd's pie. Why can't all days be the same? Why do we have to have days when everything goes wrong and days when nothing goes wrong? I'll have to ask George about that. He'll have an answer, too. He has for everything else.

Terry wants to go for a walk, saying what a warm evening it is, but I'm in no goddam mood tonight to do anything except grab a beer out of the fridge, go to bed and read the other book that George left.

Terry listens to the radio, but not so loud that it'll disturb my reading, and I start on chapter one of *The Theory of Terrorism*.

She's sitting at the foot of the bed leafing through a magazine I swiped from the Club and humming a tune that's playing on the radio.

Chapter one's all about a group of finks in Russia who called themselves nihilists and threw bombs at their king so that they could get more freedom. All they got was a rope around their necks, like George and his buddies will if they start pulling off the same stuff here.

They sure meant what they said though, these nihilists. Not only did they knock off the king, but most of his ministers, and a lot of cops and army guys got it too.

And the day they were all taken out to be hanged, one of them broke down and started crying and the rest in the bunch called him a coward and rat fink and refused to be hung beside him, they were so ashamed of his breaking down like that. How's that for guts?

The funny part of the story, though, was when it was revealed that the head of the terrorist group was also a police spy! That's politics for you. Here's the guy getting paid for finking on his buddies and letting the cops know everything that they're planning and at the same time bombing and killing the very people who pay him. That takes a bit of figuring. If the fuzz knew that the king was going to get splattered all over the countryside with a bomb, why did they let them do it? Bombs are dangerous things. When they go off in your face, they pick up what's left of you with an ink blotter or a spoon.

I guess it's like the cops here. They act like they're trying to put down crime, and when you see them off duty, or even on duty, they're hanging around with the hoods who commit these crimes. And sometimes they're committing a few crimes themselves. Take Janie. She does her business at a bar on Jarvis Street, on the west side of Allan Gardens. One night the morality boys follow her to a hotel with a john she's lined up. Just when they've both stripped and are ready to go at it, the cops bust in the door, tell the john to get dressed and go home, pull their pants down and make Janie do to them what she was going to do to the john. She had no choice. It was either that or the can for thirty days. That's the Law for you, and from what I'm reading, they're the same in every country.

But what really bugged Janie was that she was paying some of the morality cops off so that they'd leave her work in peace. These must have been new ones on her beat and they hadn't got the word yet. And as Janie said, they smelled like they hadn't taken a bath in a month.

Terry's in bed by now and I'm too tired to read any more. I tell her to turn the light out and in the dark I put my hand on her left breast and ask her if she thinks her parents will start looking for her one day. I mean, if they'll go to the cops and get a search on her. Of course, she says no and reminds me that she's eighteen. I answer that it doesn't matter what age she is. If they want her back badly enough, they'll get the Law on her.

She lies very still and I feel her shiver. Poor kid, her folks must have been real hard on her. She puts her arm around my waist and asks me to tell her that I'll never leave her. Boy, she's a drag with this don't leave me bit! That bugs me just about as much as her small boobs.

"Of course I'll never leave you. You're my woman."

Nice thing about her, though, is that it's all over with her as soon as you tell her what she's waiting to hear. Some broads go on and on till you've repeated it a thousand times, and even then they're not sure you mean it. Terry, she believes it. One more proof that she doesn't know guys. She'll learn though. She'll learn.

July 22

I spend half the night dreaming about guys getting hung and me there with them. They put the rope around my neck and I feel myself falling. I kick with my feet, trying to find a piece of ground, and I'm screaming, "Don't let me die! Please, don't let me die!" Wake up around twelve covered in sweat and the sheet on the floor. I'm real scared and it takes me about an hour and three glasses of water to get back to sleep.

As I go out the front door on my way to work I notice a dried puddle of puke on the porch steps and I wonder if that was Himmel or Cowboy. It reminds me of something real funny, and I laugh out loud.

It was the first time I got really drunk. I was with Spike and Timmy the Wart and we'd bought a twenty-sixer of rye from the bootlegger up the street. We were only thirteen at the time and about the only thing we'd drunk before that was cheap wine we'd taken off some sleeping bum.

We were happy as hell as we sat in a pile of thick bushes in the park, downing the stuff like it was water. At first it burned right down to our assholes and none of us was really enjoying it, but we kept drinking so that the word wouldn't get around that we couldn't take it. It took us about three hours, but we finished the bottle and got up to go home, since it was dark and we hadn't had supper yet. I'll be damned if we weren't drunk as truck drivers. We saw double, our legs wouldn't hold us up, the park was going around in a circle. This was no good. If we got caught on the street like this, we were dead. We sat down again and decided what to do about it.

Spike: "Lesh go sleep."

Timmy the Wart: "Lesh puke de shtuff up."

Me: "Lesh get noder boddle."

Timmy's idea won out mainly because we were starting to feel sick as dogs. Spike agreed, but only under the condition that we make a bet out of who could puke the farthest. Spike's like that. He can't see doing something for nothing.

We said okay and staggered arm in arm over to the street, lined up on the edge of the sidewalk, stuck our fingers down our throats, and threw up. Right then a white car drove up and we never did find out who won. The driver stopped a few feet down the street and got out to see what had happened to his car. Hell, was he mad. The whole side of the car, windows and all, was covered with vomit. All colours too. He came towards us like he was going to kill us, but Spike, who was pretty big for his age, pulled a blade out of his pocket and told the guy to beat it or he'd cut his balls off.

The guy got back into his white-and-puke car and drove off. We argued for weeks after who would have won if that damn car hadn't got in the way. It got so bad between Spike and Timmy the Wart that they ended up fighting it out behind the church one night. Me, I'd be damned if I was going to let that worry me.

Thinking about the rye gets me thirsty and I sneak a drink at the Club. Just an ounce with a bit of ginger ale. They think they're so smart when they take stock at the end of the month. "We can account for every ounce." Sure, but they can't tell when you've put an ounce of water into the bottle to make up for what you've drunk. Use your head and they'll never find out. Make sure it's a nearly full bottle, so that afterwards when you serve a customer a shot, he won't notice any difference in taste. And only do it once or twice a month. Doing it too often you might get careless, and somebody'll see you, or you'll forget about the water. A simple matter of using your brains. Something most people don't do.

Mrs. Waddling's caught a cold and every time she blows her nose she reminds me more than ever of a duck. Honk. Honk. Waddle. Waddle. She better not leave the city in duck-hunting season or they'll get her for sure.

July 23

Walk to work again today. It's good exercise and helps keep you fit, which is what I need cause already I'm starting to get a pot. Not much though, just a little bulge, but it's better to get rid of it now before it turns into something like Mrs. Waddling's gut, or like Big Jim's, the bar waiter.

I decide to heel it up Yonge Street to Bloor and from there over to the Club. I like Yonge Street. It's Toronto's main drag, and even though it's not as elegant as Bloor, it's a hell of a lot more exciting. It's got every kind of store imaginable, dozens of movie houses and all kinds of bars. High-class bars like the Colonial, dingy ones like the Brown Derby or the Bermuda, which caters to Negro pimps and their women, mostly white. Gay bars like the St. Charles—the smell of perfume nearly knocks you out as you walk in that place.

I went there one day with a friend. It's dimly lit and except for that perfume you'd think you were walking into a straight bar. Then, as your eyes get used to the light you see that there's nothing but guys in the place. Hundreds of them. They look you up and down as you walk towards the end trying to find a seat, and you realize what a broad in a miniskirt feels like on a windy day. It's like they're looking right through you.

We had a beer and we were just deciding to leave when somebody called out, "Mike, Jerry." We couldn't make out who it was because of the light, the smoke, and all the queers walking around. Then someone came to our table and sat down. Damned if it wasn't Ted Hill. Shit, hadn't seen the guy since he got sent to the pen three years ago for breaking and entering. Naturally, after we'd had a couple more beers and talked about old times, he got around to telling us what was on our minds.

"Yeah, I hustle. Man's gotta make his bread the best way he knows. And after three years in Kingston I know howta do it real good. That dump's just crawlin' with queers and if you're young and good-lookin', ya don't stand a chance. The first night in your cell, the boss guy there comes up to ya an' sez 'Bend over buddy,' so whattaya do? Say no and ya get your head kicked off your shoulders, or take a blade between the ribs.

"Most of the guys there got some sorta blade, usually a sharpened spoon handle, or a filed-down screwdriver. If ya got a beef with somebody, you settle it with your blades. You fight till one of ya gets cut, then ya stop. The cut guy either gets better or he bleeds to death, but he *never* goes to the doc, cause if he does that then the screws'll be turnin' the place upside down lookin' for weapons, see?

"There was one guy in there for wrapping a tire iron around his broad's head. He was a real nut. One day, a screw starts buggin' him bout somethin' or other, and the guy gets so uptight that he sinks his blade in the screw's gut.

"Christ, ya couldn't believe the fuckin' uproar over that craphead screw gettin' shanked! Man, like ya couldn't even piss without one o' them lookin' over your shoulder to see if ya had a machine-gun or somethin' taped to your balls.

"They threw the guy in the hole: solitary. That was two years ago an' they ain't let him out yet. Fuck, he'll rot in there; one meal a day, no smokes, nothin' to read, no radio, gettin' the shit beat outta him every day.

"So like I said, whattaya do, man? This kid wasn't fixin' to croak in that lousy dump. I bent over. Besides, after a while ya get used to it, and if ya play it right there's money in it for ya."

We drank all afternoon and we were getting so stewed that we ended up pretending we were all faggots out for a good time. At one point we'd just finished cutting up a thin, black-haired guy with long eyelashes and a swinging butt ("Oh dearie, isn't he just *too* much") when Ted turned towards Jerry and put a hand on his leg. A minute later they both headed for the can.

I had another brew, waiting for them to come out, and finally Jerry comes up to me from behind, taps me on the shoulder and says, "Let's go."

Outside the sun nearly blinded us after all that time spent in the dark bar. We didn't say a word on the way home and I knew I wouldn't be seeing him again for a long time. I wanted to tell him what he did was his business, but I was falling asleep from all that booze and couldn't be bothered.

I told George what had happened between Jerry and Ted when I saw him later on and just like that he pulled out a pencil and paper that he always carried with him and wrote a poem about it. I still have it.

Sitting in a bar reputed to be gay,
I'd had a few beers, was feeling mellow,
And it was such a lovely warm day—
How could I refuse that poor little fellow
Sitting beside me with a sad, sad face,
His sad, sad eyes filled with disgust
That he had to be in such a place
To appease his unnatural lust.
And when his quivering hand touched my leg
(Ever so gently, ever so light),
I was saddened at how he was forced to beg
For a bit of love in his world of night.

And I said, smiling, "I know
That though I'm not queer,
My prick you can blow
If you buy me a beer."

My pants lying on the floor,
His face buried in my crotch,
Reading graffiti on the locked toilet door,
Wishing I'd made him buy me a Scotch,
And meditating on the fortune of life
(His lips so soft between my thighs)
That has given me a beautiful wife
And two handsome children with sky-blue eyes.

And thanking God, as I step out in the sun,
That I'm no faggot, forced on my knees,
That I can walk proudly like a man,
My head held high and my mind at ease.

Not bad, eh?

Terry wants to go for a walk again tonight, so this time I agree. We walk through Allan Gardens, down Jarvis past the whore bars like the Westmoreland, which is opposite the Harmony Hotel, west on Dundas and north on Yonge.

Yonge is full of people and all the stores are open. We stop at a couple of shoe and dress stores and I can see Terry's eyes light up as bright as the neon signs. She asks me if I'd mind if she bought a new dress and maybe a pair of shoes and a handbag to match. I say no, I don't mind. And I don't as long as she's got enough money left over to pay her half of the rent.

We turn east on College and head for home. Funny city, Toronto. Just walk a block either side of Yonge Street and it's so dark and quiet you'd swear you're in the country. No bright lights, no music blaring out into the street from the bars and the record stores, no crowds of people pushing at you from every side. Nothing. Without Yonge Street there'd be no Toronto.

We're going down our street hand in hand like two kids on their first date when we hear some voices in front of our house.

"Hey, you old bastard!"

"Come on out you old bastard!"

It's two little girls about ten years old, with dirty blonde hair and dirty dresses and legs. They're yelling across the street towards the second floor where we live. An old guy lives there. I see him sometimes at the park, but he never talks to anybody in the house. Minds his own business and pays his rent on time and doesn't make a racket, which is all anybody here cares about.

The little brats giggle for a minute then yell again, louder than before.

"Old bastard! Old bastard!"

By this time we're so close we can hear them talking to each other.

"The old fucker, he's pretending he doesn't hear us."

They give a real yell, their voices cutting through the air like knives.

"Old bastard child molester *come on out!*"

Christ, you could have heard them all the way up to Bloor Street. The window on the second floor opens and a bottle goes sailing towards the kids, who duck out of the way as it crashes on the side-walk a few feet away from them.

Old bastard child molester sticks his head out the window and yells down at the kids.

"Get the hell home before I go out there and beat your heads against the wall, you brainless little sluts."

The brainless little sluts laugh in the direction of the window and walk off up the street.

"Cocksucker."

Having got the last word, they duck into an alley a few houses up, their laughs following them.

Terry is shocked, the whole mood of the evening destroyed by these kids mouthing off. Later in bed she asks how kids can get to be that way while they're still so young. I try to explain to her that those words come naturally around here and nobody pays any attention to them. Like saying gee or golly. Kids grow up fast in Cabbagetown.

That's all they hear at home and in the street so what can you expect from them?

She says, "If I had children, I'd spank them every time they spoke like that. It's bad enough to hear a man speaking like that, but a poor little child!"

I say, "If you spanked these kids here every time they swore, your hand'd be worn to the bone in a week."

What I mean to say is that I don't give a goddam what she does with her brats. Just make sure they're not mine, too. The last thing I want in this world is to be saddled with a screaming monster in my arms. Not this kid. If she wants to drop a baby, she better go out and find some other guy.

She's quiet now and more relaxed and I'm willing to bet a jug of beer that she's thinking about kids cause she's lying there with a half-smile on her face and a faraway look in her eyes.

Kids, for Christ sake! Who wants them? Pissing all over the place. Screeching all hours of the day and night. Tying you up, so that you never get any free time of your own. Your woman yelling at you that she needs more money cause the little slob's getting bigger every day. No sir. Stay single. Lay all the chicks you can, but don't take on anything that's going to bugger up your life. Hell, you're only young once.

July 24

Tonight I'm taking Terry to see Yorkville. Her reaction: "What is it?"

"Just a place where the hippies hang out," I answer. That's not saying much, but then again, Yorkville's a hard place to describe.

Before we get there, however, I take her for a walk along Bloor, since it's only two blocks south of Yorkville. Just like I thought, we stop at least fifteen minutes before every shop window there, Terry's eyes popping out of her head at all the clothes for the well-dressed broad.

The style is Bonnie and Clyde, with long dresses and berets. Long dresses! Just when the chicks are finally starting to show what the guys like to see, they decide to cover it all up again. Probably the Salvation Army is behind all this.

And the prices! Thirty dollars for the kind of stuff my mother used to wear. I'll never figure women out. Clyde styles are coming out for the men too—double-breasted suits, and hats with a brim two feet wide that you can pull down over your nose. Man, if I walked down Cabbagetown with something like that I'd have the whole neighbourhood throwing stones at me.

If they're going to put out styles because of that movie, how about a C.W. Moss style? Dirty blue jeans, rag shirt, running shoes and one of those Mickey Rooney caps.

Terry's still gawking at dresses so I walk over to the next store, a shoe store. There's a stunner of a blonde fixing up the display in the window. Miniskirt and long legs. Her back's to the sidewalk and she's bending over to pick up a high-heel shoe as I walk up. She bends over so far that her skirt lifts up her legs until I catch a glimpse of red panties before she straightens up.

This looks like fun and I'm ready to spend the rest of the night leering at her when Terry catches me by the arm and says that she's going to buy a dress next week. That breaks that up. I mean, I can't stand here with her at my side watching another chick's rear end, now can I?

Of course, Terry's never seen anything like Yorkville. ("I was at a bingo game one Sunday at the church, and I thought I'd never seen so many people in my life. But this!")

Yorkville Avenue. Two blocks of discotheques with the music blaring out onto the street; sidewalk coffee houses where you can watch people who watch you as you drink a fifty-cent coffee; art galleries full of modern painting that looks like the stuff we did in grade one; a poster store where George got his posters; and about half a million people and cars moving up and down like a permanently flowing river.

Teeny-boppers—ten to fourteen-year-olds who make the street look like a nursery corner. Hippies sitting on the sidewalk or on the steps of houses, their blank faces disappearing behind a curtain of hair. Beads, bells, buttons, tied and pinned onto the blankets and rags they call clothes. High on speed, LSD, grass and anything else they can lay their hands on. Black with dirt. Broads and guys all looking alike. Incense in the air. Getting up to walk slowly a few feet down the street till they find a new place to sit down. Tourists taking photographs. Greasers looking for a fight—black leather jackets and boots (most of them are from the suburbs). Cops walking in pairs while a paddy wagon waits at the corner of the street. College kids walking hand in hand and pretending they're part of the scene. A man and a woman with a photo in their hands approaching the hippies and asking them if they've seen their daughter who's only fourteen and who ran away from home last week with her girl friend who's fifteen.

A roar of motorcycles and a gang wheels up the street, *Satan's Choice* written in red on the back of their shirts or jean jackets. Tough babies who'll stomp you if there's nothing else to do. Riding their cut-down bikes in groups of five or six and never looking to right or left. It's you who's got to move, not them. Sometimes I dream what it would be like to ride with them, the hair tied with a scarf, leather boots and swastikas and a broad riding behind me.

But then, they're always getting busted by the Man, and most of them are stupid as hell. They want respect, but the only way they can get it is by acting tough. And their pigs look like they all got VD.

Yorkville's a great place to come looking for tail, though. But you got to watch out who you're conning. Most of the chicks here are jailbait. One night we picked up one who looked at least seventeen, built like a brick shithouse, and just when we get her into the car she comes out saying that she's thirteen. We dumped her on the sidewalk again. Man, no broad's worth getting arrested for, especially when they don't take a pill or nothing and next thing you know she's a mommy. They throw the book at you for that.

We thread our way through the people and Terry's holding my hand so that she won't get lost. Something with hair down to his feet walks by.

"What was that, a girl or a boy?" she asks.

I look back and I can't even tell by looking at the ass, and it's got bare feet so no telling there either.

"Don't tell me he's a hippie too!"

A little old guy with a hat full of feathers walks by with a button on his shirt saying 49ers. He looks like the winos at Allan Gardens.

"He's a pippy," I answer, laughing at my own joke.

The coffee houses are full and the dance halls are jammed wall to wall. The street's full of cars and the sidewalk's crammed. This is enough for me. Not much use sticking around here, since the only reason I've ever had for coming is shot to hell because of Terry.

We walk back towards Bloor Street and it takes a few minutes to get used to the quiet again.

Terry's going on about how dirty they are and how they dress. I don't say anything, but as far as I'm concerned personally, they can do whatever they want. Hell, they're the only people in Toronto who'd rather give you a flower than a sock in the kisser, and that's all right by me. Live and let live, that's my motto.

Even though she's bitching about them, I can tell she got a real kick out of going to Yorkville cause she's talking a mile a minute and her eyes are wide open with excitement.

Later in bed she holds on to me real tight and says, "You know, they reminded me of George." Then she adds, "I'm glad you don't have hair like that."

Silence for a while, then, "But even if you did, I'd love you just the same."

July 25

I wake up this morning with the right side of my face swollen, and a temperature. Terry gives me a couple of aspirins and puts a cold cloth on my head, but it doesn't help a goddam. I drink a beer, thinking that might do the trick, but no luck. Maybe what I need is two. No luck either, so I have another. By the fourth one I'm feeling a bit better, so I get dressed and tell Terry we're going to the park. She says I shouldn't because the sun will make my fever worse, that I should stay in bed and drink hot lemonade. I get kind of peeved at that. I mean, if I want a mother I can always go look for mine, wherever the hell she is now, the old bitch. So I give her a whack on the ass and tell her to get ready and this time she doesn't argue. She'll do anything rather then have me get mad at her. She's always got in the back of her mind that I might blow my top one day and boot her out of the place.

Mrs. Himmel's on the porch with (I can't believe my eyes) a bottle of wine and—Cowboy! Good Jumping Jesus, he's still here. Talk about miracles.

I give Terry a pinch on the back of the arm, which means get that sad look off your face, as we step over the creeps and I say my usual "Good morning" bit to them.

Himmel answers, "You're using too much light. Keep it up and I'll raise your rent."

I'm about to tell her to watch herself with me cause one night I might just sneak into her room and cut off Cowboy's prick while they're sleeping, but Terry takes my hand, gives it a little squeeze, and practically drags me up the street.

Funny, I think after, how Terry and me help each other out like that. And we don't even realize it till after it's done. As if it was natural. I mean, the broads around here would be the first to tell you to do it just to see if you had the guts or not, and not caring a damn if you got jailed after or if you got the hell beat out of you.

I'm sweating something fierce and my head isn't feeling any too good, but I'm the one who said we were going out and I'm not backing down now. We cross the street and who should I see but old Banana Peeler walking ahead of us.

He's an old guy who spends all his time picking newspapers and things out of garbage cans, and he's dressed in his garbage-picking uniform: old top hat with a big hole in the back and half the rim gone off one side, an overcoat so thin and worn that you can see he's wearing no shirt under it, and a pair of baggy old trousers held up by a string. His shoes got no soles and they're also held up by a string tied around each one.

He's stumbling along bent over, dragging behind him an old wooden wagon full of bug-ridden newspapers, and muttering to himself in a loud voice. As we pass him I yell out "Hi Banana Peeler," but he doesn't even notice, he's so busy talking to himself.

Terry laughs and asks why he's called that. I tell her because when we were kids at school he used to come at recess and say, "Hey sonny, you want your banana peeled?" We'd say, "What banana?" and he'd say, "This one," and touch our peckers.

"Oh, that's horrible, didn't you complain about him to your teachers?" Terry asks.

"Hell no," I answer, half laughing, "we thought it was a great game and sometimes we even showed him our bananas. Used to give him a real thrill. Then one day the cops picked him up and we never seen him again, until five years later there he was with the same clothes he's got on now and the same wagon. We found out they'd put him in a mental hospital all those years. It sure cured him of his banana kick, but I'd love to know how. Hell, look at him now, he can't even talk straight."

We get as far as the park when the sight of all those people and the noise they're making puts me off and I'm really feeling lousy. Terry holds on to me under my arm and we head for home, but just as we get around the corner of our street we bump into George and some floozie he's with, and I fall flat on my face on the sidewalk.

I wake up in the evening with a lump the size of a good-sized tit on my forehead and it takes me a few minutes before I realize that the three blurs in front of my eyes are Terry, George and his floozie, who's got her hair cut so short it looks like she's the man and George is the woman.

After a couple of brews I'm feeling better and George introduces me to his broad as Terry gets up to make supper. Her name's Myra, and George met her at one of his political meetings. They've obviously been shacking together because she's giving him the same sort of sickly love stare that Terry gave me after I'd had her the first time, and I'm surprised at that cause George has always said that he never mixes politics and love. He must really be hard up.

He asks me what I thought of the books (just like him, too—never mind asking if I'm feeling better or anything), and I tell him that the bit about making bombs will come in handy if they don't give me a raise at the Club next year.

"Yes, that's fine," says George, waving his arms and looking annoyed, "as far as the theory of urban insurgency goes, but I'm particularly interested in finding out what you think of the practice as described in the other book. Do you think their aims and methods are applicable here in Cabbagetown?"

"You mean like the nihilists and the OAS?" I ask.

"Exactly," he shouts, his arm doing a dance in front of my face, which nearly gets me sick again. "Exactly."

"Well, uh, they were all right I guess."

Hell, I don't know what to say. If those people want to kill people and blow things up, that's no skin off my ass. Like the OAS. Those cats would drive past a line of people waiting at the bus stop and machine-gun the whole lot of them, or throw a grenade in a bar and then shoot down the customers who managed to survive as they staggered out the door. Some of them were doctors and they'd let patients die in the hospital if they were Algerians—let them bleed to death.

I ask myself, why can't people just learn to live with each other?

Over sandwiches (George and his floozie have invited themselves) he keeps asking me what I thought about all those guys, and how we should try and change the source of our troubles, "from the barrel of a gun, as Chairman Mao said."

I like George very much, in fact it's thanks to him that I'm writing this diary. He told me I was a good talker and that I should be able to write down what I say. So I am.

But tonight I'm in no mood to listen to any talk about revolution in Cabbagetown or anywhere else. My head aches, I've still got a fever, and I'm uptight about fainting on the street, so I tell him, "I'm in no mood to listen to any talk about revolution in Cabbagetown or anywhere else."

Terry puts her two cents worth in. "Michael's very tired."

Thanks a pant load kid, as if I didn't know that already. Floozie says, "That sandwich was good. Do you have any more?" George stops waving his hands around long enough to pull some sheets of paper out of his pocket.

"Here," he says, handing them to me, "see what you think of a speech I'm preparing for a future meeting. It's on the revolutionary struggle in Latin America against U.S. imperialism."

"You mean Yankee," says Floozie. She's flat as a board and I'm beginning to wonder just what George sees in her. Maybe she does something special that makes up for her lack of tit.

"I've written this survey of the Latin American battle against Yankee colonialism in a light-hearted vein, in fact you could say cynical, retaining, nevertheless, the essential element basic to an educational speech or forum—awareness of the motives leading the imperialists to continue their exploitation of the underdeveloped peoples of the Third World."

She's got a full-lipped mouth, though. Maybe that's it.

"Anyway, you read it and let me know what you think about it," he gets up, brushing bread crumbs onto the floor with his hands. "I better warn you, though. It's not finished."

Great. The damn thing isn't even finished and still he wants me to read it. Oh well, I've got nothing else handy to read right now, and Terry's got some of my things to iron, which should keep her busy for an hour or two.

As she's getting the table ready I tell her to iron my suit. It's a navy blue suit and the only one I've got, so I always like to keep it neatly pressed even though I don't wear it very often.

She smiles and comes over and gives me a kiss and I give her one back. Isn't that lovey-dovey.

Now for George's speech. By the way, you know why he gives me all this garbage to read? He's sure that one day he's going to convert me into a real, live revolutionary.

When I think about that, I laugh almost as hard as I did the day my old man got ten years in Kingston for rape, and that was goddam funny in itself, cause after it turns out that the bitch he was supposed to have raped was a part-time whore who laid that charge on him cause he paid her only half of what he'd promised, that being after he'd screwed.

This is the speech.

The Neighbourly Stick or 40,000 = 52

Once upon a time when the U.S. of A. was a young and vigorous nation just beginning to discover and exploit the natural resources in its huge land, a president by the name of Monroe came out one day with the doctrine which he modestly named the Monroe Doctrine.

This doctrine was a very simple one—it merely told the rest of the world to forget about South America, it's ours! And to prove that they meant what they said, the Americans kicked the Mexicans out of their states of Texas, Arizona and California; chased the Spaniards out of Florida, and bought Louisiana from the French.

This land that they took soon became part of the U.S. of A. and although it had little to do with the Monroe Doctrine, as none of it was in South America, it did prove that even then the United Stateseens were great believers in real estate.

This tremendous land grab kept the boys in Washington quiet for a while, and apart from a civil war in their country and a naval bombardment of Japan (which somebody thought was part of South America), they hardly bothered anybody.

Then came 1898, and the Cubans were fighting for their freedom against Spain. Uncle Sam, feeling sorry for these poor Cubans, blew up one of his gunboats in the port of Havana, declared war on Spain, and set the Cuban people free—as well as the Philippinos and the Puerto Ricans—which had nothing to do with Cuba.

However there was one little hitch. The U.S. soldiers, having liberated these countries, showed no desire to leave. They even set up their own governments and administrations.

Soon the "liberated" peoples began wondering what the score was, and before you knew it, Uncle Sam's fighters for freedom were busy fighting the people they'd just set free.

Not until 1912 did they finally leave Cuba, and then only on the condition that they could send in troops any time they felt like it. (This was known as the Platt Amendment, which was added to the Cuban Constitution.)

In the Philippines they fought until 1930, and in Hawaii they built a great big naval base—Hawaii being another fortunate land to be taken over by the United Stateseens.

Then along came FDR and

That's all he's written and I'm kinda mad about that. Why the hell didn't he wait till he'd finished before showing it to me? And what the hell does he mean by 40,000 = 52 anyway?

I throw the sheets down on the floor, and Terry's bending down to pick them up when there's a great goddam crash and a thump outside. Terry gasps with fright and you can hear Mrs. Himmel and the rest of the boarders running out the front door to see what the noise is about.

I'm curious about what's happened, so I put on a pair of shoes, grab Terry by the hand, and push my way through the mess of people on the front porch to see Dottie, an Indian woman about forty years old, with pockmarks on her face, lying on the front yard of the house next door in a pool of blood. She's moaning and groaning, so I guess she's not hurt too bad.

Somebody asks, "What's happening?"

Somebody answers, "She was thrown out the window."

I look up and sure enough, there is a big hole in the window of the room she shares with her husband, a white guy.

"Dog-gone," drawls Cowboy, "she fell two stories."

"That bastard husband of hers should be thrown in jail," screeches Mrs. Himmel, her beer-red face drawn tight in a grimace.

In the distance there's the sound of sirens getting closer.

"Yeah," pipes in some mousy woman who lives on the third floor, curlers in her hair, "drinks all day, that's all he does. And his wife working at the factory, slavin' for forty or fifty hours a week."

Why not seventy or eighty? If there's anything that bugs me, it's a broad that can't keep her trap shut. Some slaving that Indian does. Hell, go over to Harry's Grill any night of the week and you'll see her there hustling the Newfies and the blacks at two bucks a throw.

A cop car pulls up followed by an ambulance. The cops start throwing their weight around. "Okay, okay, what's happened here? Everybody move." Nobody says nothing and nobody moves. The ambulance attendants aren't too happy about all this because the Indian doesn't look like she'll be able to pay. They talk together for a minute and then bring out a stretcher and throw her in the back of the ambulance and drive away, siren blazing.

The cops have found out what's happened, thanks to Himmel, and they strut up the stairs of the house next door as if they were kings.

"Do you remember when he chased her down the street with a broken bottle, screaming he was going to cut her head off?"

"He's an animal. Worse than any Injun just off a reserve."

I'm starting to get bored and I turn to Terry to see what she thinks of all this when the cops march back out of the house and into their car with the guy between them. His hands are handcuffed behind his back and there's tears all over his face. He's mumbling something, but I can't hear what it is. Poor bastard, what he's done is good for two years at least, and in spite of what all these jokers are saying, he's not a bad head. I don't know him that well, just had a beer with him now and then, but he's always got a joke to tell and he doesn't mind paying a few rounds whenever he's got enough bread. As far as I'm concerned she got what she deserved, and besides she probably got out of it with just a bone or two busted. Nothing serious.

Back inside Terry carries on like the rest of them. What a brute the guy is. How he deserves a good long jail term. The poor woman; and so on so forth.

Me, I'm really getting cheesed off. First my fever and hitting my head on the sidewalk, then George's unfinished speech, now this.

"Shut up, or I'll do the same to you one day."

I'm immediately sorry for what I've said cause Terry gets a shocked look and turns white. She's gonna cry in a minute, so I take her hand, lead her over to the bed, and tell her I was only joking as I stroke her hair at the same time. Her head nods sideways and there's goose pimples on her skin. Poor kid. She takes things too seriously.

There's my sleep buggered up for another hour or more while I convince her that I still love her with all my heart, and all that jazz.

July 26

My fever's gone down to normal (wonder what it was?), but I phone up the Club and tell them I won't be in today because of the summer flu. It's Mrs. Waddling I'm talking to and she tells me to sweat it out and take hot lemonade and lots of aspirins and cover up. I say yes Mrs. Waddling, thank you Mrs. Waddling, and hang up on the old cow.

I spend the morning sitting around doing nothing, which by noon gives me a real appetite, so I put on a shirt and go over to Blow Job's for one of his dogburgers. The place is crowded with people coming and going, and it's a few minutes before I find a seat.

Terry, who hasn't seen me come in, is hopping around like mad serving about twenty tables at the same time. There's sweat on her forehead and her red hair is hanging in strands from the roll she makes out of it when she works. Funny how work makes people look ugly.

"Michael, what are you doing here?"

She's got that same surprised look on her face that Timmy the Wart had when we put a tack on his seat one day at school.

"Can't you see?" I smile at her with all my teeth. "I'm waiting to be served."

She smiles back and brushes her hand against her forehead, then she gets serious again.

"I hope at least you phoned them and told them you were sick. It would be terrible if you got fired."

I smile at her again and don't say anything but I'm starting to get mad. What does she think I am anyway—a dummy or something? I mean, hell, I think I've told her a thousand times already that I like my job. On top of which, they need me in that place. They couldn't do a thing there without me, and if I ever left, they'd have a goddam hard time trying to find somebody as good as me, especially with all the chickenshit you got to put up with there. It's no crime to take one day off once in a while, is it?

But I keep my cool with her.

"Look, Terry, I came here for a hamburg and a large Coke, not a speech, so hustle and get them for me, okay?"

Naturally, she hustles. All broads are the same, act like a man and they appreciate it, and if you don't think that's true, then you tell me why they live with us then. It's not for the tail cause they don't enjoy it that much. It's because they like a man telling them what to do.

I finish the hamburg, wishing at the same time that I'd gone to work after all. That's how bad the food is at Blow Job's. On the way out I give Terry a hard pinch on the butt that almost makes her drop a bowl of soup on a customer, wave at the great BJ himself, who's sitting behind the cash register like he's Al Capone, light up a smoke and drop the match in a flowerpot near the door, and step outside whistling "Let's Spend the Night Together" to nobody in particular. I feel great. Just look at all those clowns rushing off to work with their food splashing about in their guts. Hell. Not even any time to digest the stuff. Rush. Rush. Rush. And what for? An ulcer or a heart attack at forty. Enjoy life while you can, that's my motto. There's other things in life besides work. Look at George, he hasn't worked a day in his life, and he's happy, with his politics and bombs and things. Look at the hippies, they sit around all day screwing each other and popping bennies in their mouths, and they're happy.

I got to admit, though, that's not the answer either. After all, you got to have some money in the bank if you get sick or you got to raise bail in a hurry. Me, I got a hundred dollars, and now, with Terry here, I can always count on her if I need money in a hurry. Security, baby, that's what's in. And that's why I'm neither a bum or a convict today, like so many of my buddies. In other words, I got a head on my shoulders.

All this thinking's tired me out, so I go back to my room and have a little sleep, which turns out to be four hours long and is only interrupted by Terry coming home from work and waking me up. She takes her dress off to change into something more comfortable and the sight of her boobs, milk-white in her brassiere, gets me so horny that I throw her onto the bed and have a go at her, which afterwards makes me so hungry that I eat three ham sandwiches with mustard and pickles.

It's two in the morning before I manage to fall asleep again. Every time we finish making love, Terry always asks me if I love her. Sex is one thing and love another, but just to make her happy I always say, "Sure honey, you should know that by now," and then she holds me tight for a while. It's a real ritual and sometimes I get tired of it. The truth is, though, that I do love her. A little, that is. Let's put it this way: I don't mind having her around, and that's quite an improvement over the other chicks I've shacked with. She's clean, too, and she shaves her underarms.

Mrs. Waddling asks me if I'm feeling better. I say yes Mrs. Waddling, I mean that's obvious or I wouldn't be here. Maggie's on the day shift and we got spaghetti for lunch and "Did you know that Tony Curtis is a woman? He had an operation in Denmark." I feel like saying that at least he's got *something* in his favour, what about you?

Miss Virgin rushes in at five as if someone had shoved a cigarette up her skinny butt, gives me a I-know-you-weren't-sick look and disappears into the office. This evening there's a Club Special Dinner, whatever the hell that means. Not that the ladies care. Any excuse to get out of the house is a good one, especially if there's food and booze involved.

There's about seventy of the old bags come in, including the one that thinks that my blue eyes are "adorable." She tells that to all her guests whenever she brings them in, and makes me blush. *Blush.* That really grabs me cause I haven't blushed for so long I thought I'd forgotten how to do it. But I got one up on her. She's stupid. She always orders a Manhattan "and not too much gin in it please Michael." Now whoever heard of a Manhattan with gin? I tell her not to worry and make the thing like it should be made—rye and sweet vermouth. It goes to show about people, though. This poor broad has been going through life thinking that there's gin in a Manhattan. Christ, she doesn't even know what the hell she's drinking!

There's a new waitress on the night shift. Her name's Mrs. Russell and she's Estonian—that's around Russia somewhere. Yeah, Mrs. Russell. And she talks like this: "Vat yu sa yu name iz agen? Mikeel?" It's a shame I can't understand her cause she's built like a ten-ton truck—wide strong hips, wide shoulders and two giant breasts like balloons. Not too old either. I'd say about forty, which makes it right as far as I'm concerned. Women that age got lots of experience in bed and they're not shy like the young chicks. But there's one nice thing about a young one, though. You can train her. Take Terry. The first few nights she was so scared it was hardly no fun at all, but after a week or two of showing her how it should be done, she became a real pro. Even doing it with the light on, although I got to admit that she does go red in the face when we do it that way.

Thought for the day: Love is like a shot of Johnny Walker. It's good while it's going down your throat, but when you piss out an hour later, it's all over.

July 28

It's a real humid day today and the sky is gray, which means it's going to rain.

There's a pile of newspapers lying in the middle of the park and the noise of someone snoring under it. Some bums are so lazy they can't even get up early enough to grab a free breakfast at the mission. Another bum walks towards the newspapers, looks around for a minute to see if anyone's watching, then bends over and takes all the papers off Sleeping Beauty. Stealing your own bed off you while you're sleeping on it!

There's an Indian sitting on a bench over by the other end and he's feeding a squirrel with some pieces of bread he's holding in his grimy hands. The squirrel hops right up and takes them out of his hands. That makes the guy smile and there's no teeth in his mouth. It looks like the entrance to a cave; or a hairless cunt. When the last of the bread's gone, he reaches into his overalls, which are so old and dirty you wonder how they stay on him, and pulls out some more bread, scrapes the scum off it, and offers it to the squirrel who rushes right back to him. Togetherness. Indian and Squirrel. Each one as intelligent as the other.

Real excitement at work. One of the waitresses, a mean old hag who's slightly hunchbacked—she reminds me of Dopey in *Snow White and the Seven Dwarfs*—can't find her purse when she's getting ready to leave for the day, so runs up and down the stairs screeching and screaming that it's been stolen. All the other women in the place start screeching and screaming, too, and before you know it there's so much hollering going on that Mrs. Waddling and the caretaker both waddle in as fast as they can to see who's been murdered.

"My purse! My purse!" she screeches. "Somebody's stolen it!"

"Now, now," honks Mrs. Waddling. "Let's not accuse anybody of theft before we've had a good look for it. Where did you leave it?" But Screecher is too uptight to hear what Waddling's saying. "My purse! I had five dollars in it and someone's stolen it!"

Everybody's looking all over the place trying to find the goddam thing—except me—and it's finally turned up in the can, where she'd left it when she went there.

"That's it! That's my purse!"

"There, you see now. There was no reason to accuse anyone here of theft, was there?"

"I didn't accuse anyone of theft! Who says I accused anyone of theft?" She grabs her miserable little purse that's got more years than her, and walks out the door glaring at everyone. I wink at her as she goes by, which makes her glare all the harder, her makeup all screwed up in the lines of her crow's face.

I go up to the bar and pour myself a vodka, making sure to put the right amount of water back into the bottle, and wonder if all old women turn out like her or Maggie. They're all so hung up, they shouldn't be allowed to walk the streets with ordinary people. One day they might flip their biscuits and knife somebody.

All people, when they get to be sixty, should be put to sleep like they do with the dogs. That way they're not a bother to nobody.

Like the woman I saw once leaving the Harmony at one in the morning, so stoned she couldn't even walk, so she crawled across Jarvis Street on her hands and knees. Lucky for her she was wearing a yellow dress. The cars went around her and she got across safely. We were standing on the sidewalk and we'd made a bet as to whether she'd get nailed or not. The guy who bet that she would was egging her on.

"Come on Grannie, just another few feet. Don't stop now baby. Watch out for that car!"

The rest of us were laughing so hard we thought we'd piss our pants. She looked so funny: crawling on the white line with her stockings ripped by the concrete, her purse open and dangling from her right arm, trailing bobby pins and things along her path, her head bobbing up and down and her mouth moving a mile a minute, although we couldn't catch a word she was saying. The cars slowing down as they noticed her, the drivers sticking their heads out the windows as if they couldn't believe what they were seeing, then speeding up when they got past.

On the other side she reached a lamp post and managed to get up. We all crossed as well, and the guy who'd won the bet took her arm and raised it in the air like you do to a boxer when he's won a fight.

"Here she is, ladies and gentlemen, the world champeen road-crawler!"

Talk about laughs. Man, we just couldn't laugh any louder. Our ribs were splitting and we couldn't even stand up straight.

Granny was still mumbling to herself and we shut up for a minute to catch what she was saying, but we still couldn't get a word. It must have been Polack or something like that. The guy who'd raised her arm said, "How does it feel to be champ? Tell the fans how it feels," and that broke us all up again cause her mumbling was getting louder.

We left her there and went over to Jay's place (he's a bootlegger) and got a bottle of rye off him and sat in the park drinking it till the Law made their rounds looking for bums and queers.

That was one time I didn't mind losing a buck. The laughs were worth it.

I tell Terry about the deal with the purse and she thinks it's terrible that the waitress should accuse us of stealing it before she even looked for it.

"At least I know you wouldn't have done it."

How right you are, kid, I thought. I sure as hell wouldn't risk six months in jail for five lousy bucks.

July 29

It didn't rain yesterday, but it's making up for it today. A real tropical storm. The wind's howling and the rain's coming down in sheets. I have my raincoat on, but even so when I reach the streetcar I'm practically soaked right through, that rain's coming down so hard.

Of course Mrs. Waddling, who should be swimming around outside enjoying the weather, asks me if I got wet. I'm stupid. I should have said "Of course not, Mrs. Waddling. On a nice sunny day like this?" instead of "You bet I did." What's the word George uses for people like her? Mediocrity, or something like that. Well, that's her all right, mediocrity.

One satisfaction today, though. Miss Virgin got even wetter than me. She was so soaked that even her bones were splashing around in her frame, and her hair was hanging all over her face so that you couldn't see it. An improvement, to say the least. Just to cheer her up, I say, "Is it still raining outside Miss Patterson?" with a dumb look on my mug so that she doesn't think I'm kidding her.

She doesn't even answer me, which shows that her manners are worse than mine, and squishes into the office leaving a trail of water behind her which one of the waitresses has to clean up with a rag after.

Terry got wet too and she's hung her clothes to dry over by the window. She hangs mine up as well, although they don't really need it now, and afterwards presses them. I spend half an hour reading a magazine I swiped from the Club. It's got an article in it on Latin America. It tells how happy the natives are in Mexico and what a great place it is to go on holidays. There's a couple of photos of a beach called Acapulco with some brown-skinned chicks lying on the sand trying to get even browner. They'll end up looking like niggers. They're real cute, too, and I close my eyes and imagine myself lying there on the beach beside them with the waves rolling in towards me and a chick on either side. I snap my fingers and one of them brings me a tall cool rum and Coke while the other one runs her fingers up and down my body and her lips tickle my ears.

Mrs. Himmel and her Cowboy are bashing around upstairs and the noise brings me back down to earth.

Sometimes I wish I had a million bucks just so I could do all the things that I see in the photographs and have fun like the women do in the Club who take off every winter for Bermuda and the Bahamas and all those other places around there.

But then, what's the use of dreaming. I'll never have a million bucks and I'll never be doing those things. I don't really give a damn, anyway. I can have just as much fun right here.

In bed Terry tells me about a dog she had at home called Rags, a mongrel they'd found one day outside the house. It used to follow her everywhere and she loved it very much, and one day it got run over by a car and she cried for weeks after. Her old man dug a little grave for the thing near the barn and every morning she'd pick some flowers and leave them on its grave. She said it was the best friend she ever had.

I'm not really listening cause thoughts of Acapulco and the chicks there are still going through my mind, but I notice that she's making some sobbing noises all by herself and I realize that she's crying over this mutt she once had. For some reason, I feel sorry for her dog, too, and I cradle her in my arms until she stops crying. Poor dumb Terry, all feelings and no brains. She won't get far in this city like that. Maybe she realizes that, though, and that's why she doesn't want to leave me. Old Daddy Michael. Tear-wiper for young girlies. Ha-ha.

July 30

Friday. Payday. On the way home from work I stop off at Silverstein's Second Hand Clothes Shop and pick an almost-new sports shirt. It's real sharp, with blue leaves on a white and brown background, and after arguing with Silverstein for fifteen minutes over the price, I get it for a buck.

"But you're going to drive me out of business," he bitches. "How I'm supposed to make a profit at this price is beyond me. And with a wife and two teenage sons at home, counting on me to bring home the food every night."

Silverstein's a little Jew with a scrawny face that looks as if he sucks lemons all day long. He carries on like this with everybody in Cabbagetown and if you didn't know the guy better, you'd end up paying him his price for the junk he's got to offer in his store. He gets it for practically nothing, too. Other salesmen use smiles, he uses tears.

One thing's for sure. It's not with creeps like him that Israel won the war.

George was burning mad when the Arabs and the Jews had a go at it in June. He was saying that the Jews were acting like Nazis and attacking innocent farmers and taking their land and killing them, and that the West, which is so ready to attack the Americans for what they're doing in Vietnam, was backing Israel all the way, even though they're doing the same thing.

The papers, and the women at the Club, were saying the opposite, that it was the Arabs who were trying to wipe out the Jews and that they were only defending themselves.

I usually take George's word in these things cause he knows what he's talking about and he's always got an answer for everything. He was brown from the sun at that time and with his long hair and that red silk scarf around his neck, he almost looked like an Arab himself.

"Watch out Silverstein doesn't see you," I joked at him, "or he'll send his army after you."

George even wanted to go and fight with the Syrians, who he said were the toughest Arabs there. All I said to that was that it's a long way to go just to get your brains blown out.

That day we got drunk in a bar near Yonge Street. We'd had about twelve beers each and we were so stoned that it took us about five minutes before we got up off the table and into the street. It was rush hour and the sidewalks were full of office people going home from work with that sour look office people always have when they're walking.

We staggered and stumbled our way up Yonge, bumping and knocking into people for about three blocks, with George yelling now and then into some startled face, "Palestine for the Palestinians!" or "Vietnam for the Vietnamese!" or "Yankee go home!" or "Louis Riel, where are you now that we need you?" Me, I wasn't saying anything cause I was having a hard enough time just keeping on my feet trying to keep up with him.

Suddenly George stopped dead, right in front of a skin store. You know what I mean, one of those places where they sell nothing but girlie and gay books and mags.

He turned to me and said, "Let's go in and have a look."

Inside there's about ten million colour magazines of naked broads standing in the sun, or sitting in their rooms, or sailing boats, or getting spanked, or kissing other broads. All of them smiling, with their tits in the air and their arms pointing at you, telling you to come over and play with them. I'm smiling back at one of them that must have at least a size sixty when George yells at me from across the room.

"Cowboy Queer!"

I bump my way over to where he is, ready to tell him to fuck off, I'm no queer, when I realize that he's beside the pocket book section and that he's just read out one of the titles.

I go over to the next section and yell back at him, "Video Virgin!"

He yells back, "Hot Hands!"

I look at the next title in the row, "Sex Peddler!"

The owner of the place, a skinny fairy with ears as big as an elephant's, looks up at us with one of those dirty looks you reserve for shoplifters or cops. He's reading this week's issue of *Flash*.

"Flesh Parade!"

"Creature of Sin!"

"Any Man Will Do!"

"Passion Pirate!"

"Love Mother, Love Daughter!"

"Stag Stripper!"

By this time the half-dozen sex fiends in the place have all stopped trying to get an orgasm by thumbing through the books, and are looking at us in a definitely pissed-off way. That just makes us try all the harder.

"Instant Love!"

"Wild Whip!"

"A nymph who turned men into candles and burned them at both ends!"

"All right, you guys," Fairy gets up from behind the counter, "what the hell are you trying to prove? If you're not going to buy anything, get the hell out of here." Man, he's so mad that his ears are flapping and his fairy face is all red. Some of the customers are leaving the dump and we start to walk out with them. Fairy keeps his bloodshot eyes on us as we leave.

"Sub-teen Sex!" George hollers out as we get near the door, and I put my arm behind a row of magazines and send the whole pile crashing to the ground.

We go out the door laughing our heads off, and I look back for one minute and see the fairy picking up the magazines and shaking his fist at us at the same time. I put my hand on my crotch and shake it back at him. His ears flap all the harder.

Anyway, that ended George's plan to go and fight for the Arabs that day and we walked home, our arms around each other's shoulders, singing "Roll Me Over in the Clover" and other popular songs.

Terry thinks my sports shirt is the greatest and it'll go well with my gray slacks. I think it will too, and just to prove it, we'll get dressed up tomorrow night and go out and have a drink.

July 31

Terry's done her hair up in some sort of a roll tight up on top, which makes her look older, and she's shortened the hem on her green dress, which makes her look sexier, so with my good slacks and my new shirt on, and her looking like a swinger, we make quite a pair as we walk into the Top Hat Tavern, which is smack in the middle of Cabbagetown.

It's a huge old wooden building pretty well the same as the Harmony House, except it's ten times as big. It's got a bouncer at the door, which gives it some sort of class, a guy seven feet tall and about as wide, with a scar running from his mouth to his ear. The place is packed and he makes us wait near the door until there's an empty table.

There must be at least forty thousand people in here and the noise is deafening. So deafening that you can't even hear what the group over near the end of the room is playing. You know it's Country and Western, though, cause they're dressed up in cowboy suits. There's three of them—two guys with guitars and a woman singing.

Terry says something to me, but I can't hear her due to the noise.

"What did you say?" I yell in her ear.

"I said, do you think we'll get a seat?" she yells back.

"Sure we will," I shout. "Won't we?" I yell at the bouncer, who's standing in front of us.

He looks at me. "What do you think I am, a fucking mind reader or something? I don't know buddy, just wait and see."

After that little speech he turns his back on us and glares at the crowd. Any other guy saying that to me, I'd bust his head open, but Little Ernie (that's all he goes by) doesn't mean anything by the way he talks, it's just that's the only way he can express himself. He's been a sailor on cargo ships most of his life.

Finally, there's an empty table and we run over to it before someone grabs it. It's in the middle of the room and the noise here is worse. A loud roar that goes on and on without stopping.

Beside us there's two truck-driver-type guys with their Sunday suits on and their wives beside them, two frowzy blondes, one fat, one skinny, and both with last week's makeup still on. They're stoned already, and God knows, it's only ten o'clock.

I look around for the waiter but I don't see him anywhere. Terry looks kind of stunned. She turns towards me and says, "I hope this bar isn't like the first one you took me to."

"Hell no," I answer back. "This joint's much classier."

Splash. Splash. The waiter dumps two draughts on our table and holds his hand out waiting for the money. I give him fifty cents, and he pockets the change before I've offered to give it to him and moves on to the next table. Splash. Splash. Splash. Splash. It sounds like you need a raincoat around here.

One of the blondes has stuck her leg out from the table and has lifted her skirt right up to her ass so she can adjust her stocking. The two guys keep talking together as if nothing has happened. She gets kinda mad about that and shouts to the other blonde so that everybody can hear her, "Look at that, a run in my stocking, and I just got them yesterday." The other blonde looks at the run and says, "Gee that's too bad." The guys keep talking to themselves. Everybody else is looking, though, and that gives blonde number two, the fat one, the guts to lift up her skirt and tell the whole world, "I bought these a week ago and they're still as good as new." Finally one of the guys turns to the broads and tells them to go up to the stage if they want to do a striptease. That makes them pull their skirts down a bit and the guys go back to their conversation.

By that time we've finished our beers, and the waiter comes by again to slop two more glasses on the table, which is so wet by now it looks like the Don River. Terry says she doesn't want any more cause she's scared of getting drunk like last time. I tell her not to worry about it, that two beers never hurt anybody. The waiter keeps the change again and that's starting to bug me. The least he can do is let me offer it to him.

Terry sips her beer, pretending not to notice the skinny blonde, who's dragged her other leg out from under the table and is looking for runs on that stocking.

The noise in here is beating on my ears. Terry's talking again, but I can't catch a word. She leans over the table. "Why don't we go somewhere else, Michael?"

"Oh come on, baby, we just got here," I answer, smiling at her, and she leans back on her chair without saying anything else.

Behind all that roar I can actually hear a few snatches of song now and then. That means that my ears are getting used to the racket. I smile at Terry again and hold out my hand to her. She takes it and smiles back. That should keep her quiet for a while.

Two frogs walk by, small heavy guys with black hair and eyes, and leer at the skinny blonde, who's still got her skirt hiked up her legs. They say something in French to each other and laugh. That makes the fat blonde start hiking her skirt again, and the only thing that stops her pulling it all the way up is a belt on the side of her dumb noggin from her man, who's interrupted his conversation long enough to let her have it. The other guy turns to the skinny blonde and tells her to pull her skirt down before she makes the customers puke. That cuts them right down to size, and they both sit there without saying a word and drain their glasses.

Behind us there's an Indian woman sitting alone with a beer held between her hands. She's talking to herself and it goes something like this: "De wite mans, dey only wan me when deys wanna fuck.

Dey sez dat's all Injun womans good for. How come all de wite mans like dat?"

She takes a swig out of her glass and looks up for a minute. I guess she's about fifty. Her hair looks like it's never seen a comb and there's pockmarks on her face like Dottie has. VD probably. All Indian women get that some time or other. She's sort of fat and she's wearing a man's shirt and an old skirt with a rip down the side, men's socks and a pair of house slippers. Her clothes are dirty, she's red-eyed, and she smells.

"Dey all tells ya dey loves ya when dey wanna fuck ya, and after dey tells ya dirty Injun."

Terry's looking shocked at the woman. I feel like telling her that that's all they're good for anyway, but she wouldn't understand.

The waiter comes by again and we have two more beers, although I can see that Terry's not feeling like having any more. She looks at the full glass of white foam and yellow liquid with disgust.

"Really Michael, I don't think I can take any more," she says, looking at me with her sad doggy eyes. Me, I pick up my glass and bash it against hers, saying cheers (which is what they say in England) and winking at the same time.

I down half of it with one gulp and she takes a small sip out of hers. You can see she's not really in the mood. Guess I better cheer her up.

"It's Saturday, honey. Hell, I've been working hard all week and this is the only day I get a chance to have a ball."

She gives a half-hearted smile.

"Besides, I can't help but drink, having the swellest-looking chick in Cabbagetown sitting at my table."

She smiles with her teeth showing and says something like "Oh Michael."

"I mean, there's guys that'd give their right ball and maybe their left ball too, to have a doll like you to keep them company." She blushes and chuckles at the same time and picks up her beer for another little sip. Way to go, Mike kid. You done it again.

A glass falls to the floor where the blondes are sitting and the fat one, who dropped it, turns to her old man and tells him to order her another beer. He answers that she's had enough and she gets in a huff over that, says to her girl friend, "Come on" and they both get up off the table and head for the ladies' john. The two guys don't even look up.

Out of the corner of my eye I spot the two Frenchmen, who are sitting further down the row, get up on their feet and swagger off after the blondes. As they pass my table I notice that one of the husbands gives them the eye for a second and points them out to his buddy.

"Why do de wite mans call me squaw alla time. My name Helen. He call me squaw, but he fuck me jus same as a wite womans."

The frogs have caught up to the blondes and they've just said something funny to them cause all four are laughing. They're standing in a corner by the john and the guys have got them on the inside of the corner with their backs to the wall. One of the blondes is pretending to adjust her brassiere strap and her hand on it is making her right tit jerk up and down like a rubber ball. The frogs are looking at it like it was a fifty dollar bill and the broads are getting a real kick out of it.

"At least you've got good stockings," shouts the other blonde. "They're not ripped like mine. Just look at them," and up goes her skirt again.

The Frenchies figure they've got it made for the night. They move in closer to the broads and wink at each other. And that's the last thing they do.

The husbands, who've been keeping an eye on the whole show, get up when blonde number two starts the bit with her stockings. They march up the aisle and just when the Frenchies wink at each other, the heavier of the two, who's the husband of the fat one, picks up a chair from the table nearest the john and slams it down on the head of one of the Frenchies. He slides against the wall and rolls to the floor, his eyes still full of the sight of the blonde's tit. Man, like he never knew what hit him. The second guy grabs the other Frenchie by the throat and opens his face with a broken glass that he's got in his hand. Frenchie screams and puts his arms in front of his face to protect himself. The glass twists into his crotch, and when his arms drop towards his cut balls, he gets another swipe in the face.

Jesus, this guy's a pro. Talk about a cut job. That's one of the best I've ever seen. Frenchie didn't stand a chance. Face, crotch, face. He's sitting on the floor beside his buddy, who's still knocked out, bleeding like Niagara Falls and crying like a kid. The whole bar's in an uproar. Everybody's got up and rushed over to see what's happening and it takes Little Ernie about five minutes of pushing and hitting people before he gets to the scene of the massacre. Some women are screaming and just everybody else is yelling. Some of the smart ones are getting out before the Law comes. Terry's sitting stiff as a board, her face pale as a ghost, her hands held together so tight her knuckles are turning white, and her eyes wide open in horror. Like a scene out of *Psycho*.

Everybody's up and milling about except Terry, me, and the Indian woman, who acts like nothing's happened. That's when the cops come barging in, two at first and five more a few minutes later. They push the crowd out of the way and bend over the two Frenchies. I can't see a thing from where I'm sitting because of the people but I can tell that the frog who got carved up is in a serious state cause there's the sound of a siren, and a couple of ambulance attendants come whipping in the bar. The cops and Little Ernie make room for them by pushing some people against the wall and the ambulance guys put the Frenchie on the stretcher. He's groaning something terrible and for a second I get a glimpse of him: blood on his face, on his shirt, on his pants, running down his legs. He won't be hustling the girls for a while. Then the crowd moves forward again and all I can see is the heads of the attendants as they whip the guy out of the place. The other Frenchie's up on his feet by now. He's holding the back of his head and apart from a little blood on his hair, he looks okay. Then the cops hustle him and the two guys who did the damage out to a waiting paddy wagon.

Everybody starts to sit down again until someone yells, "Hey, look at that! They're fighting the fuzz!" The herd jams the hall and the exit door and in sixty seconds the dump's empty, which gives me the chance of draining a few glasses on some of the other tables, since mine's already finished.

I gulp down two or three nearly full ones and sit down again before they start coming back in.

Terry's still got the same look on her face. Christ, you'd think she'd been raped or something. I reach over and separate her hands before she breaks every bone in them.

"Hey baby, what's the matter?" I ask her. "Don't tell me you're all shook up about the fight. Hell, that was nothing, you shoulda seen the ones we got into when I was running around with the gang."

She blinks her eyes and looks at me, tries to smile and gives it up as a lost cause. She puts her hands back together again. Then she says, "Please, Michael, let's get out of here. Let's go home. Please. I'm feeling sick."

"Sure honey, anything you say," and I get up. It's a good idea cause in the first place they'll probably close the place for the night, and also some of the joes outside will be coming back soon and they're going to notice that someone's drunk their booze.

The Indian woman's still sitting there with the glass between her hands. I help Terry up cause she really does look sick. A few minutes of fresh air outside will clear that up.

"If I had some moneys, I go back to de reserve. Dere's no wite mans dere."

Outside the crowd's breaking up, but it's easy to see that there was a fight, like the guy said. There's still a couple of cops hanging around, and groups of people are talking in loud voices. Someone yells from across the street, "Every cop kicked in the nuts means one less cop who's going to have cop kids." I take it from that, that a cop got booted. Probably by one of the guys who got arrested.

Haw. Haw. Haw. Everyone laughs at that and one of the cops looks across to see who said it, but there's a bunch of guys all together and after trying to scare them with a hard look, he goes back to the door of the bar where he was standing before with the other cop.

I know who it is, though. It's Jerry and I haven't seen him since that afternoon at the faggot bar, so I grab Terry by the arm and steer her across the street to where he's standing with half a dozen buddies.

They're still laughing and talking together, so I have to punch him on the shoulder before he turns around and spots me.

"Mike baby!" he puts his arm over my shoulder. "Hey how're you doing man! Geez, haven't seen you in a month of Sundays. What happened, you tried to make a butch one night and she cut your knockers off?"

He slaps me on the back, nearly knocking my lungs out the front of my chest, and laughs. Real funny, I think. About as funny as a truckload of dead babies. That's what bugs me about Jerry, he's got a mouth like a sewer—it's always spewing out loads of shit, but I stick around, clowning with him and being introduced to the guys he's hanging around with, because he's always got something to drink at home and I'm still feeling thirsty.

Terry, who's starting to look half human again, asks me what a butch is and I look at her without believing what I've just heard. "It's a lesbian," I answer and wonder if she's putting me on or if she's really that stupid. Everybody, but everybody, knows what a butch is. Except, of course, if you're brought up on a farm and got nothing to play around with but the chickens and the cows.

I talk about old times with Jerry for a while and crack jokes with the guys. Hell, it feels good. Been a long time, all right, since I've done this. That's what happens when you get tied up with a broad. You drop all your buddies, and that's a bad thing cause you never know when you might need them. Like tonight, with the bar closed and the Harmony House too far away.

"Who's the chick?" Jerry asks, noticing for the first time that I've got one with me.

"Her name's Terry," I answer. He gives her a good up and down look for a minute then turns back to his buddies just as Terry's raising her hand to shake it with him.

We all stand around for about ten minutes and I'm getting tired of just standing there and I'm ready to admit that there'll be no party at Jerry's tonight, which means no more booze for the night, so I say to Terry, "Well let's hit the road," when Jerry puts his arm around my shoulder again and says, "We got some tail waiting for us in the car. Wanna come over to my place and have a party? Bring your chick." He winks at me.

It's about goddam time.

"Hey," I say, "that sounds groovy. Yeah sure, we'll come, won't we Terry?" Terry nods her head and looks like she's going to drop dead on the spot. So what if she doesn't want to drink, she can sit there and listen to the radio.

So me and Jerry and Terry and another guy pile into Jerry's bomb, a '56 Ford with a '62 Thunderbird motor and no muffler. Jerry lays about fifty feet of rubber right past the cops and we all laugh as they run out to the middle of the street and try to get the number of his licence plate. Hell, by the time they got their notebooks out we're already half a mile up the street, the bomb making a roar like an atomic fart.

By the time we hit Dundas we're doing seventy and I'm starting to get nervous, not cause I'm scared of an accident, but because we've all been drinking and if the cops pull us over we've all had it. The two broads are in the back seat with Terry and me. One of them's Indian and she's got a face that shows what she's been doing the last thirty years of her life—drinking and screwing. She's wearing a faded blue skirt and a tight sweater and her black hair hangs down past her shoulders. Ten years ago she probably looked all right but now she's just a has-been. She's been through the mill, and ten years from now she'll end up like the other Indian broad in the bar tonight.

The one beside her sitting next to the window is about the same age. She's white, with close-cropped hair like someone who's just got out of prison, and wearing a pant suit that's about a size too big for her.

They're both stoned right out of their minds and they're having a ball shouting out the window at other cars.

"Hey, fuckface, you wanna drag?"

"Whassa matter, you got no balls?"

The Indian, her name's Delia, puts her arms around Jerry and says "C'mon honey, step on it."

"Yeah, stuff this car right up their fat asses," squawks the other one, who goes by the name of Doris, though I'll bet a buck that's not her right name.

Terry huddles in closer to me and throws me a look that says what are we doing here Michael, we should be home. Jerry wheels around a corner on two wheels and everybody piles up on top of everybody else.

"Jesus Christ, what you trying to do, get us all thrown in the can?" I yell at Jerry, who's laughing his head off with the other guy, and the broads in the back seat joining in. Stupid bunch of clowns.

"Don't worry bout it Mike," Jerry answers over his shoulder, "we're almost there."

"Whassa matter, you scared?" pipes in the other guy. Greasy little bastard, if I lose my cool tonight, it'll be with him. He's got a bony face and so much Brylcreem on his hair it shines in the dark. Hairy arms and a beak like a parrot's. Thin lips and two black eyes that turn around on the seat now and then to look up Terry's dress.

I ignore him for the moment and turn to Jerry again. "I hope you at least got a driver's licence." He passes a car, crossing the white line and just missing a car driving the other way.

"Sure I got one," he answers, laughing, "but it's in the cop shop right now. They took it off me for six months."

Great.

Suddenly he brakes to a stop, throwing us all forward, which makes the broads squeal, and says, "Everybody out, we're here."

I step out on the sidewalk and look around and say to myself, Hell, after all that driving we're only half a mile away from my place. That crazy bastard, at least he better have lots of booze.

"Geez, what a dump," says the Indian, holding on to Jerry like he was the Rock of Gibraltar.

"It better have a good bed," giggles the other broad. "After two years in Mercer sleeping on a board, I'm ready to give my right arm for a bed with a real mattress, clean sheets and a soft pillow."

"Shit," says Greasehead, "it's not your right arm you'll be giving tonight to get on a bed, you can be sure of that."

Doris giggles again and runs her hand up the jerk's pant leg. "Well, what are we waiting for?" she says.

I was right, she *has* been in prison. Probably tough as nails, too. Just spent two years without a man, and that barrel of Brylcreem's getting her. I'm starting to get seriously pissed off, and we haven't even begun drinking yet.

His room's bigger than mine and he's got a carpet, too. And a double bed, right smack in the middle of the room. Two chairs and a table with three legs. A light bulb hanging from a single cord and a table lamp. Greasehead and the two broads pile on the bed and Terry and me grab a chair each while Jerry fishes a twenty-sixer of rye and a mickey of rum out of the closet.

"Sorry, gang, but I got nothing to drink it with, unless you want water," he says as he passes each of us a glass.

"So, who needs anything? Just hand that bottle over, cutie," says the prison broad, "and I'll show you how a real woman drinks." She grabs the bottle out of his hands (the rye) and guzzles about a quarter of it before stopping to get her breath.

"Hey," screams Delia, wrestling the bottle out of her hand, "leave something for us, eh."

"Up yours. Haven't had a decent drink in so long I forget what the stuff tastes like."

Greasehead puts his hands on one of her legs and squeezes. "You sure know how to hold the stuff," he says to her, slobbering as he talks. "That's nothing Dino, wait'll I really get a few in me. I'll show you what I can do," she answers and uncrosses her legs so he can get a better hold of them.

So the guy's a lousy wop. What the hell's he doing around here? This isn't his district. He's still grabbing a look at Terry's legs, too. Christ, the sonafabitch's got two pieces of snatch next to him, what else does he want?

We've each got a full glass of rye and Jerry's sat down beside Delia. Terry's taken a little sip and that makes her cough. We all laugh and she gets red in the face.

Jerry turns to Greasehead and says that's the first time he's seen me with a broad who can't drink. Greasehead answers that broads that can't drink can do other things and they all go into hysterics over that. Terry's face is so red it looks like a baby's ass after a good spanking. Someone turns the radio on and switches the light bulb off so there's only the table lamp to see by. We finish our drinks and

Jerry fills us up again. Terry's still got her first drink but she gets some more poured in anyway. "Gosh, Michael, I'm going to get drunk again," she whispers in my ear, and I tell her, "Don't worry, I'll carry you home if you do." There's some real cool R. and B. on the radio and Jerry's grabbed Delia and is dancing with her, their hips together and their asses rotating in unison. She's kissing his ear and he's got his right hand cupped over her butt.

Greasehead gulps his second drink down, waits for Doris to finish hers, pushes her across the bed and lays down beside her. Their legs dangle over the edge of the bed.

Terry looks kind of embarrassed. She sips her drink slowly and smiles at me once in a while without saying anything. Me, I'm busy trying to imagine which of the two broads would make the best lay.

My guess is Doris. When she came in she took off the jacket of her pant suit and showed off a nice pair of tits. Also, she just got out of jail and she's got hot pants. But Delia's got a nice ass, and from what I've heard she doesn't mind using it either, and full lips like a Negro woman. I'm sure she knows more tricks than Doris, but then Doris'll probably give you a wilder ride for your money.

"Ouch!" squeals Delia, "don't bruise the merchandise." Jerry laughs and pinches her ass again.

"You gotta know what you're buying these days, and the only way to tell is by touching it."

Delia stops dancing, takes a swig from her glass and tells Jerry that seein's as good as feelin'. Jerry answers, "Yeah, when there's something to see," and Delia says, "Well take a look at this," turns around, bends over, and flips her skirt over her waist. She's not wearing anything underneath. Jerry whistles and Greasehead stops feeling his broad so he can get a good look. He whistles too and says he hasn't seen a nicer pair of cheeks since his sister got married and moved out of the house, which makes Delia so happy she shakes her butt up and down and right and left like a stripteaser, which excites Jerry so much that he pinches it again which makes her squeal again and move her butt all the faster.

Terry puts her hand on my arm and tells me with her eyes, let's go home, but I pull my arm away and give her a dirty look. I want to tell her that this is the first party we've been to together and she should enjoy it, but I'm too busy watching the Indian. There's a fast R. and R. on the radio and the guys are clapping their hands to the rhythm and telling Delia "Faster baby, show us what you can do," and Delia bends down lower and pulls the skirt higher till it covers her head and the only thing you can see are her enormous cheeks bobbing and twitching on top of her legs, which are spread wide apart so you can see her cunt if you bend down a bit. Jerry pinches them again and Greasehead gives them a pinch too and Delia's going faster and faster till it seems that her ass is really a mouth and she's talking to you. I'm starting to sweat and I light up a cigarette and offer one to Terry who takes it and starts coughing again after the first drag, but this time no one notices.

Doris, who's been watching, propped up on the bed with her elbows, finishes off her fourth or fifth glass, stands up and says, "Shit, is that the best you can do?" Her face is flushed as she takes off her blouse and pants and stands in her underclothes in front of the guys till they turn around to look at her. God, but she's got a nice pair! And slim legs and a real tight little butt. Greasehead puts his hand on her left tit and pats her bum with his other hand and says to Jerry, who still hasn't made up his mind which way to look, "How's this for a real piece?" which makes Delia bounce her bum harder still, but it's Doris's turn now and after a couple more twitches she stands up straight and pours herself a drink. "Come on," says Greasehead, "whattaya waiting for, Christmas?"

"Up yours," she answers, then pops her tits out of the top of her brassiere, so that they stand out straight ahead like the women you see in the *Playboy* cartoons. "You like them?" she says to Greasehead, pushing them under his chin, and as he leans over to get a mouthful she backs off giggling and pushes them under Jerry's face, "and you?" "Not bad," Jerry answers, lifting his glass to his mouth, "but I seen better."

I think Jerry likes an ass more than anything else cause Doris's boobs are really delicious. They look like they'd melt in your mouth. She comes over to me and says, "And you, baby face, you ever had a real woman's tits in your hands?" I says, "Ever since my mother all

I've had is real tit." I'm dying to grab them, put them in my mouth, squeeze them so hard they'll burst, but what can I do with Terry there? She struts past Terry and laughs at her embarrassment, then faces the guys who have sat down on the bed with Delia between them and says, "Ready fellows? Watch this," takes off her brassiere and starts bouncing her tits in the air. They go around, sideways, up and down, every direction possible and then some, and her hardly moving at all, like those things got a life of their own. Man, I never seen anything like it, not even at the Victory Burlesque where they got pros. (We got kicked out of there once for throwing a water bomb at one of the strippers. Got her right square on her tummy. She jumped a mile.)

Terry's closed her eyes. Jerry and Greasehead are so horny that one of them's put his hand up Delia's dress and the other one's jerking off with one hand and feeling her tit with the other. He's pulled it right out of her dress and it's hanging there like a ripe melon and he's pinching her nipple. Her eyes are closed too. The music seems to be getting louder and the only other sound in the room is the wheezing and panting over on the bed. I finish the rest of my glass and pour another, filling up Terry's at the same time. "I couldn't take any more," Terry says, trying her hardest to avoid the scene in front of us, her eyes looking straight at me. "Drink," I answer, "drink."

She takes another sip and while the glass is still to her lips I tip it up so that she gets a whole mouthful. She chokes and part of the rye dribbles down her mouth and on her dress. She takes a hanky out of her purse and tries to wipe it up before it makes a stain. She's coughing.

"Oh Michael, what did you do that for?" she cries, her eyes open wide for the first time since we got here.

"Hell," I smile at her all friendly-like so she won't think I'm being mean, "if you don't learn to drink now while you're young, you'll never learn. And you can't go through life like that."

"Oh, you're always teasing me," she says and smiles back. One of her real cute doggy smiles which makes her look about twelve years old. I pull her chair closer to mine and give her a soul kiss, tongue and all, till she gasps for breath. My hand's on her tit.

"Not here, Michael," she gasps, drawing away after a minute or so. "Please not here."

Jerry and the dago have lifted Delia's skirt up and they're pulling some of her hairs out. "Hey, cut that out," she tells them and tries to put her hand over her snatch, but they each grab one of her hands and hold it behind her back while they pull hairs with their free hands. She squeals, she shouts, she wriggles all over the place. They laugh. They pull hairs, counting them as they tear them out—"fifteen, sixteen, seventeen."

"You guys are gonna leave me like plucked chicken," she complains, but she's loving every minute of it. Terry looks sick again.

Jerry looks up at Doris, who's stopped throwing her breasts all over the place since nobody's paying any attention to her, and tells her to get them a drink. "A working man needs a drink now and then, just so he can keep working," he says, laughing as he pulls out another hair—"twenty-eight."

"Up yours," she says as she fills up two glasses with what's left of the rye and hands it to them, which makes them stop pulling Delia's hairs. They gulp down the stuff and Doris opens the rum, takes a stiff swallow, burps, and jumps on top of them on the bed. For a minute there's nothing but a tangle of legs, arms, tits, screams, laughs and curses. There's the sound of something getting ripped and Doris's panties go flying towards the floor.

"Cocksucker," she shouts, sitting up, "you tore my only pair of pants."

"So, be like Delia," Greasehead shouts back, dragging her back to the bed. "Don't wear pants."

"Right," giggles Delia, "they get in the way when you feel like a quickie."

Jerry's pants fall down to his ankles and he straddles Delia. They bounce up and down on the bed like two rubber balls. They groan, they gasp, her fingernails leave marks on his back, his ass goes up and down, and it's all over.

Doris is saying to the wop, "What about us honey? I haven't had it for two years. What about us, huh?"

The wop, he's too busy looking at Jerry and Delia. I pour myself some rum and turn around to see him looking at Terry again, his eyes blazing. Terry, she don't notice a thing cause she put her hands over her eyes when they started balling.

So that's why he hasn't banged the prison broad yet!

I go over to him and Doris and say to Doris, "Maybe he thinks you're not good enough for him." He throws me a dirty look and says, "Go worry about your piece buddy, I'll worry about mine." But that's done the trick. He's either got to do something with her or tell her to fuck off.

She pulls his zipper down and sticks her hand inside, and he's touching her tits, and they're both kissing after a minute. Jerry grabs Delia's dress and wipes himself off with it. She doesn't even seem to notice. Her eyes are still closed and her mouth is open. That girl sure likes her sex.

The radio's blaring another fast R. and R. and I'm not feeling so hot any more. That fucking Greasehead eyeing my broad like that has given me the bugs and I feel like zapping him. No fights for me tonight, though. You never know if somebody will call the cops. Hell, we're making enough noise as it is.

"Hey Terry," she looks up at me, "wait'll I go piss and we'll go home right after, okay?"

She nods her head and says, "Yes. Oh yes, please." Man, did you ever in your life see anyone as eager as her to leave a party? It shows what farm living does to you.

The john's at the end of the hall, and as I go out the door of Jerry's room the door next to his opens and an old bald-headed guy in his pyjamas steps out and gets in front of me so I can't get past him, and me wanting to piss so bad I can taste it.

"Y-Y-You, you, you g-g-g-guys-s-s m-mak-k-ing s-s-s-o-o m-m-m-uch noise-e-e, I-I c-can't s-s-s-sleep."

Oh Christ almighty, he stutters yet. I'll be pissing my pants for sure before he's finished whatever the hell he's going to say.

"Look pop, grab me after, eh? I gotta go to the john right now."

No use, he doesn't move. His mouth starts making strange sounds and his lips twist around like a bowl of boiled spaghetti. "One,

one s-s-s-econd y-y-oun-young m-m-an, do y-you re-re-re-alize th-th-that it-it's thr-three o'o'clock i-i-in the-the mo-mor-morning?"

"Hey pop," I yell and point towards his room, "there's a fire in your bed!" He turns and looks and I slip behind and whip into the john like a bat out of hell. Man, does that feel good. I'll bet I pissed at least ten gallons. I comb my hair with my hands, splash some water on my face cause I'm starting to feel a bit hungover by now, and head back for the room. I'm almost there when old fuckface jumps in front of me and blocks the hall again, his mouth moving a mile a minute.

"Y-Y-Y-Y-Y" (Oh great, he's so mad he can't even get the first word out) "Y-Y-You y-y-young p-p-p-unk-k, th-th-th-the best" (Way to go pop, you got a whole word out) "cu-cu-cure for-r pu-pu-punks-s-s l-like y-y-ou is-is a-a-a-a-a g-g-ood-d th-thr-thr-thra-*shing*!" He spits out *shing* like it was a bad tooth.

Christ, what a way to end a Saturday night.

"And you know the best cure for a guy who stutters?" I ask him, putting on my best smile. That catches him off guard and he steps back, his goggle eyes wide open. "W-W-What?"

"Shut up!" I scream in his face and dodge past him and into the room.

Of course, I knew what was bound to happen if I left Terry alone for five minutes. She's still sitting on the chair just like I left her, but Greasehead, that fucking Greasehead, is standing over her trying to pour a glassful of rum down her throat. She's moving her head from side to side trying to avoid it, but that mother-fucking wop is pouring it over her closed lips anyway, and the stuff's running over her chin and onto her dress. The two broads and Jerry are watching the show with ear-to-ear grins, lying there naked, smoking. Nobody's noticed me come in.

Terry looks really scared, but since they're all laughing she's trying to treat it like a joke too.

"Come on now, a big girl like you can take a few drinks, can't she?" He's right in front of her so close that his legs are straddling her knees, and he's holding a cigarette in one hand and that fucking glass of rum in the other.

"No really, I-I don't think I'd like any more thank you," she answers, so weak I can hardly hear her. She tries to smile, but what she wants to do is cry.

"No really, I don't think I'd like any more thank you," he shouts out, mimicking her voice. "Just try, sweetheart, just try, just close your sweet little eyes and imagine it's that gearbox boy friend of yours who's offering you a drink." He slops some more rum down her face. The creeps on the bed are howling like they been given a dose of laughing gas, and that's when I let him have it.

He never knows what hits him. I spin him around real hard and right at the moment that he's face to face with me I chop him in the windpipe and boot him in the shins twice real fast, and he pitches to the ground like a pine tree, gasping for breath, his hands around his throat, his face turning blue, his eyes popping out of his head. I jump in the air and land heels first on his balls and he doubles over like a toothpick snapped in two. There's no sound out of him now, just his face twisted out of shape, looking like the fucking ape he is.

The whole bit's taken about thirty seconds and it's all happened so fast that nobody's even moved. I stand there staring at that thing on the floor for a moment, and then look at the rest of this sad crew. The two broads are just lying there with their mouths open a foot.

"Geez," says Doris when she gets her breath back. "Geez." Delia says nothing, and Jerry's just getting off the bed now.

"You haven't croaked the guy, have you Mike?" He's sweating and he's real scared.

I feel like spitting in his face. "If I did, it's your own goddam fault. What the Christ did you let him do that to my girl for, you stupid prick?"

"Hell, Mike, it was just a joke. You don't kill a guy over a joke."

"Yeah, it was just a joke," mumbles Doris.

Christ, I'm so uptight right now, I'll murder all three of them if they say one more word. "Come on Terry, get up for Christ's sake!" I yell at her cause since I went to work on this greasy piece of sewage lying here on the floor Terry hasn't moved, like it was her I'd creamed. But she hears my voice and slowly, very slowly, she gets up on her feet and walks over to my side. "Get your purse," I tell her and when she's done that I open the door and push her out into the hall. Before I close it, I look at the guy and his eyes are rolling around in his head and there's a hiss coming out of his throat, so I know he's not dead. Jerry's still standing there and Delia hasn't moved. Doris is pouring a drink into her glass. Her hand's shaking.

"Tell that piece of wop shit that if I ever see him again, I'll finish what I didn't do tonight," I yell at all of them, pointing my finger at him, then I slam the door and push Terry down the hall and out the front door.

I'm mad, real mad. I walk up the street so fast that Terry can't keep up with me, so I have to pull her along by the arm. She almost trips once on a curb, but I yank her arm and she's on her feet again, half-running, half-walking. The wind's blowing and her hair's all over her face, and I walk fast so she's running and I can hear her breathing hard, but I keep going fast and finally we get home. Inside I open a beer and guzzle it down in ten seconds flat and open another one and light up a cigarette. Terry undresses, puts on her nightgown and goes to the john with a paper bag in her hand, and by the time she gets back I'm in bed and the lights are off. She gets into bed and says the first thing since we left the party: "Michael, all that's happened tonight, it-it scared me so much that my period's started."

Jesus Christ, is that all she has to say?

August 1

It's about six in the morning before I get to sleep. Tossing and turning and wondering just how bad I hurt that guy.

When I wake up it's twelve o'clock and I'm tired as hell and feeling hungover, but I get up anyway and pour some water on my face. Terry's up, too, and she hands me a coffee she just made. It's scalding hot, but I drink it down fast and I feel better after.

I eat some cornflakes and have another cup of coffee while Terry's washing. She looks better now that she's combed her hair and washed. She says, "Good morning Michael," and comes over and gives me a kiss. That makes me nervous and I stop eating my cornflakes. She pours herself a coffee and sits down opposite me, all smiles as if nothing had happened last night.

"What's so good about it?" I snap at her.

She says nothing but she looks at me in a real queer way. Her eyes are bright with excitement, like she's just made love or something.

"I said, what's so good about it?" I yell at her, her smile bugging the ass off me.

"Michael," she hesitates, "I was scared last night. I don't think I've ever been so scared in my whole life. What happened in that bar was just horrible." She stops again, fingering her cup, looking puzzled. "And after in that party, I really don't know what to say. That fellow was disgusting and I didn't know what to do. He kept pushing that glass against my lips and laughing at me, and you weren't there."

"Yeah, but I came back, remember?" I cut in to get her to finish her little speech before I really blow my top.

"Yes, you came back and what you did to him was—was, well it was wonderful! Oh Michael," she gets up off the chair and throws herself against my chest, her arms around me, "nobody has ever defended me before like you did last night. I felt like a little rag doll sitting all alone in that room until you beat him up and then, I-I felt like a queen, like a queen who's loved so much by her king that he dies for her honour. Oh, I don't know how to explain it," she kisses me hard on the lips, "I can only say thank you a million times. I'll never forget what you did for me. I love you. I adore you." She kisses me again and again, her hands fly up to my face and stroke my cheeks, my eyes, my lips. She smiles, she stares with a love look like you see in the movies. She kisses me over and over. "Oh, I didn't think a man could love me so much that he'd risk his life for me."

For a minute there I'm beat. I mean, how can you get mad at a broad who's calling you the greatest guy in the world, but when she says that bit about risking my life for her, I'm myself again. Dammit, I didn't risk my life over that dumb wop, I didn't give him a chance to touch me, but the point is that maybe I've killed him or busted him up real bad and the Law comes looking for me. And the Law comes looking for me. *And the Law comes looking for me!*

I push her off me and she asks what's the matter, did I say something wrong? I want to tell her a million things, everything that's bugging me since last night, but how in hell can you expect a dummy like her to understand? It'd be like talking to Miss Virgin about sex.

Like how I quit school in grade nine, mostly cause most of my buddies were doing the same thing, or they'd got kicked out; and my old lady yelling that I'm gonna turn out a bum like my old man and the old man yelling "Whattaya mean I'm a bum," and them fighting; and me going over to Blow Job's and spending the day with the gang drinking Cokes, playing the juke box, standing on the sidewalk watching the cars and telling each other what we'd do if we had one, like putting double mufflers and fuel injectors and things on it so it'd go faster than any cop car around, and whistling at the chicks and asking them if they wanna screw, and combing our hair and dusting off our shoes and saying gotta blow when it's supper time; and going back home and the old man asking "Well, ya found a job yet?" and the old lady saying I'll turn into a bum like him and him saying "Whattaya mean, like me?" and they're both stoned.

Eating whatever the hell's in the fridge and buggering off as fast as I can ("Don't stay out all night, ya hear?") and meeting the guys in front of the restaurant again. Always the same guys—Spike, Timmy the Wart, Handsome Harry (who looks like a boiled potato), the Kid, and sometimes, when he's not doing thirty days for something or other, Dirty Doug. Lots of other guys, too, but I've forgotten their names, or they're not here any more. And the chicks—Jane, who's so goofy she got kicked out of grade four; Marilyn, who swears like a truck driver and who's got the fastest boot in Cabbagetown; Ladeda Linda, who's stuck up and won't go with anyone except Spike; Hairy Mary, who won't screw cause she's scared of having a kid, so she gives hand jobs (she's only twelve); and Sally the Squaw. She's half-Indian and thirteen and has two boobs the size of footballs and she's been screwing since she was seven and she's good at it. Doesn't tease around like the other ones. Once we had her drop her pants in the men's john at Blow Job's, and she did it standing up cause the place was too small to lay down.

At night, going over to the Gardens and bugging the queers for a while and maybe punching out a bum or two for the hell of it, or if we got tired of that, going over to the boys' club in a church near the park and busting up whatever they're doing. Breaking the pop bottles, feeling up the chicks in there, thumping a couple of guys (they always bawled, and that'd make us hit them harder), and blowing the joint before the cops came.

We were always scheming ways of making a fast buck, like we always needed the bread for booze or Mary Jane or safes or a new comb.

Drinking a lot in those days, sitting in the park or behind a church. Three or four of us with maybe Hairy Mary with her hand down our pants while we passed the bottle around. Almost got caught once, too. A cop comes up the alley with his flashlight and shines it right in our eyes. Spike was with us that time and he's a fast thinker. He throws the bottle at the cop, and as he ducks we jump over a fence and run like hell down another alley, over another fence, and into Blow Job's. When we get there we see that Dirty Doug and Hairy Mary aren't with us.

Hairy Mary we don't ever see again cause she was sent to a girl's reformatory and she fell down some concrete stairs there one day and broke her neck. We sure missed her. Nobody could jerk off like she did. Dirty Doug came back after doing his thirty days and we asked him what happened. "Shit, you'd never believe it. When you guys all hightailed it over that fence, there I am sitting like a bump on a log cause Hairy Mary can't get her hand out of my pants. It'd got stuck on my belt and the more she pulled to get it out, the stucker it got. So we're still sitting there when the cop spots us. And that guy was one mad cop! He yells at us to get up and I end up having to take off my belt before she can pull her fat hairy hand out."

One night we stole a car, a real sharp '58 Olds, and bombed around for a while and pissed on the seats and had a ball before dumping it in the schoolyard. That was so much fun that the next night we get together, me, Timmy the Wart, the Kid, Sally the Squaw and her kid sister who's only ten but she's already got two little boobs sprouting out, and cross the wires on a '57 Caddy convertible parked over by Maple Leaf Gardens and head for Wilcox Lake with a case of beer.

The Wart's driving and he's doing sixty up Yonge Street and saying "Man, these Caddies really go," and saying it again, and saying it right up to the moment that a squad car starts honking at us to pull over.

We're all under sixteen so they throw us in the juvenile detention jail at 311 Jarvis. Timmy and the Kid both been there before, but it's my first time. It doesn't look like a jail. Ordinary wooden doors with windows, four beds to a cell and a big window near the ceiling. I tell the guys, "Let's bust the window with a chair," but they say, "Forget it, we tried before." It's got that special glass in it that can take up to five hundred pounds pressure.

We spend two weeks in there and there's nothing to do but play checkers and dominos and listen to the radio and sweat. Sometimes a cop or a social worker or a parent comes in and that breaks the monotony, but most of the time we're bored. There's about twenty guys in the place and most of them are in for breaking and entering, or car theft. One, a blackie by the name of Digger, is in for assault— he beat the living shit out of his old man, "cause he was beating up on my mom." He's big for fifteen and we're wondering if he's as tough as he's strong, so one day three of us corner him in the shower and call him nigger and black bastard.

He's tough all right, but three against one is too much for any guy. The guards, who are dressed in ordinary clothes, no uniforms, but are still guards, break it up and cuff us around a bit. That's not as bad as the cops though. When they pulled us into the station that night, all handcuffed like we were the Mafia or something, they slapped us all over the place and punched the Wart so hard in the gut that he puked right on the floor. They gave him a mop and told him to clean it up and whacked him on the head with the handle when he'd finished. Me and the Kid, they cracked our heads together and told us we were lousy punks and that if we opened our yaps about getting hit they'd really work us over. Dirty bastard cops.

Nobody came to see me all the time I was there, and one Friday morning it was court time for me and I had to go before the judge with the same clothes I'd had on for the last two weeks. There were other families there and one mother was crying, but for me there was nobody, and my clothes were dirty and I stood there in front of the judge, who read off what I was being tried for. He had a moustache and a nice kind face and a sharp suit on and he asked me if I had anything to say before he passed sentence. I wanted to say "Fuck you" cause there was nobody there and I felt so goddam alone, but he was smiling at me in a way that my old man had never done—as if he liked me or something—so I just shook my head and said nothing. I wished I was home reading a book.

"Michael Armstrong Taylor" (what'd he have to say my middle name for? I hate it), "the court believes, and allow me to add that we have only come to this conclusion after long talks with your parents, former teachers and Dr. Morton, the court psychiatrist, that it is in your best interest and in society's that you be sent to a reformatory for an undetermined period of time.

"We all feel that although you may judge this an unusually harsh sentence at the moment, you will, in the years to come when you have reached manhood, thank us for giving you this opportunity to learn a trade and lead a productive life."

Thank you.

He was still smiling as they led me out of the court and back to the cell. Reformatory for me, and Spike had got off with six months' probation when he got caught stealing a car last year! It's my goddam parents that put the judge up to this. The bastards. I didn't ask to be their son. The dirty rotten bastards. The lousy drunks.

I'm an RC so they sent me to St. John's Training School, which is about forty miles out of Toronto, near a hick town called Uxbridge.

As you drive in there's a barn which makes you think it's a farm they've sent you to, then you pull up to a huge three-story building and they leave you in the hall sitting on a chair beside an office.

The guys that run the place are called brothers. They're a religious organization like the priests, only they can't say mass, and except for

Sundays and holy days when they put on those long black robes that look like housecoats, they dress just like us.

One of them comes over to me, flashes me a grin, and pulls me into an office where he reads me off the rules of the place and asks me if I've got anything to say—hell, that's all people are asking me today. After, he calls someone on the phone and a guy about my age with blond hair and jeans and work shirt comes in and says, "Yes Brother?"

"Mike, I want you to meet Mike." Mike shakes hands with me, and Brother George (they only use their first names) tells him to show me around.

As we're going through the dormitories and the kitchen and dining room he asks me where I'm from and what I done. I tell him, and he says play it cool here and you'll be out in six months. Six months! Christ, that's like saying six years. I notice there's no bars on the windows and the doors are ordinary doors.

He takes me outside and says, "This is the yard." There's about five hundred guys standing around, all dressed like Mike in those damn work clothes that make you look like a DP. "Is that all you guys do here all day, stand around?" I ask him, and he laughs and says, "Hell no, we're working and studying and playing sports all day long. It's just that it's supper in a few minutes and the guys are waiting for the whistle to line up." He points to a long building behind the main one and says, "Those are the workshops. There's a print shop, a shoe shop, a carpentry shop and a barbershop and in the main building there's the bakeshop and the kitchen. Everyone here works in one of these shops some time or other during the day. Out behind the main building there's about ten acres for playing football and baseball and all the other sports. It takes a bit of time getting used to, but you'll like it here," he says as the whistle blows and everyone runs to form a line for supper. Mike slaps me on the back and we run as well.

I notice that there's practically nothing to stop you from busting the joint if you want to. No walls or anything like that.

The brother who's blown the whistle waits till we're all formed in three lines and standing straight, one behind the other.

"He's Brother Lawrence. Watch out for him. He's the one who'll decide when you can go home." Brother Lawrence—a face tough as granite and gray eyes that can look right through you. A build like a football player.

"Okay you guys, get those lines in order or you'll be eating your supper at midnight!" he barks at us, and there's some shuffling of feet and somebody yells, "You're stepping on my foot, prick." Brother Lawrence tells the guy, "Come here, Randy, so I can slap your face," and Randy steps out of line, walks up to Lawrence and gets a slap that you can hear all the way back to Toronto. He steps back to his place in line, and we march down to the dining room and get served like in the serve-yourself places. You walk up to the front and the food's thrown on your plate, and you say a prayer and eat while Lawrence and another Brother walk up and down and dining room supervising, which means slapping a kid if he's done something he shouldn't have.

After supper they give me jeans and an old shirt and tell me to change in the locker room, which is near the dormitory.

For some groups there's basketball in the indoor gym and for ours there's television. We sit there watching some movie on the TV set till nine o'clock when they march us up to the dormitory. There's about fifty beds in it and a shower room close by where we're supposed to shower every night. By ten the lights are put out, and that night for the first time in years I cry. Friday night in prison! What are Spike and the others doing tonight? When will I see them again? Hell, I'll probably be here a year, maybe two. That crap about six months was just that: crap.

So help me, as soon as I get to know the layout of the place, I'll blow the joint. I want to go back and see my buddies. I don't want to spend a lousy year or two rotting in here. Hell, I'm only fifteen.

Next morning we're up at seven (I think it's the first time in my life I've been up that early). Lawrence comes into the dorm and blows that whistle of his, and everybody's up like a shot, except one guy who sits up on the bed and rubs his eyes. Lawrence walks over to his bed, grabs hold of one side of the mattress and tosses mattress, sheet, blanket and guy on the floor. We splash some water on our faces, get dressed and make our beds. Mike shows me how it's done, "And if you do it any other way, you lose points." Points? What's that?

"You get so many points at the end of each month, depending on how good you've been. Since you're new, you start at Good. Then it's Very Good, Excellent and Honour. When you've hit Honour they let you go home. If you run away or something like that they drop you right to the bottom which is Very Bad. Then it's Bad, then Average and then Good again. Like I said before, play it cool in here and do everything you're supposed to do and after a couple of months here you'll go up a grade each month, which means only six months."

"How long you been here?" I ask, and he says, "Eight months. But I took off my first month here."

"What are you in for?"

"Auto theft."

"The same as me."

"What'd you steal?"

"A '57 Caddy convertible. And you?"

"A dump truck."

"A dump truck?"

"Yeah. Stupid wasn't it? I did it on a dare and I ended up crashing it into a parked car."

"Where you from?"

"Me? From Kenora—and you?"

"From Cabbagetown."

And that's the way the conversation goes during breakfast. Scrambled eggs and coffee and bread and jam. After, it's school for the morning and Mike shows me where the class is. Some laugh, that is. We sit all morning doing nothing and every time the teacher goes out for a minute everybody's throwing compasses at each other and ripping up each other's notebooks. Before noon the guys who are fifteen get a smoke. You get ten minutes to smoke it and you got to throw the butt in a pail of water when you're finished. "That's so nobody smokes the butt after. We call it butt-banging here."

We line up for lunch when that goddam whistle goes off, and somebody gets a goddam good hoof in the ass from Lawrence cause he's not moving fast enough. We eat stew and potatoes and after we line up outside again and it's our turn for the shops. Mike takes me to the shoe shop, where they make the boots that the guys here wear.

So that's the great trade I'm going to learn. The great opportunity I'm getting by being sent here. Making lousy work boots! No man, this isn't for me; I'm getting out the first chance I get.

The guy who runs the shoe shop looks me over, says, "You look like a smart kid," and gets me sorting out different size laces. At three o'clock we march out, reeking of glue and leather, and it's sport time. Baseball today, which I can't stand. They put me on the field and I miss a fly and everybody boos and the brother who's umpiring says I shoulda been sent to St. Mary's, the girls reformatory. They all laugh and I feel like sitting down right there on the field and bawling my eyes out again, I got the blues so bad. Then it's smoke time again. I'm getting the knack now—you smoke the cigarette down till it's burning your fingers and then you hold it between your finger-nails cause there's still a few good puffs left in it, and by the time you heave it in the pail there's almost nothing left.

Line up for supper and somebody gets beaned on the head with Lawrence's whistle cause he's slouching in line. It's some sort of meat and lots of bread. After, it's our turn for the basketball gym. Some game. Everybody's kneeing everybody else in the nuts, they're kicking the ball with their feet. If you run two feet with it, you get tripped. Two guys end up punching each other out over a penalty. The brother in charge, a tall wiry guy with a bald spot on the back of his head, separates them by booting one in the ass and grabbing the other one by the throat, slamming him against the wall and slapping his face. Then they're marched off upstairs.

"That's good for five whacks." I'll find out later what those whacks are given with.

Shower and bedtime. We've got about half an hour at bedtime for reading and most of the guys got comic books. Lawrence calls me into his room, which is next to the dorm, and asks me what I think of the place (I'm supposed to say super-keen maybe?) and tells me he hopes I'll get along here all right. He asks me if I like to read. I say "Yes Brother" (whatever you do, don't call them mister; they blow their cool over that), and he points to a row of pocket books on a shelf by his head and tells me to take one. I choose *Shane* cause I've seen the movie and I liked it, and he tells me to hit the sack. Man, those eyes of his, they really look right through you. They look as if they'll jump right out of his head and kill you dead if you say something he doesn't like. I'll never forget them. The only guy in the world I've never been able to look straight in the face.

Fifteen minutes later lights out, and my first day in jail shot to hell. And the second day. And the third. And the first week. And the second week. And the only thing to break the routine is Sundays when it's sports all day (Mass in the morning. First time I ever been in my life), and we get candy in the afternoon. And parents and friends can visit on that day, but nobody comes to see me.

After the first month, I can't take it any longer and I bust out with a French kid from Timmins. Like I said before, there's nothing to it cause there's no walls. Behind the shop building there's a small forest, then a creek, then the road. We wait till before smoke time in the afternoon, make sure no one's looking, then run like hell through the trees, wade across the creek and head the same direction as the road but along a field a hundred yards in from it, ducking every time a car goes by. By night we're in Uxbridge and we wait till after midnight before stealing a car and heading up north. I took the French kid with me cause he says once we hit Timmins way they'll never find us: "I know every tree up dere. Day never fine us in a milyun year." Our plan is to spend the rest of the fall up there and head for Cabbagetown in the winter when the heat's died down. Hell, I don't want to spend eight months freezing my balls up there in the North Pole where he's from.

Around five in the morning we run out of gas in a small village I can't even remember, except it is somewhere up north, and we get caught trying to steal another car. It's the OPP and they treat us nice. They don't hit us or nothing and they even give us coffee and a smoke before one of the brothers arrives to pick us up. Too bad all cops can't be like them.

"Well, did you have a nice drive?" Brother Harry asks us on the way back. He laughs as he says that, and we can't help but laugh with him, even though we're so tired all we want to do is sleep.

We get back around lunch time and are hustled up to the second floor (or was it the third?), told to strip, given a shower and thrown into a ten by ten room built of concrete, painted green, and a heavy grille on the window. There is a pail on the floor in one corner which is our toilet. Meals are handed to us through the door and half an hour later the plates taken away. That night they give us mattresses as thin as Graham wafers, dirty with piss and shit stains. We stay there for a week with nothing to do and nobody to talk to except each other. After the second day I tell Frenchie to shut up, I'm so sick of hearing stories about the bears and wolves he'd hunted and about his uncle, Gros Pierre, who's so strong, once he picked up two guys who were bugging him in a restaurant, one in each hand, lifted them over his head and heaved them through the plate glass window onto the sidewalk outside.

Big deal. Even the strongest guy doubles over with a good boot in the nuts.

We pass the time by counting how many concrete blocks are on each wall (some two hundred, I think) and how many holes in the grille covering the window (over nine hundred and I remember that well cause Frenchie and I had a fight over it). On the tenth day Lawrence tells us to get up and we're marched into another room further up the hall. Wait here, he tells me (as if I'm going anywhere) and he takes Frenchie somewhere else with him.

Five minutes later he crooks his finger at me and I follow him into a little room at the end of the hall, empty except for two chairs and a bed with a mattress on it. Brother Harry, the guy who drove us back, is sitting on one of the chairs, and Lawrence tells me to pull my pants down and lie face down on the bed. I do that and look out of the corner of my eye at him. He's got a leather strap about two feet long and six inches wide, with a wooden handle at the end. He raises it over his head and sends it whistling down on my left cheek. Crack. Oh Christ does it burn! My ass rises about a foot in the air and my eyes sting with tears. "One," he counts out loud. He raises it over his head again and I hear it whistling and crack! "Two," and again, "three, four, five!" I can't take it any more. My ass is on fire and the tears are spilling down my cheeks. "Get up," he says—thank God it's over—"and lie the opposite way on the bed." Oh no, no, no. Crack! "One." Now it's my right cheek and I'm biting the mattress to keep from screaming out loud. "Two." My teeth dig in harder, my jaw threatening to crack. "Three, four"—just one more, just one more—"five!" He sends that one down extra hard and I can't help myself, I bawl out loud. "Okay, get up and put your pants on." Christ, it burns, it burns, it burns. Just the feel of the jeans against my ass makes me grit my teeth. I wipe my nose against my hands as Lawrence marches me down the hall. "You're starting off at Very Bad, and we're going to keep our eyes on you for a while, so don't take another notion to go for a walk."

We reach the yard and it's baseball time and he tells me to join my group.

When I look back on it now, I guess I learned from that cause I never pulled off another blooper the rest of the time I was there.

Fall became winter and the snow came, and a hockey rink was set up, and the monotony went on. Shovel snow, class, hockey, basketball, whistles, TV, line-up, shower, make your bed, breakfast. Sundays, Mass, and still nobody sees me. Smoke in the butt pail, lights out. Slap. Boot. "You're on dishwashing tonight." Sneaking a butt now and then behind the rink. Having a fight now and then. New guys escaping and being brought back. Learning from each other how best to steal a car or break into a house or store; talking about guns and broads and how we won't get caught next time and how we'll see each other when we get out; and guys leaving and new guys coming. Having my best friend in the place, Randy, the one who got slapped my first day there, get beat up by O'Sullivan and spend a week in the hospital with twenty stitches in his head. Ganging up on O'Sullivan in the room where we put on our skates. Turning the light off as soon as he walks in and heaving skates at him, and him grunting every time he's hit and heaving them back at us, and those skates flying in every direction and it's so dark you can't see who's next to you. The light turned on again, and Williams, who's about four foot eight, sitting under a pile of hockey sticks holding half his teeth in his hand, and O'Sullivan with a gash along his forehead swearing at us, "I'll be gettin ya for this, ya chickenfaced bastards," and everybody losing a month over that. I was up to Good at that time.

And grabbing Williams one night while he's still waiting to get some false teeth put in, and forcing him to suck us while we're showering, the noise covering up the sound of his lips. It was my turn when Lawrence walks in and we break up the party. He looks in, but we're all taking our shower like good little boys, the tears running from Williams' eyes mingling with the water spraying on his face, and I say to myself good thing Lawrence walked in then before he started on me. That would have busted me to Very Bad again and probably the strap too.

Line up, whistle. Slap. Scrambled eggs. I've read almost all of Lawrence's pocket books, most of them westerns, and it's spring and I'm up to Very Good. I might be home (Home! That's a laugh) in two more months. Classes will be over in June and I haven't learned a goddam thing and I've got so many holes in my back from thrown compasses that I feel like a sieve, and the only guy who took class serious, Randy, who was real smart and always got A's and B's had his Math notebook glued up on him page by page and he threw a fit and had to be locked in solitary for two days till he calmed down. He was in for fighting. Every now and then he had to go and beat someone up, he didn't know why, and his parents had talked with their priest who suggested sending him to St. John's. I thought we were all court cases and I was surprised at that. The poor bastard came from Penetang and I heard from one of the guys who'd done time a few months after I left that they'd finally sent him up there—to the hospital I mean. His parents were probably happy cause that way they could visit him every week, not once every two months. Wonder if he met Sonny there.

June, and I've been here ten months. Still nobody has visited me, but I'm used to it by now. I've seen guys come after me and leave before me but I know my turn will come soon cause next month I'll be in the Honour grade.

No more classes so we spend mornings cleaning out the barn and afternoons in the print shop (they finally took me out of that goddam shoe shop), where the boss boots me all over the place on my first day for spilling a case full of type on the floor. It isn't my fault, I was tripped, but I spend the whole morning on my hands and knees picking up about ten million pieces of type and getting booted every time the boss passes by. I swear I'll get the guy who tripped me, but next week he goes home. Smoke. Whistle. Run to line up. Run to the sports field. "You were talking in line. Eat supper standing up!" Slap.

A new guy called Junior gets slapped by Lawrence for trying to hide a butt he found, and Junior punches him in the face. Baff. Baff. Two swift ones to the head and Junior hits the ground. Lawrence drags him up by his shirt collar and gives him two more and Junior hits the ground again. He's pulled up and knocked down for a third time and there's blood running from his nose and mouth. Lawrence tells him to start running around the field and he's given a hard kick to send him on his way. For a few seconds he hobbles, holding the top part of his leg with his hand, and Lawrence comes running up and boots him again and barks in his ear, "Run, dammit, before you end up carrying your head in your hands!" and Junior runs. And runs. And runs. The field's about five miles each lap around and Junior runs and runs till he's drowning in his sweat and his tongue's hanging out and he's tripping every ten steps, his feet barely able to get off the ground. Then the supper whistle sounds and we all run to line up and are hustled in, and we hear Lawrence barking at sonny "Just keep running. If I come out and see you've stopped, consider yourself dead." By shower time, Lawrence finally lets Junior come in and boots him up the stairs and tells him to shower, and after boots him into the dorm.

One Sunday after breakfast, Lawrence calls me into his room and I'm scared shitless cause I'm on the Honour grade, been there a month, and I'm scared he's found out that I was butt-banging in the john. But all he says is "You're going home tomorrow."

I can't sleep a wink that night and I even get to thinking that he's pulling a trick on me, that they're going to send me to Guelph cause I'm sixteen now, and then the morning whistle blows and I'm the first out of bed and the first in line for breakfast. After breakfast, just like yesterday, he calls me up to his room again and says that I'll be leaving at eleven with the laundry truck, and to go down to the office and check with Brother Simon, the secretary.

I do that and after he's given me a speech on being a good boy, he shakes my hand and wishes me luck. I go out to the yard and it's ten o'clock, so I shake hands with Randy and some of the other guys, and at eleven Lawrence accompanies me to the truck, shakes my hand and says, "Hope you don't end up in Guelph."

Don't worry about that, dogface, it's been seven years and I haven't done a thing to cross me with the Law since. Like they say, I learned my lesson. I'd rather die than put up with another year like that, being treated like a dog and having to kiss everybody's ass, and running when they tell you to run and eating when they tell you to eat and farting when they tell you to fart. Never again baby, never again. Oh sure, I've been in a couple of fights, and I've got dead drunk on the street, and I swipe newspapers out of the newspaper boxes whenever I got nothing to read at the Club, but never anything serious.

At least, not till last night. Hell, maybe that guy's dead. Maybe I was just imagining that he was groaning. Or maybe he's in the hospital with his nuts on a sling and he's taken out an assault and battery charge on me and the fuzz's on its way over to pick me up.

All these things are going through my head while she's asking, "Did I say something wrong?" and I can feel beads of sweat rolling down my forehead. I could get up to ten years for this, all because of her, and here she is saying what a hero I been to her!

"No baby, you didn't say nothing wrong," I say to her as I walk out the door, cause I think I better get some fresh air before my head blows to pieces.

"Wait Michael!" she runs up behind me and grabs my arm and I turn to her and say, "Get the fuck back in the room before I break every bone in your face!" and walk down the front stairs leaving her standing there. What I need right now is to be left alone.

Mrs. Himmel and Cowboy are sitting on the porch with a bottle of wine between them, and I walk past them and send the bottle flying down the steps with the toe of my shoe.

"Doggone, look what ya done," says Cowboy, wiping off some wine that's splashed on his boots. "And that's the only bottle in the house," screeches Himmel, standing up. "That was a buck-fifty bottle, too, and we'd only taken a few sips out of it."

Yeah, I'll bet. "I'm putting that onto next week's rent! And last night when you came in you were making so much noise you woke us up. If that happens again you can find somewhere else to live!"

Sing canary, sing.

I walk down the sidewalk towards Allan Gardens with a smile on my face and I'm feeling better already. "And next time excuse yourself," she yells at me so hard it's a wonder all the windows on the street don't break, "and don't leave the bath so dirty either!"

I light up a fag and remember what it was like my first day back. I walked up the stairs to my "home" and the old man was there, drunk, and a fat scraggly woman with a butt in her mouth was changing a baby's diaper. The baby was screaming and the woman telling him to shut his mouth up and the ashes from the cigarette were falling on the baby's head, making him scream louder. "So you're back, eh?" said the old man, taking a swig from a beer lying on the table. "Hope you learned your lesson. I don't want no kid of mine turning out like his mother, a useless tit." He took another swig. "Where is she?" I asked. "She took off with a guy," he answered, "and this is your new mother and that's your little brother. His name's Arnold. Go say hello to them." I looked at that pile of lard and the screaming thing with a face like a monkey's ass and I walked back down the stairs and over to Blow Job's.

He looked at me like I was there yesterday and said he dunno when I asked him if Spike or any of the other guys were around.

I walked over to the park and spotted Dirty Doug talking to some broad I didn't know and he said, "How's it going Mike," and I said, "Fine," and he walked off with the broad saying, "See you at the restaurant tonight," and I said "Sure," and sat down on a bench feeling blue. No buddies. No family. Nothing. I sat there for a couple of hours till I was hungry, so I went back to the restaurant and ordered a hamburg and Coke.

Around seven Dirty Doug came in, followed by Spike and his brother and Ladeda Linda. They all clapped me on the back and said it's great to see me, and Dirty Doug'd told them I was back, and how'd it go there, and we chewed the fat for an hour drinking Cokes and smoking. Christ, it felt great to smoke whenever you wanted to and put the butt out after in an ashtray, and no whistle blowing in your face.

"Some haircut they give you in that place," said Spike, running his hand through my hair and everybody laughing and me feeling great cause my buddies remembered me after all.

"I couldn't talk to you over at the park," said Dirty Doug, "cause the chick I was with had to get home by supper time so that only give us a couple of hours to ball."

"That's okay," I answered, punching him in the arm. "I knew I'd catch you later."

"Guess what Mike," Spike cuts in, "Linda's working for me." Ladeda smiled, all proud. "I got her hustling over by the Harmony and she's doing real good bringing in the bread."

I didn't say nothing and after a minute Spike went on, "Anyway, when Dirty Doug told us you were back, I told Linda and we decided to give you a welcome home present." Ladeda and Spike smiled at each other and I was imagining something stupid like a pair of falsies. He started to say something else, stopped, grabbed Ladeda by the arm and said, "Here it is." Ladeda got up and came over to my side of the table. I didn't get it. "What is it?" I asked. Don't forget I just did almost a year in jail.

"It's Linda, man, Linda. She's yours for the evening. Go over to her place and have a ball. It's free," he said, looking at me like I gone right off my nut.

For a minute I sat there without saying anything. Isn't that something, I thought to myself. Isn't that just something. The guys have bought me a fuck. God, isn't that really something. I said, "Gee, guys, I don't know what to say," and really I was stuck for words. Spike's own broad. Man, that's buddies for you. I got a lump in my throat and I lit up another fag and the lump was getting bigger. Spike and his brother and Dirty Doug get up and said, "See you around," and "Have a ball," and to Linda they said, "Don't tire him out too much," and I was left sitting there with Ladeda. She said, "Let's go lover," and we went over to her place and that's where I spent my first night back in Cabbagetown. She wasn't bad either, once you got used to the smell.

It's not too hot today but everybody's out there anyway. The kids around the ice cream truck still pushing and yelling and sticking their grimy hands at the driver who's still going nuts trying to serve them all at once.

Mouth over in the usual corner and his wife with her sign:

WE ARE ALL
GOD'S
LITTLE CREATURES

---

and a couple dozen of God's little creatures standing around listening to what God thinks about them.

Hell, I'll be damned. Mouth's wife's pot is getting bigger. Don't tell me he's knocked her up and we can expect a tiny Mouth in a few months' time! Ha, that's a good one. Mouth fornicates too, just like everybody else, unless it was the Holy Ghost pulled it off. I wouldn't put it past him to try and tell that to his grubby flock.

The old guys are back straddling their usual bench and playing their game of chess. Nothing, but nothing, bothers those guys. I wish I knew how to play. I'll have to ask George to teach me cause I'm sure he knows. There's an old woman sitting beside them and she's wearing this black cape that almost reaches down to her feet. She looks like Batman's grandmother.

I have a drink of water over by the fountain and sit down on a free bench to listen to some Newfies playing a guitar and singing. They're much better than One-eye and they sing pretty good. There's about ten of them, and a lot of people hanging around and joining in. They're passing a bottle around, making sure first there's no cops around.

My head's starting to clear and apart from the fact that I'm hungry, I'm feeling a lot better and I've almost stopped thinking about last night. A bum sits down next to me, smelling of wine and puke and dirt. I'm about to get up when he says, "Pardon me imposing myself upon you in this manner, but I can tell by your dress and deportment that you're a college student and I wonder if I might have a word with you."

Jee-sus, I think, did you ever hear a bum talk like that in your life?—and pegging me for a college student! Although it's easy to see why he did. I cut my hair once a month and put on a clean white shirt every week for work and my shoes are always polished (more now since Terry came; she does them every Friday), so instead of getting up I stay put and see what the rub's got to say.

"I realize that your natural inclination on being approached in this way is to get up and leave, but I beg you" (he begs me yet!) "to bear with me for a moment and hear the sad but, alas, true tale of the misfortunes that led me to live the type of life I'm leading now."

Shit, he sounds like something out of a fairy tale. Maybe he's just escaped from 999 Queen.

"Go ahead, buddy," I say to him, lighting a fag. "I got lotsa time." He looks at the fag and when he sees I'm not handing any out, he talks again.

"Like you, I was once a college student, studying for my BA in philosophy, and in love with a young lady who had golden hair that would sway in the wind like fields of wheat" (wheat, for Christsake) "but I was filled with a certain restlessness" (with a certain amount of bullshit too) "that impeded me from marrying her on graduation, as we had originally planned, and instead made me rush and join the Army when the Korean war broke out and the Government was asking for volunteers to serve there."

I take another drag. He looks at it like he's going to die if he doesn't get a puff soon.

"Rather than continuing to bore you any further, perhaps you would prefer that I leave?" he asks, hoping I'll say no.

"I don't care, pop," I answer, "you do what you want."

The Newfies have just broken out in a fast song and they're clapping their hands to the beat.

"Well in that case, allow me to terminate my sad story by recounting briefly that Korea was not what I'd imagined warfare to be like.

"It was cold, very cold, and days and nights we sat huddled in our trenches waiting for the Chinese to attack. We were lonely and our clothes were always crawling with lice and other parasites. We would clean our weapons and wait. Then one night"—he raises his hands

in the air and his face takes on a faraway look—what a con man—
"they attacked!" His voice trembles. "Thousands of them, blowing
whistles" (sounds like Brother Lawrence was leading them), "tooting
on horns and screaming like banshees" (like what?). "We fired and
fired on them till our weapons jammed from the heat, and still they
came. Thousands of them lying on the ground with our bullets in
them, and waves of them still rushing up the hill, screaming at the
top of their voices, until they overran our advanced positions."

He stops for a minute and looks at me with his eyes wet. I take
another drag and say, "Well, what happened?" He looks at the cigarette again, at me again, and goes on.

"We pulled back, firing at them with the few remaining bullets
we had, and still they came on, wave upon wave of little yellow men
with quilt uniforms, and the courage of Richard the Lion Hearted.

"We retreated step by step, relinquishing every foot of ground at
the cost of one dead enemy soldier. They were almost on top of us
when we heard the sound of airplanes over our heads, followed by
the thunderous detonations of bombs. We were saved!" He smiles
and looks up at the sky as if the planes were going to fly over any
second now, his smile splitting his beard in two. "We were saved," he
repeats, like I didn't hear him the first time or something.

"I turned to my comrade in arms, Stanley Wilson from
Vancouver, B.C., to congratulate him on a fight well won, when I
noticed for the first time that he was lying on his face in the mud of
our trench. I trembled, and prayed to all that was holy that nothing
had happened. I shook his inanimate body and turned him around.
He was dead. Shot between the eyes. Stanley, my true friend, who
had trained with me and shared with me all the pleasures and toils
of army life. Dead. And a wife and two lovely children at home who
would never see him again.

"I cried openly, unashamedly, over my fallen comrade" (I thought
a comrade was a communist, like George's friends. He calls them all
comrade), "picked up my rifle, and walked amongst the bodies with
hate in my heart for those Chinese who had killed him.

"Halfway down the hill I noticed a body that shook, and as I
approached it I distinctly heard a whimper escape its lips. He was a

young fellow and his eyes were filled with pain. I noticed no immediate wound and only on closer scrutiny did I ascertain that half his back had been ripped open by a grenade fragment.

"Suddenly the thought of poor Stanley, who would never see the green forests and blue lakes of British Columbia again, leaped before my mind like a rabid beast. I raised my rifle above my head and thrust my bayonet into the wounded Chinese's chest with all the strength that my hate could muster.

"The poor fellow attempted to protect himself with his arms but the blade, sank deep into him and with a gurgle escaping his lips, he died. I stood there staring at the blood seeping from his shattered chest and slowly the horror of the act I'd committed in a moment of hate and folly overcame me and I threw away my rifle and sat down beside the man I'd just murdered and cried to myself as I thought that he, too, would have a family crying for him."

He stops again, and you know something? There's tears in his eyes! Yeah man, real tears, flowing down his face, making furrows through the grime and disappearing into his beard. Man, oh man, this guy takes the Oscar for acting. I'm really impressed. I put out my cigarette and his eyes drop to the smashed butt on the ground.

Two kids walk by in their Sunday best, their hair combed and everything. The boy's about ten and the girl maybe a year older. They're walking hand in hand and there's a great big button on the kid's suit coat that reads:

LEGALIZE
PROSTITUTION
NOW!

Why, the little bastard, he's too young to even get a hard-on. They're eating Eskimo Pies and I look at the ice cream truck and there's not too many people around it now, so I get up and tell the bum it was a great story and I really dug it.

"Wait," he says to me, wiping his face with his hands, "I haven't finished yet."

"Yeah, well tell me the rest next Sunday. I got to blow now."

"Well, at least have the decency to bestow upon someone less fortunate than you a small token of your material prosperity," he says, kind of vexed. I don't quite catch what he's said but I figure he means a handout, so I give him a cigarette and leave him there waiting for me to give him a light. Hell, maybe he wants me to put it out for him afterwards too.

I got to piss.

I whip over to the washroom beside the hothouse and walk down the stairs. Inside, it's dark and the stench of piss gags you. There are puddles of the stuff on the floor, half-covered with leaves of toilet paper. One of the pissers is empty and I go over to it. The one beside me is taken up by a guy who keeps looking around to see who's coming in. His hand's moving back and forth. I look over and damned if the guy isn't whacking himself off. He spots me looking at his pecker and smiles. Most of his teeth are black and full of holes and he looks like a bulldog, with about three foreheads, one overlapping the other. His eyes look right into mine and then descend to his pecker, then come up to me again. His hand moves a bit faster. Another guy comes splashing through the piss and I zip up my fly and move so he can get in. The queer looks at him and smiles and his hand moves faster again. I walk up the stairs and the sunlight blinds me for a moment after the darkness of the washroom.

A young kid about eight with short pants on and freckles scurries out from within the group watching the Newfies sing, and runs into the can. Queer in there'll blow his load for sure when he sees him.

There's a pile of red hair running towards me and when it gets closer I see it's Terry. She rushes up all out of breath and says, "I thought I'd never find you. Do you know today's our first month together? I just had to find you and tell you. Gosh, who's that singing over there? I bet you didn't even think of our anniversary, did you?"

"Hey, slow down," I tell her, "you're not helping my head any." That's women for you, the harder you treat them, the more they love you. Guess she was scared I'd kick her out when I got back.

A gray cop car drives slowly up the walk, forcing people onto the grass. One of those unmarked jobs with two plainclothes cops inside. They look from side to side and stop in front of the Newfies

(I'm behind them). Sweat breaks out on my face and I pick my nose. Christ, I'm scared. They're probably looking for me. The Newfies stare back at them and the guy with the guitar starts off a song about cops and how stupid they are. Everybody that knows the words joins in and in a minute half the park's surrounded the car and everybody's laughing at the cops, who start off again and drive out to the street, the song getting louder as they get farther away.

"Gee that was funny," says Terry, who's been laughing like everyone else.

"Look kid," I say to her, "has anyone come around looking for me?"

"No, why?" she answers. "Were you expecting someone?"

We walk over to the ice cream truck and I buy two Eskimo Pies, and we walk around eating them.

"Just like the day I met you. Remember, Michael? You bought me an Eskimo Pie," she gurgles at me, her mouth full of ice cream.

"Let's go home," I say when we've finished. "I'm hungry."

Himmel and Cowboy are still sitting on the porch and there's another bottle of wine between them. I remember my manners and say, "It's been a beautiful afternoon, hasn't it, Mr. and Mrs. Himmel?" and Himmel throws me a dirty look. Cowboy slaps his hand on his knee, guffaws, and says, "Doggone, she ain't got me hitched yet," so Himmel gives him a dirty look and says, "What makes you think I wanna marry you, you hunk of horse turd?" and Cowboy says "Doggone," and they start arguing and I hit the bed while Terry's cooking up some ham and eggs.

After, she washes my socks, and I can't sleep because Himmel and the cowboy are yelling and thumping around upstairs. And I'm waiting for the cops to come crashing through the door any minute.

Finally it's midnight, and Terry's asleep. She's on the rags, remember. And upstairs it quiets down, and no cops, and tomorrow I got to work.

So I go to sleep.

And I wake up about four in the morning.

I've been dreaming my old man was a judge and he was smiling at me and saying "You gotta hang, boy." And I'm saying "I don't want to." And he's saying "It don't matter. You gotta hang. It's best for you and it's best for society." These goddam hanging dreams. I'm getting tired of them.

August 2

Work for me today even though for everybody else it's a holiday. That's one of the chickenshit deals I don't like about the place, but when I think of the job I got a week after leaving St. John's, it helps me cut down on my beefing.

It was with a moving company and I'd have to be there at six in the morning so that when the drivers got their job orders we'd be ready to go out with them. You'd spend all day moving fridges and stoves and beds and everything else in the house out to the truck, till you felt every bone in your body was broken, and the woman of the house saying every five minutes, "Be careful, don't scratch the furniture," till you felt like sticking the armchair you're carrying down her yap, or dropping the sofa on her foot, and you'd get home at night dead. Real dead. And your hands and clothes dirty and too tired to even light a smoke. And the next thing you know you're asleep and it's six in the morning and time to start again. Hell, it was just like jail, man. And to think that that's all some guys do all their lives.

Mrs. Waddling asks me if I've had a good weekend and I choke over that. Mrs. Russell, the Estonian, asks me, "You hav a gud veekend, yah?" and I answer, "Ezellent veekend, yah." I mean, a guy can only take so much. We get boiled chicken for lunch and Maggie tells us that Raquel Welch wears falsies. Pretty mild for her. Maybe she's not feeling good today. Rice pudding for dessert, floating around in a bowl full of milk and looking like—never mind.

I grab a white jacket, slip my black bow tie on, and get the bar ready upstairs. Today lunch is a real gas. Two old bags come in and I go over to them (I serve the booze, as well as pour it) and ask what they want. They say, "Martinis please, on the rocks and with a twist of lemon." Then one turns to the other and says, "How do they make them here, Agnes, the three to one method or Madame Vanier's famous recipe?"

Huh? What in God's name is that thing talking about? Hell, I pour in a shot of gin and slop some dry vermouth on top of it, stir it and that's that. If they want it extra dry I put in less vermouth and stir it faster so that the ice melts more and makes up for the vermouth.

They both look at me for an answer.

"Well," I answer, giving her one of my world-famous smiles, "we don't have any particular method here. It depends on the customer." When I want to, I can speak real well. That's what reading does for you.

"I was merely curious because Madame Vanier's recipe calls for four parts gin to one part vermouth."

"I see." I smile at her again. Jesus, four parts gin to one part vermouth! What's she want—a bucket of the stuff?

That's like the night when one of the members comes in dragging her husband behind her. When I ask them what they want, she says a gin gimlet, and her husband, who looks like one of the rubbies at the park except that he's well dressed, says to me, "You know how to make a vesper?"

Now I've heard of a lot of drinks and I know how to make most of them, but a vesper!

"I'm afraid I don't, sir."

Nothing to it, son," he answers, falling forward a bit in his chair. His wife shoots him a dirty look. "Nothing to it. You just get the biggest glass you can find, pour in four ounces of vodka, one of gin, just a breath of vermouth and top it off with an ice cube. Just one."

The only glass I can find for a drink that size is a wine glass. When I bring them their drinks, he picks his up, sniffs it and pours half of it down his throat, looks at me and says, "I'd be surprised if you'd told me you'd heard of it, it's my own invention," drains the rest of the glass and orders another. I'm not kidding, that guy's got a cast iron gut. Christ Almighty, four ounces of vodka and an ounce of gin! And he drank three of them before going for supper downstairs! Tell that to the winos and they'd never believe it. His wife sure looks like she doesn't. Guess some women never get used to their husbands being alcoholics.

Around two, Mrs. Waddling waddles up to the bar to make sure it's still here and tells me that I should be taking the sun because I look white and pale. "Yeah," I feel like telling her, "like at eight at night, maybe, when I get off." Besides, she's exaggerating a bit. I go to Allan Gardens every Sunday and my face is always red after.

Supper is this morning's boiled chicken heated up and some kind of goo plastered over it. Miss Virgin's got no new pimples. Maybe her boy friend's cut her off. A party of fourteen tonight and most of them want whiskey sours. And you know why? Not because they really like it, but because the first one says "A whiskey sour, please," and all the others ask for the same thing. Like a bunch of chickens. One clucks and the rest cluck. Cluck—whiskey sour. Cluck—whiskey sour.

Ann's on tonight. She's cook and real friendly. She always gives me a piece of pie when I close up for the night.

Like tonight it's Lemon Meringue, which I like almost as much as Eskimo Pies, so I eat two pieces and she says the place might go broke if you have another piece and we both laugh and Miss Virgin bounces out of the office, sticks her empty sweater out a few inches and glares at us, her hands on her bony hips. What a sweety-beauty. What a sweety-cutie-beauty. The pie curdles in my stomach.

The cops weren't around today, so I got nothing to worry about on that point now. The only thing is to keep my eyes open in case Greasehead comes looking for me with some of his buddies.

That's the trouble with fights. The guy who's lost is usually dying to make up for it and if he does manage to get you, then you're gunning for him after, and it goes on till one of you is either dead or in the pen. And me only wanting to lead a nice, quiet, happy life.

There's no justice in this world.

August 3

Today's a hot sonofabitch of a day and by ten when I leave, I'm already sweating. Himmel steps out in her nightgown as I go out the front door. God, I didn't think anybody could look so awful—hair in curlers, cream all over her face, bleary eyed. Maybe that's the reason nobody can put up with her for long, not because of her yelling and bitching. I wonder what Terry'll look like twenty years from now. Who knows, maybe I'll see her one day on the street and thank God I never got hitched to her. On the other hand, maybe she'll still be a cute number and I'll be mad as a wet hen cause I didn't keep her with me. Twenty years from now I mean. Things are going all right so far. I wish sometimes she'd wise up about life, though.

On the way home tonight I decide to whip over to the pool room, since I haven't been there since I met Terry and it's no good to keep to yourself like I've been doing. After all, a guy needs a bit of fun sometimes.

It's hot as a camel's ass inside (What a day! Sweat. Sweat. Sweat. And no sign of it getting any cooler tonight either) and Jake, a frog from Quebec who's been in Cabbagetown so long he's forgotten how to speak his language, greets me with "I hear you got permanent nooky now." "Yeah, that's right," I answer, kind of pissed off (it's probably the heat). "Beats having to go out every night looking for it. And what about you, still beating the old meat cause the chicks run every time you open your beak?" Jake's got two buck-teeth that stick out a mile when he smiles. That's why he never smiles.

He throws me a mean look, so just to set things right I ask him, "What's Smokey the Bear's middle name?"

"I dunno."

"The," I answer. He looks stupid for a minute, like a squirrel when you hold out what looks like a piece of bread or a peanut in your hand and he zips over to you all happy, grabs it out of your hand, flips it in his mouth, and spits it out two seconds later cause it's a stone. That kind of a look.

Finally he gets it and he laughs. His front choppers stick out and I laugh too. Christ, he's a regular squirrel himself. All he needs is a tail.

"Hey, I got one for you."

"Let's hear it."

"Why wasn't Christ born in Newfoundland?"

"I dunno."

"Cause they couldn't find three wise men and a virgin."

Where the hell did he pick that one up, the dumb gopher? Not in this hole, that's for sure. That was good, that one. I'll have to remember it for George.

"Not bad, Jake. Keep it up and we'll send you to Newfie country for the summer."

Yeah man, it feels great to be with the gang again. I got to do this more often in the future. Imagine Jake telling me a joke I didn't know. That's embarrassing.

There's only two tables taken. One by a couple of kids, and the other by Glen and some guy who I seen around a couple of times at Blow Job's. I go over to them.

Glen's just bending over to make a tough bank shot into the side when I get behind him and goose him and wreck the shot. He whirls around, mad as hell, recognizes me and breaks out laughing.

"Mike, you whore son! I haven't seen you since you conned that tail into your pad. How're ya doing playboy?"

Jesus, everybody and his uncle knows about Terry already.

"Not bad, Glen. Keeping fit."

"Yeah, I'll bet. Lot's of sexercise, eh?" He laughs again and it's obvious he's happy to see me. As he talks the butt he's got in the corner of his mouth flips up and down, spreading ashes all over my shirt. I don't think I ever seen him without a butt in his mouth.

He was born with a butt in his mouth.

"Mike, this is Baby Bill."

Baby Bill and I shake. He's a tough looking guy. His shirt's rolled up to show a pair of muscles like Charles Atlas never had.

We start a new game and after a while I'm winning by about ten points. I hook Junior, and fuck up Glen's chance to get anywhere by sinking a black and leaving him up the other end of the table, and I'm feeling great since Glen's a damn good pool shark. He's been playing since he was old enough to see over a pool table. His old man used to bring him in cause he wanted him to have a career and not be a bum like the other kids. And that's how he makes his living—by sucking in guys at a buck a game, letting them win the first and then when they figure they got it made, beating them at the next five, or as long as the guy can stand it.

But when times are hard, he does other things too.

"Hey Mike, we got something cooking, Baby Bill and me, want to hear about it?"

"Sure."

Hearing don't cost nothing.

"We been casing the liquor joint up on Parliament for the last week and we figure we can pull a job there on a Saturday night just before closing, when they're standing up to their asses in dough. We got it all figured out."

Baby Bill, who's about to plop a red into the end pocket, comes over to where we're talking on the other side of the table.

"It's all right to let him in on this deal, eh?" he asks Glen. "Shit yeah, man. Mike's okay," he answers.

Baby Bill looks like he'd bend you over his knee till your back snapped like a twig if you ever finked on him or crossed him. I better set him straight.

I shout, "Me and Glen known each other for years. I was even screwing his sister for a while."

I mean, how close can two guys be?

"That's only when I wasn't having a go at her."

Poor Linda. She was whoring at fifteen and scoring H at seventeen. Today she's twenty and you can see her down by Jarvis and Dundas at night, selling herself at a buck a throw. Even less. It doesn't matter as long as she makes enough to get her dope. She looks like she's fifty, all white and bent over and skinny as a needle, her eyes sunk so far in her head that from a distance you'd swear you're seeing a ghost. She's so hooked, she'll do anything for the bread. I heard she blew a dog at a party for ten bucks once.

She was a good lay before she got that monkey on her back.

Having established myself with King Kong, Glen tells me the whole plan.

It's a simple one and from the way he explains it, it'll probably work. They need a third guy, but I tell them "No thanks." The idea and the money both sound good but I'm not their baby. I'm tempted to write their plan down in my diary, but they haven't pulled the job yet, and I don't want to be accused of being a rat fink and having Baby Bill come over one day and rip the head off my shoulders like it was a blade of grass. And besides, Glen got pulled in for being drunk about a month ago and in the back of the cop car he booted the cop who was driving in the head, so when they got him into the station they gave his legs a going over with their night sticks and at court he got a good lawyer who claimed police brutality and false arrest and all kinds of other things and he got off. But the fuzz was so put off about that, that for the next two weeks he couldn't leave his place to get a pack of smokes without some cop following him.

Like they're just waiting for him to make some false move so they could really bust him. After all, you don't boot a cop in his fat head and hope to get away with it. If I were him I'd wait till the fall. Maybe the heat'll be off him by then.

Anyway, Glen says, "Too bad. We could have used a guy with brains" (He could at that too. There's not too many around here), "but never mind, I guess you got enough problems of your own right now keeping Red there happy." I tell him about the wop I wiped out on Saturday and he says, "Don't worry, if they come looking for you, you know we're always around." Baby Bill flexes his muscles at that. A regular Tarzan. He must be a ditch digger or something.

I get home after eleven and there's Terry sitting on the bed and listening to CHUM and waiting for me to get home. Just like my dog. He wasn't happy till I was back either. Funny thing about Terry and me, we both had dogs when we were kids. Hers died and mine was stolen by somebody one night when we let him out. I always suspected Blow Job's cousin Bum Bum. He's the one that keeps the restaurant supplied.

Terry gets up to kiss me (I guess she was worried that something had happened to me cause she looked real sad and hung up as I walked in). Right when her lips are next to mine, I hear a squawk over by the window, turn around—which makes her miss and kiss me on the ear instead—and spot a bird on the sill. Not a robin or a sparrow or any of the birds you find around here, but a blue-coloured one with a yellow face and a beak like one of those parrots they got down at Riverdale Zoo.

"It's a budgie," she says, all happy. "Do you like it?"

The thing squawks again.

"Just dandy. What's it for, a midnight snack?"

"Oh Michael, you're so funny," she laughs. "I thought it would brighten up the room a little. They're so cute and you can train them to talk, and they'll go on your finger, and—"

"And they crap on your head as they fly by," I cut in. This bird's got no cage or anything, it's sitting on a piece of wood in the corner, which she's nailed up about five feet off the floor.

I go over to it and it squawks and squeals and looks at me with one eye, its beak open like it's going to eat me or something. Little blue bastard.

"Look, kid, we can't have that thing in here. Like I said, it'll crap all over the place, or it'll fly out when we open the window."

I'll get a cage then," she says. She looks kind of hurt, but she's still trying to keep the smile on her face. "I thought it would be nice to let it fly free about the room. It's such a shame to keep it in a cage."

"Yeah? You get a cage," I tell her and let the matter drop cause I'm tired and I want to finish the *Saturday Evening Post* I borrowed from the Club. "But if it starts squawking at six in the morning, it's going."

The article is pretty good. About Negroes and how they live in New York. The rats chew the babies' faces when the mother leaves the room for a minute. That means that there's some pretty hungry rats down there, and some pretty ugly niggers too. Too bad Bum Bum hasn't heard about all those rats, he'd be down there on Friday and have enough rat steaks by Sunday to keep the restaurant going for the next six years. And New York would give him a medal, too.

Squawk!

Terry says, "Isn't that cute, he's saying good night," and I say "Real cute," and I'm thinking, say good morning too early tomorrow, creep, and I'll pour a gallon of glue down your beak.

Wish to hell she hurries up with her period. One of the reasons she's here is so that I don't have to go out looking for my tail, like Jake said.

August 4

The bird says good morning at six when the sun's straining to get through the curtains, and I throw an ashtray at him, which misses and clangs against the wall and makes a hell of a racket. This gets the squawk box all excited and he doesn't shut up for five minutes, so

Terry gets up and rushes over to see if I was lucky enough to bean him, giving me a mean look and talking baby talk to it.

Birds, they're all the same whether it's feathers or skin over their bones. She puts some seed she bought in a jar top and places it on the window sill along with some water, and bird walks over to it, looks at it, then at us, and starts eating, looking up every now and then to make sure there's no more ashtrays coming his way.

He finishes—there's seed all over the floor (which'll make the cockroaches happy)—squawks and goes back to the middle of the perch.

Terry says something like "Don't be mad Michael, it's his first day here and he's not used to us yet, but he'll be quieter after a week or so, and isn't he lovely (look, he's preening his feathers!)" and I turn over and go back to sleep.

Squawk!

Nine thirty only and that undersized chicken's woken me up again. That's it. I whip out of bed, open the window (she thinks maybe we're going to leave the window closed the rest of the summer, and because of him die of heat stroke!), grab him and throw him out, followed by the perch, seed and water.

No use sleeping any more this morning. I make a coffee, smoke a cigarette and walk to work. There's some pigeons at the park grubbing around looking for food. I kick at the nearest one and they hit the air. Damn birds. An old woman sitting at a nearby bench with a *True Romance* in her hands, looks up and curses me for cruelty to birds.

"You animal! Don't you dare touch those poor pigeons or I'll call a policeman!"

I thumb my nose at her and head up the street. The old witch, she's just liable to start screeching for a cop over those goddam pigeons.

A couple of bums shuffle by. They look like Mutt and Jeff and they have a bunch of celery in their hands. Mutt stops me and asks me if I want to buy one bunch for a dime, or three for a quarter. Jeff—he's got a scab on his nose and he stinks worse than Mutt—says I can have the whole lot for a buck.

"Wow," I answer, "just what I always wanted."

"Celery's good for your eyes," says Mutt. He's got some yellow matter all over his eyelids, so I tell him to eat it himself if it's so damn good.

Jeff tries another angle, "You'd think the stuff was stolen, it's so cheap, wouldn't you."

"But that ain't so," says Mutt, nudging Jeff in the gut with his elbow. "We're owners of a celery ranch outside of town and we sell our own stuff, that way we got no middleman and you get it cheaper." Jeff nudges him back and gets Mutt right in the yap, making him drop his celery. It falls in the gutter and he picks it up and tries to scrape some of the scum off it with his fingernails, which are longer than a girl's. And blacker than an Indian's asshole.

"We'll sell it for seventy-five cents seeing how it got slightly mussed up." If I remember right, that's the cheapest a bottle of wine goes for.

A yellow cab comes up the street, and they think it's a cop car and try to hide the celery under their shirts, but the leaves stick out from under, and one of the stalks is jammed up against Jeff's scab.

"Hey, we better go find us a paper bag," says Mutt.

"That way it keeps fresher longer," Jeff says to me as they shuffle off down the street, looking like two walking gardens.

When I see Mrs. Waddling I realize that what I should have done with the bird is give it to her. They would have made great company together, one honking and the other squawking. Too bad. Spaghetti for lunch.

As I walk past the waitresses' changing room on my way to the bar, I peek in for a sec and get a good eyeful of Mrs. Russell (I keep forgetting her first name). She's got nothing but her slip on and when she bends over to slip on her uniform her two balloons jiggle in her brassiere and threaten to flop out. I'll have to get friendlier with her, no doubt about it. I've always thought how nice would be to have a piece of tail here at the Club when there's nothing doing. It would make the day go faster.

Naturally, when I get home Terry's crying her eyes out. She's crying so hard that she can't even ask what happened, so I tell her. "I opened the window and it flew out."

She bawls harder and I think tonight's as good a night as any to go over and see how George is doing.

"Did—did you try and catch him?" she whimpers. "Did you try and catch him after he flew out?" Her eyes are red and there's about fifty thousand Kleenex on the floor. She looks like my dog when the old man booted him because he'd chewed up one of his shoes.

"Yeah, I run all over the place after him, and I was almost on top of him over by the fence behind the house when this cat grabbed him in its mouth and took off with him."

She starts bawling again, harder than before, so I light a butt and sit down beside her on the bed. "Don't feel bad honey. He died fast. Cats break a bird's neck. They don't like eating them while they're still alive. It gives them indigestion."

I thought my little joke would make her feel better, but the opposite happens. She flops face down on the bed and really has a good bawl. "Poor little bird," she sobs.

"Tell you what. I'll get you one for your birthday." Her birthday's in February.

But she keeps on bawling like she never heard me and says something else about that damn bird. I turn CHUM on, but it's the Speak Your Mouth program, which isn't bad if you like to hear people being insulted by that Givens guy, but I figure music is what this place needs right now, so whip the dial over to CKFH. A baseball game. I switch it off.

I'm too tired to go to George's tonight, I decide, so I get undressed and sit on the bed thinking whether I should take a bath or not, since I already had one on Saturday, decide I'm too tired for that, too, and grab this morning's *Globe and Mail* that somebody left behind at the Club, and read the front page. All it's got on it is Vietnam and some riot in the States so I turn off the light and hit the sack. Terry's still crying and I'm thinking about Mrs. Russell.

She gets up, turns the light on again, blows her nose, picks up the Kleenex all over the floor and goes to the bathroom with her paper bag in her hand. Dammit, I'm cut off tonight, too.

Later, she snuggles into my arms, half-laughs, half-sighs, and says, "Isn't it terrible, Michael?"

"What, the bird?" I answer, half asleep. "Hell, it's got nothing to worry about any more."

"No, I meant that if I cry like that over a budgie I lost, wouldn't it be terrible how I'd cry over a baby I lost?" She snuggles in even closer when she says that her head on my chest and her eyes warm and wet.

What the hell's a baby got to do with a bird? Suddenly I think, she's not knocked up, is she? Then I remember she's having her period.

Still, why did she put that in about a kid anyway?

August 5

Great not having that bird squawking at six in the morning. There's some thumping and screaming upstairs followed by the sound of cowboy boots down the hall and a door slamming. Wonder who'll be on the porch with her on Sunday?

Terry doesn't say a word about last night. Just sits there humming a song on the radio and sewing something up. Sometimes I'd really like to know what goes on in her head.

Around ten we go for a walk around the park to cool off. It's pretty quiet, only a queer walking his cat ("Oh! A Siamese. Isn't he beautiful?") wearing a pair of white pants and a powder blue sweater, and wiggling his ass like a beauty queen. Enough to put half the broads around here to shame.

There's a couple of old Indians sitting by the flower bed in front of the washrooms and a little kid—can't be more than six, with a T-shirt black with dirt, jeans that look like his great-grandfather's hand-me-downs they're so worn, and running shoes with holes in the front and his toes sticking out through them—walks past the two old guys and says "Kemo sabe," lifting up his right hand, palm forward like an Indian salute, at the same time. The old men laugh and the kid goes on his way proud as a cat with a mouse in his mouth.

It's full moon, and the moon's rays make the grass look like it's silver-plated or like there's a dew on it. Real pretty.

We sit down on a bench over by Robert Burns and have a smoke. That is, I do. She only smokes when she's drunk, and she's only been doing that since she met me.

I put my arm around her like we're high school lovers or something kooky like that, and she gives me a little peck on the cheek. We sit like that for about half an hour without saying anything, just looking at the moon, watching the first queers start coming in for their night's fun, and behind them the headlights of cars speeding along to wherever they're going.

But it starts getting cool and I run out of matches so we head for home, but slowly, and holding hands—we've only done that a couple of times since we been together—thinking our own thoughts and at the same time feeling close together like we're one person. A fantastic feeling. One I've only had once before in my life and that was so long ago I even forget what her name was.

A rat races across the street, followed by a mutt barking like all hell, and two kids with sticks in their hands yelling at the top of their lungs.

A minute later the rat races back across the street in the direction he's just come from, the dog still right on its heels and the kids behind it. Man, that rat's going to get its money's worth tonight. It'll be so pooped tomorrow, it won't even be able to go over to Mrs. Himmel's back yard, which serves as the neighbourhood garbage dump, to get its breakfast.

No one on the porch tonight. Not that I expected any different. It usually takes her about two good drunks in the Harmony before she can get some poor slob to come live with her. Too bad about Cowboy. He was more intelligent than what she usually has. At least he'd say doggone when you passed him.

August 6

Miss Brown's an old bag of bones who comes into the Club once in a while. I really like her (she's a retired school teacher) cause she's always got something nice to say like "You're a very intelligent boy. Too bad you never finished school," and she'll pat my shoulder and say, smiling, "If I'd been your teacher, you would have." She's about seventy and she wears at least six inches of makeup on her face, but she's the one woman I'd like to have had as a mother.

Sometimes, though, she can be a real pain in the ass: like she's always promising to get me a bartending job in the King Eddie Hotel cause she says she knows the owner there, but that's the last I ever hear of it. Not that I care, though. I'm happy here.

Also, she invites a lot of university girls in for sherry parties (I figure she's lesbian because they're pretty sharp looking tricks some of them) and sometimes she'll say right in front of them, "Michael's an adorable boy, and so intelligent too," which sets them all off giggling and makes me want to jam the tray down her mouth. Like the other one who's always talking about my blue eyes.

Take today. She's got ten sharp looking pieces of tail, and I mean sharp. As I come up with the tray full of sherry glasses she says, "Aren't these girls beautiful?" and I get red in the face and don't say anything and start serving out the drinks. Three of them are sitting on a sofa and they're sunk so deep into it that their legs are almost up to their chins and, naturally, they're wearing miniskirts. As I bend over to put the sherry on the low table in front of them I sneak a look up the first one's legs. Christ, she's sitting so low that I can practically see her belly button. I serve the second one, but she's seen what I'm up to and crosses her legs, which still doesn't stop me from seeing what colour panties she's wearing. The third one's crossed her legs also, and put her hands by the side of her skirt, so nothing doing there, besides she's fat anyway.

As I leave Miss Brown says, "Isn't he a darling boy?" and they all giggle again and I feel like saying to her that she brings the nicest collection of tail in here of all the members of the Club.

I look back at them and the three chicks on the sofa are whispering to each other and giggling. One of them looks up and I wink at her and she whispers something to the other two and they all look at me, which makes Miss Brown and all the rest look at me too. Christ, do I feel stupid with the whole gang of them staring at me like I'm naked or something. Miss Brown picks up her sherry and says, "Drink up, girls, leave Michael alone to do his work." Giggle, giggle.

As they're going downstairs after, she comes up to the bar and says, "I'm trying to line up an interview for you with the owner of the Royal York Hotel. His daughter is one of my guests—she's the one who was sitting between the other two girls on the sofa."

Yeah, the one with the blue panties.

"Thanks, Miss Brown," I answer, and she trots off down the stairs with her little chickadees.

This afternoon I hear Miss Virgin talking to Anne.

"Yeah, I think I've got piles," she says. "I was sitting on the toilet and it was hurting like hell."

Good old lovable Miss Virgin, about as feminine as Sonny Liston. Her and her boy friend (whoever the madman is) must have a ball talking about her piles in bed at night. I'll bet he kisses every pimple on her face, too, before they go to sleep. Passion, man, passion.

I drag a case of beer home, have a couple, look at the movie section of the *Telegram,* which I took from the corner box cause I feel like seeing a movie tonight, wait for Terry to get fixed up and off we go to see *In the Heat of the Night.* We get there in time for the last show and there's a line-up about ten blocks long to get in. All these office creeps who live out in the suburbs and come down on a Friday night with their scraggy wives for a drink and a movie! Pricks. They could come any time of the week, but no, it's got to be a Friday night, so that guys like me got to spend an hour in line before we get in. Pricks.

The show's kind of expensive but I pay for Terry's ticket anyway. Sort of to make up for the bird, you know. Inside it's packed and all we get is two seats near the front, which I hate cause you got to bend your neck up, and when you leave it's so stiff you walk home like a queer, your neck in the air and your mouth open, waiting for a joint to chew on.

The movie's a gas. It's about this nigger who's also a cop and he's in Mississippi and the white cops there, who're about as stupid as any cop here in Toronto, got a murder on their hands and they can't solve it, so they ask the black guy to do it. And man, these cops are real farmers. One of them's called Shagbag, and another one's made six hundred dollars in the past twenty years or something by flipping heads or tails with quarters, and they all talk with "y'alls" and "I declares" thrown in all over the place, and there's a chick in the movie who's got the best pair of boobs I seen in a long time and she gets knocked up by a guy with an IQ of ten who works in a restaurant and kills flies with a rubber band. (George said I should see this movie because it shows up very well the plight of the black man in the southern United States. George has never got a cent but he always gets to see all the new movies in town.)

There's a part I really like, which has four guys ganging up on the nigger. They've got iron bars and chains and things and it reminds me of the time we took on some wops from over Spadina way.

They were a tough bunch. One night they came over, two carloads full of them, cause the week before we'd gone to a dance in their district and tried to con off one of their girls. They walked into Blow Job's but none of us was around just then (we were getting juiced over at Dirty Doug's place with his old man's booze), so they waited for a while outside and caught Jim, a little guy who wore glasses, had a brushcut and didn't have anything to do with us, and punched him out till he fell to the sidewalk. They busted his glasses, and dragged him across the sidewalk till his nose was balanced on the edge of the curb and stomped him on the back of the head. His nose was busted so bad that it twisted to one side and there was nothing the doctor could do. It's still twisted today and he says he can smell better when the wind's coming in from his right side, which is the side his nose is pointed.

A real jerk, Jimmy, like the day he comes into the restaurant with that goddam brushcut of his. All cut off on the side and just this strip of hair on the top of his head. Man, we razzed him about that. We even got him outside after, turned him upside down and brushed off our shoes with his head.

Anyway, after they busted his nose, they cruised around the streets looking for us, and goddam if they didn't spot us just as we're storming out of Dirty Doug's, his old man hard on our tails with a brick in his hand. We run down the street with him screaming he'll get us for drinking his good Scotch and us laughing like hell, and baff, we run right into the wops. They're standing beside their cars. There's about a dozen of them and some have got tire jacks, one's holding an air rifle, another a car aerial, and a few got brass knuckles around their fists—garbage can handles with the edges cut up and jagging outwards. They'll take half your face off with one good swipe.

Spike pulls his switchblade out of his pocket, Dirty Doug runs to a doorstep, grabs a milk bottle sitting there and busts it, and the rest of us move back a few feet cause we got nothing to fight with. Dirty Doug's old man runs back into the house and I grab the brick he's dropped.

They move towards us, telling us we're a bunch of mother-fuckers and they're going to bust us good, and we yell back that their old men suck cocks. Then the guy with the air rifle takes a shot at Spike, I heave the brick at the biggest one there, and the fight's on.

It only lasted about five minutes, but, man, it was rough. Spike had caught that air gun pellet in the side and he was hurt. Shit, those things'll take a hunk of flesh the size of your thumbnail out of you. I'd connected with the brick and the guy was sitting on the sidewalk holding his head. Spike's brother got in real close to the guy with the car aerial so he couldn't take a good swipe and his boots were flying at him. The tire iron caught Sally the Squaw across the shoulders and Dirty Doug was swinging that bottle left and right in front of him till he caught a slug from that fucking air gun in the gut and he went down and they all put the boots on him. I grabbed one of the guys with the knuckles and I'm holding him down by his hair, trying to aim his head at a car window, when I get plastered right in the mouth by another guy with knuckles. I let go of the guy and put my hand to my face just as those knuckles swing at me again. I raise my hand ahead of me and they glance off my fingers. Spike's cut one of them, cause he's headed back to their cars holding his side and swearing. Someone's trying to boot me in the face but all he's hitting is my hands, so he goes to work on my ribs. Sally the Squaw's got her hands around the crotch of one of them and she's squeezing harder and harder and he's screaming.

We hear a siren and the wops jump back into their cars yelling they'll get us some other time, and me sitting there against that car bleeding like a stuck pig. My lower lip's hanging down. It's been cut in two by those knuckles and my right hand's bleeding too. All I see everywhere is blood. On the sidewalk, on the parked cars, on us, everywhere.

Somebody helps me and Dirty Doug up. Sally the Squaw's still holding onto that wop. They're both lying on the sidewalk. We pull her off the guy just as a cop car turns up the street, sirens blazing, and duck down between two houses and make it to Dirty Doug's old man's place, where we try to wash off some of the blood.

That poor wop when the cops found him. His balls must have looked like a plate of mashed potatoes.

I'm bleeding so much that they take me up to Wellesley Hospital when the cops have left and have my lip and my big finger stitched up. Those goddam garbage can handles, they're vicious. It took six stitches on my lip to close the thing up and two on my finger, which had been opened right to the bone. When I got home that night my mouth was swollen like a balloon and there was dried blood all over my face and hands and clothes. The old man looked at me and said, "That'll teach you to lick a broad when she's on the rags." My old woman was out somewhere getting drunk.

Yeah, great times we had in those days. Two months later I was sent to St. John's and that ended the deal we'd organized to get those wops. We were going to get about two hundred guys and burn the whole wop district right to the ground.

Terry thinks the movie is great and says it's terrible the way they treat the Negroes down there, and I say I don't know about that, they were picking cotton and everything and they looked pretty happy to me. There's lots of Indians down here who would give their right arm to have a job picking cotton.

Tonight I get my first go at her since Saturday. Damn broads and their periods. Every time I mix a bloody Mary at the Club I think of that.

August 7

Saturday at last. As soon as I get home I guzzle down two beers, burp and finish off a third, then I stop cause it's a good idea to leave a few for Sunday. My original plan is to take Terry to a nice quiet beer parlour over on Sherbourne Street, but on second thought I decide against it. I don't want her period starting all over again. So what are we going to do, being Saturday and all?

"Let's go over to George's."

"Okay Michael, as soon as I finish combing my hair."

Half an hour and two beers later we're off. It's kind of humid and the mosquitoes are biting and I'm in a sweat by the time we get to his place. So is she.

I pound on his door and wait. Nobody answers. I pound again and put my ear to the door. There's some noise inside.

"Maybe he's gone out."

I'm about to say, don't worry, he's just getting his pants on, when the door opens and there's the one and only George, standing there with his hair all over his face, no shirt on and his pant belt unbuckled. That's what I like about me, I'm usually never wrong when I give an opinion.

"Oh-hi-Mike-Terry-come-on-in."

He's talking in that tone of voice with no expression, like a tape recorder, and his eyes are wide open and bloodshot. Inside, the room is full of smoke that smells like a bonfire of dry leaves.

Where'd he get the money for the Mary Jane?

"Where'd you get the money for the Mary Jane?"

"That's not Mary Jane," he answers, "that's kef."

"What?"

"Kef, man, kef. Straight-from-Tangiers."

"Arab Mary Jane, yet," I think to myself.

Terry's waving her hand in front of her as if that's going to scare the smoke away. She coughs. Over on the bed there's something laying down and when I get closer I see it's a chick. One of the Yorkville chicks, with hair down to her ass, tight jeans with paint all over them, and beads around her neck. She's nude from the waist up—not that it matters much, she's so flat—and her feet are dirty. She's holding a joint of kef in her left hand.

Terry and me sit down on some newspapers on the floor cause the chairs have got cups and things on them. George walks over to the edge of the bed and sits down.

"Mike-Terry-this-is-Yvonne. Yvonne-this-is-Mike-and-Terry."
He's laughing after he says that and Yvonne doesn't say anything.
Just lies there looking at the ceiling. There's a cockroach walking
across it.

Terry looks kind of embarrassed at the sight of Yvonne but she
smiles at George like there was nothing wrong. I pull his speech out
of my pocket and hand it to him.

He asks me what I thought of it and I say, "Great, but what does
40,000 = 52 mean?" He laughs at that and looks up at the ceiling as
well. Terry and me sit there like two turds in a sewer. I look around
the room now that my eyes are used to the smoke. He's got a couple
of new posters, but they look homemade. One of them's got LBJ
sitting at a table with McNamara and Rusk beside him and under
it there's the title, "The Unholy Trinity—Three Boors in One." The
other one's a photo of Lamport with his mouth open and his hands
raised like he's going to hit somebody. Title: "Brutus Canadensis."

George and Yvonne are grinning and mumbling to each other.

"Hare-Krishna."

"Hare-Krishna."

"Hare-Krishna."

"Hare."

"Hairy who?" I cut in cause I can't place who they're talking about,
but the broad just keeps on saying that, and George only laughs.

"Hey George!" I yell at him, loud enough so he'll pay attention.

"Yes-my-dear-Michael?" he asks, with a queer smile on his face.

"What happened to the chick you had last time I saw you?"

He sits there for a minute thinking, then he says, "Oh-that-one.
I-found-out-she-had-Trotskyite-leanings-so-I-had-to-tell-her-to-go."

Hell, man, who cares what leanings she's got? A piece is a piece.

He lights up and offers me a drag. I pull in deep so the smoke goes
right down to my gut, hold it for a few seconds and let it out slowly. It's
kind of dry on my throat, but that's because I haven't had any for a hell
of a long time. Terry says "No thanks" when George offers her a puff,
but I say to her, "Go ahead, kid, have a puff, it'll do you good," and she
draws some into her lungs and coughs so hard that even that boobless

blob on the bed stops watching her cockroach and turns to see what's the matter. I bet she's as much fun as a dead body.

George stretches out on the foot of the bed. Her feet are beside his face, and his beside hers. That's what they do for kicks. They suck each other's toes. Wow.

"Hey man," I yell at George again, "throw me a butt, eh? I didn't come here just to look at you all night." George laughs at that like it was the funniest thing he ever heard in his life, and throws me one that he's pulled out of his pant pocket. All crushed and flat. I light it up and take a couple of good deep drags. Terry says no when I offer her some, but I make her have a drag anyway, and she coughs all over the room again. Hell, I'm not wasting any more on her, besides just the smoke in here is starting to get her high. I can tell cause she giggles after that last coughing spell. She leans against the wall and stretches her legs out. I'm starting to feel good, too. Terry and me look at each other and laugh. That's the first time I've been affected so fast by the stuff. Must be cause it's kef. George says it's stronger than Mary Jane. Also the fact that the room's full of kef smoke.

"Did-you-know-that-Sir-John-A-Macdonald-was-a-dipso-maniac?" George asks, his voice floating around the room like the smoke.

"No-I-didn't-what's-a-dypsimanawhatchamacallit?" my voice floats back at him. Christ, I'm bombed already.

"Groovy," grunts boobless from her end of the bed. Christ, she's got a voice like a man. Maybe she is, and George doesn't know it yet.

"Groovy-what?" George asks. "A-dipsomaniac-is-an-alcoholic-my-dear-Michael-Sir-John-A-Macdonald-our-first-Prime-Minister-was-a-wino."

"The-cockroach-made-it-safely-across-the-ceiling-my-soul-is-a-cockroach."

I take another deep drag and flop full length on the floor beside Terry, who takes my hand and giggles. Her eyes look all funny. I guess mine do too.

"One-day-Sir-John-A-was-giving-an-election-speech-in-Kingston-he-was-drunk-and-just-as-he-was-about-to-begin-hebarfed-right-in-front-of-the-thousands-of-people-who-had-come-to-hear-him-speak-for-a-minute-he-stood-there-without-saying-a-word-then-lifts-his-fist-in-the-air-shakes-it-at-the-crowd-and-cries-and-that-ladies-and-gentlemen-is-what-I-think-of-my-opponent."

I laugh and laugh. Terry laughs and laughs. George laughs and laughs. Boobless says nothing. This is great (I take another drag) this is just great. I laugh and laugh. Oh man, what a ball we're having tonight.

Terry puts her head on my chest, grins like a monkey, and whispers at my belly button, "Can-I-have-another-drag Michael-I-mean-Michael-please?" "Sure-Terry-I-mean-Terry," I answer laughing, "but-the-cigarette's-up-here." She laughs and turns her head and takes a deep drag and hardly coughs at all. "Oh-my-head's-spinning-but-I-feel-so-happy," she says as she lets the smoke out in front of my face. I try to grab a mouthful before it floats away.

"Groovy," grunts boobless. Hell, she's not really that bad, they're just not fully grown yet, that's all. She's really a nice kid and I like her almost as much as I like Terry. I like everybody.

Hey, there's some bottles under the bed, at least a half-dozen.

"What's-those-bottles?" I ask George, who's just had another drag and is still chuckling over the Sir John A. story.

"What-bottles?" still chuckling.

"The-ones-under-the-bed-rye-maybe-gin-wine?"

"Those-bottles" chuckle "those-bottles" chuckle "they're-Molotov-Cocktails." Laugh. "Drink-one-of-them-and-light-a-cigarette-after-and-you'll-be-Canada's-first-spaceman." Laugh.

Molotov Cocktail, where have I heard that before? At the Club maybe. Who knows. Who cares. I don't feel like a drink, anyway.

"Groovy-here-comes-my-soul-again." There it is all right. Big and brown. Big brown cockroach. I love it.

I smoke the cigarette right down to the end and take a last drag between my fingernails like when we butt-banged at St. John's. If Lawrence could see me now. I laugh, and Terry laughs, her head vibrating against my chest. I love her with all my heart.

"Oh-I-feel-like-I'm-flying-oh."

"Hey-Mike."

"Yeah-sweetheart?"

"You-know-what-LBJ-is?"

"No-sweetheart-give-me-another-joint-before-you-tell-me."

He throws one at me and it floats in the air for an hour before landing on Terry's head. She picks it up and puts it in my mouth.

"Here-Michael-sorry-I-keep-saying-Michael-I-mean-Michael," she giggles and her teeth are so white I think they're marshmallows and I want to eat them. I giggle back at her. I light a match and the flame's ten thousand miles away. She takes it out of my hand and puts it next to the cigarette, then throws it under the bed. It lands beside the bottles, burns for a second (or is it ten thousand years?) and dies out.

"Groovy—you-got-one-for-me?"

"Sure-Yvonne." He reaches over and kisses her hard little nipples, handing her one at the same time, and lights it for her and kisses her nipples again. She's got the most beautiful nipples in the world. I want to kiss them too. Terry takes the butt out of my mouth and drags on it till her head falls on my chest. I take it out of her hand and her head slides down to my stomach. I feel her mouth moving and bend over to hear what she's saying. All I hear is a hum.

The smoke is rising up and down in the room like boats at sea. I try to catch one of the boats, but it escapes between my fingers and goes sailing towards boobless. She's not really. In fact she's got nice big ones. It's just that she's stretched out and that makes them look smaller than they are. Terry's are nicer though. I love Terry and I'm going to marry her one day. I love her breasts with those rosy nipples sticking out from the middle like two little tongues. George lights up another one.

Where's he getting them from? We must have smoked a million of them already. I love George. He's my best friend. My hand falls to the floor and I'm too lazy to pick it up. It's got a right to rest on the floor just like us if it wants to. I laugh at my hand.

"LBJ-is-a-grub-just-a-grub-in-the-ground-and-eats-roots-that's-all-he-does-is-eat-roots-eating-grub-no-good-to-anybody-lying-there-under-the-ground-brown-and-covered-with-dirt-eating-roots-lies-there-for-seventeen-years-like-that-eating-roots-under-the-ground-and-one-June-night-he-comes-out-of-the-

ground-he's-got-wings-and-he's-a-June-bug-and-he-doesn't-have-
to-eat-roots-any-more-he-flies-about-till-he-comes-to-a-bright-
yellow-light-and-he-flies-to-it-as-fast-as-his-grubby-brown-wings-
will-take-him-happy-that-there's-a-light-and-he-flies-even-faster-
until-he-crashes-right-into-the-light-bulb-he's-burned-to-a-crisp-
and-he-falls-to-the-ground-right-on-top-of-the-spot-where-he-
just-spent-seventeen-years-eating-roots-and-now-he's-nothing-
a-cigar-ash."

For some odd reason, I'm hungry. Terry's conked out so I push
her gently off me (she's a great kid. I don't want to hurt her) and her
eyes are wide open but she's not seeing anything. George's still talking about grubs and Yvonne (she's a real doll) is looking for her soul
which has just disappeared into a crack in the wall.

Naturally there's nothing to eat in his ice box except a piece of
bread so hard if it fell on your foot, it'd break it. No wait, there's a
half-eaten apple. I pull it out carefully cause I don't want it to get
bruised (poor little apple) and carefully sink my teeth into it. It's the
tastiest apple I've ever eaten, red and juicy and just hard enough to
make your teeth tingle.

"Groovy. Here-comes-my-soul-again." The cigarette is burning
her lovely delicate fingers, but she doesn't notice it. I want to tell her
but I'm too happy to talk.

Her soul starts walking down the wall towards her. She reaches
up to hold it in her hand. Her fingers brush against it and it falls off
the wall.

"My-soul-it's-gone-my-soul's-gone."

"It's-not-your-soul-it's-my-baby."

That's Terry talking. She's talking about me. I'm her baby. Her
loving baby.

"Here-comes-your-baby," my voice says to her, but she doesn't
hear me.

"It's-my-baby-it's-not-your-soul."

"Please-come-back-soul-I-need-you." She leans over the edge of
the bed and looks under it for her soul, her beautiful breasts swaying
as she turns.

"Englishmen-are-the-cause-of-most-of-the-world's-troubles."

"Here-comes-your-baby," my voice tells her as my body floats down beside hers and my mouth covers hers.

"Baby-oh-baby," she holds my head in her hands and lays it against her lovely breasts. It sinks into her soft, warm, tender breasts. It disappears into her breasts. Goes right through her blouse and snuggles in next to her brassiere.

"Palestine-Cyprus-India-Pakistan-United-States-West-Indies-Malaysia-Singapore-Canada-Gibraltar-Guyana-Belize-South-Africa-Rhodesia-Nigeria-Aden-Ireland."

Yvonne's butt has fallen to the ground, and George has put his out against the wall and mine's almost had it. There's only a few puffs left in it and I get up and offer George a drag, and then Yvonne. She stops looking for her soul and lies face up on the bed as I place the butt in her mouth. I kiss her nipples because they're asking me to and they're hard and warm. Her mouth smiles at me so I kiss it too. It's wet and warm. I kiss George's toes and they wiggle and say thank you and I sit down beside Terry and give her a puff. She doesn't cough at all now. I kiss her knees and they say more, so I kiss them again.

"Wherever-the-British-have-gone-they've-left-nothing-but-trouble-and-hate-behind-them-trouble-and-race-hate."

There's no more lovely kef left. I look back at that lovely apple I've just eaten. The core is lying in a pile of newspapers and magazines like an egg in a nest. It's well protected there. Nobody'll hurt it.

We lie there for a million years until I look at my watch (it's winking at me. I kiss it) and I see it's three in the morning.

Suddenly I'm tired and want to go to my lovely room with my lovely Terry and make beautiful love to her on our lovely bed. I want to make beautiful love to Yvonne too. I want to make beautiful love to everybody.

I want to read a book.

I float over to George's library. His library is mostly about ten thousand books piled up in one corner of the room plus dozens more hidden in the newspapers and magazines on the floor.

There's a pretty one with a red cover, and one with a green cover. I'll take it too. And the one with a black cover. There. Now I have three books.

"Let's-go-home-Terry-love," my voice tells her, and slowly her delicious body gets up off the floor and follows me out the door. I've forgotten to say good night to George and Yvonne. I open the door and stick my head in the room. Yvonne's just seen her soul walking along the floor, and George has just seen Yvonne. He's sitting up pulling her to his end of the bed as I say good night. They don't answer.

The moon is so bright. It's dazzling, like gold. A golden plate. We walk home, our arms around each other, and stop and kiss every few feet.

An old woman's looking around in some garbage cans near the park. She throws on the sidewalk what she doesn't want, and puts the rest in a shopping bag. Such a sweet old woman. Bent over a garbage can. Wearing an old black dress with an army belt tied around it. Wearing a pair of winter socks with holes in the heels. She looks so lonely. I think I'll go over and kiss her. Show her that I love her.

"Get away from me, you little bastard!"

Is she talking to me? She can't be. I'm not a little bastard. I just want to give her a kiss. I love her. Her hand reaches out at me. Dirty black fingernails.

"Gwan, beat it!"

Terry's laughing. She must think it's funny. I laugh too.

"Leave me alone!"

She's talking to me. What have I done? That moon, it's so bright. Terry laughs and laughs. The books under my arm are getting heavy. Terry takes my arm and says something. The stars smile at me.

"Used to be a woman could walk the streets safely at night!"

We run through the park and play hide and seek around the pine trees. Robert Burns smiles at us. I hide behind some bushes and somebody hisses in my ears "Beat it!" Everybody wants me to beat it tonight.

Terry's searching around for me behind the fountain. I whistle and she comes running, her face shining like the moon. I wish I had my dog with me. I should go visit my father. I wonder where my mother is. And my half brother. We kiss long and hard, our tongues, our lips, our mouths become one, and that one is me. Somebody walks by. He's weaving from side to side. He walks over to a bench, goes to sit down on it, misses, and ends up on the grass. He looks so happy lying there without a care in the world. He snores.

There's our house. It looks lovely with the moon's rays reflected off it. A silver castle. There's some scuffling around in the room next to ours. That's Bertha's room. Bertha's very religious and she always dresses in black and every Sunday she goes to St. Peter's Anglican Church. She cleans houses up in Rosedale during the day and I only see her about once a month. Mrs. Himmel told me she's crazy, that every night she gets up at one in the morning and kneels beside her bed and prays till dawn. And she whips herself with an iron coat hanger. I think maybe I should knock at her door and tell her I love her. But I'm too tired now, and besides she'll probably tell me to beat it.

How wonderful to go into your room and know that you're not alone in it. I get on my knees and kiss Terry's hands and try to tell her how wonderful it is, but Terry wouldn't understand. She says, "Get up Michael. Get up. You're not my slave, I'm yours. I love you so much."

"I love you too," I tell her.

With the first rays of the morning sun creeping through the curtains, we make love like nobody has ever done it before. It's too good to be true.

We sleep.

August 8

Three o'clock. Three o'clock in the afternoon. Half the goddam day shot to hell. I kick the sheet off us, give her a boot and start the water boiling for a coffee. I boot her again. Dumb bitch. All she does is sleep.

"Get up! It's three o'clock," I yell at her. "Come on, get up!"

Finally we get around to having something to eat. She's complaining that her head hurts. She wants to know if we were smoking dope last night. God, is she stupid!

"God you're stupid! It was kef. Everybody knows that."

"Is that like marijuana?"

"Like what?"

"Like marijuana."

"You mean Mary Jane."

"Yes, Mary Jane."

"Well say it right then."

A regular farmer's daughter.

"It was so strange."

"What? Here, get me another coffee."

"So strange."

"*What?*"

"I thought I saw my baby last night."

"You thought you saw what?" My eyebrows raise half an inch and I drop my cigarette.

She stops dead, pouring water into the kettle. Her face turns red and she looks scared. Real scared.

"What baby?"

Her eyes are looking at something on the floor.

"What the hell are you talking about?" I get up off the chair and walk towards her.

"Come on, spill it!"

She shuffles her left foot. Her face has turned white. She looks like she's going to cry.

"Come on!" I yell right in her face, shaking her shoulders with my hands.

She steps back a foot, looks up at me, and runs over to the bed and starts crying.

I walk over to her and shake her again. Goddam broad, that's all she ever does is cry. She could fill up Lake Ontario with all the tears she's dropped since she's been here.

"Talk, damn it, talk! What baby?"

"Please Michael, don't be mad at me." Her nose is running and she gets up looking for her purse. It's over by the door and I pick it up and throw it to her. She takes some Kleenex and blows her nose.

I calm down a bit. As long as she's bawling I'll never get a word out of her. I light a smoke and sit on the chair and wait.

She throws me a sad, sad look. Like she's going to die or something. I say nothing.

"I—I had a baby," she stammers.

"So?"

"It was with that fellow I was going with back home."

"And?"

"When my parents found out, I told them that we'd get married." She starts crying again. I'm starting to lose my temper.

"But they said I'd ruin my life by getting married so young. They said, don't worry, we'll protect you. You just stay here and when you have your baby we'll tell everyone it's a child we've adopted and no one will know." Sniffle. Sniffle.

"Well?"

"It was a beautiful baby. Oh so beautiful."

"So, where is it now?"

"They—they," again she bawls, her head buried in the pillow, her whole body shaking like a Jello. Man, what a patience I got.

"They took my baby and gave it up for adoption. They took my baby away." For a minute the whole room's echoing with her goddam bawling.

"They said it was better for me that way. That I had my whole life ahead of me still. That it was better for the baby, too, because that way it wouldn't be a bastard. Oh, my poor little baby." She breaks down again. "My poor little baby. I came home one afternoon and it was gone. They'd taken it away. It was gone. It was gone. It was gone. My baby. My poor little baby."

That's enough for me. I get up and look around for my pants.

Now my head's aching too. Broads. Broads. Broads. You can't trust them. Here I am thinking that I got a real innocent kid with me. Here I am treating her real nice and being good to her, and it turns out she's been getting screwed since God knows when. Probably with every straw-sucking, clod-headed farmer she's ever met. Like, I been taken for a sucker. A kid, for Christsake. A goddam kid. Telling me she left home cause her folks wouldn't let her go out with some shitty little punk up there. And here she is, a mother. I'll be damned. Man, have I been taken for a ride.

How come every Sunday turns out like this?

She's crying so hard now, she looks like she'll fall apart at the seams.

I've got to get some fresh air.

"Michael, please don't be mad with me. I was ashamed to tell you before."

For some reason, I feel sorry for her right then.

"Nothing to be ashamed of, kid. Most women drop a kid some time or other."

I light another smoke while she's busy drying her eyes. Her face looks like a tank ran over it.

She sits up.

"That's why I left home. I couldn't stand living in the same house with them. In the same house where my baby lived." She looks like she's going to cry again, but she stops herself. "I came to Toronto to start a new life."

Some start.

"I hadn't thought about him too much till last night. It was horrible. He was standing there on the ceiling smiling at me and when I smiled back at him he was gone. I wanted to cry, but all I could do was stare. My poor little baby." She's starting to sound like a broken record.

I got to do something to shut her up. I sit down beside her and take her in my arms and lie her down. She looks dazed, like she's still doped up from last night.

I lie down beside her and we stay like that almost all afternoon, without saying anything. A couple of times she cries again, but it doesn't last long. I kiss her after and she's quiet again. All that time I'm trying to sort things out in my mind.

Okay, so she's had a kid. So what? That's no skin off my nose. She's a nice kid and she keeps the place clean, pays her share of the rent, and doesn't mouth off. She doesn't mess around with the other guys and she's good-looking. Well, not ugly anyway.

She's had a kid, but her folks got rid of it, so she doesn't have that on her back. Everybody makes a mistake once in a while. The thing is to learn from your mistakes. Not to get caught twice doing the same thing. I think I asked her when I first brought her here if she was using pills or a safe or something, and if I remember right she blushed. In my book that means she is. Hell, a person only blushes when he's scared to tell the truth. So why get in a heat because she lied to me? Besides, she didn't really lie, she just didn't tell me, period. As long as she doesn't have one while she's with me, she can stay as long as she wants. Just as long as she doesn't have one while she's with me. Hell, she can't be that stupid anyway. Not after having gone through that once already. Can she?

Around seven, we have something to eat but neither one of us is too hungry. We listen to the radio for a while and talk about last night. She seems happy now that she's got that out of her system.

A good cry helps once in a while.

We're both knocked out from last night and today, and tomorrow is work, so by nine we're in bed. I haven't been in bed by nine since St. John's. And I still haven't found out what 40,000 = 52 means.

August 9

Monday. Monday. Thank God it's holidays in September. I get two weeks paid, from the first to the fifteenth, or something like that.

Sherry party of twenty gibbering dames. One of them breaks a glass and I have to pick up the pieces, with Mrs. Waddling running around looking under sofas and chairs to make sure I don't miss any. Goddammit, what am I, a bartender or a glasspicker? What I'd do to roll her fat carcass around the floor till all the glass had stuck in her. Much quicker, and you don't miss any slivers either.

Maggie's sure that Sean Connery is a faggot ("you can tell by his eyes") and I get riled over that cause he's one of my favourite actors.

One of Miss Virgin's pimples has burst, which means she was really having a go at it over the weekend. Looks beat today. Got nothing to say. Her knees knock as she walks into the office and her hair's a mess. Anne gives me a piece of pumpkin pie and Virgin doesn't even bother looking.

Terry's in bed when I get home. She says she felt sick at work today and she was so weak she could hardly carry the plate trays into the kitchen for washing. I never thought she was such a sickly kid, coming from a farm and all. Last time I'll waste any of George's kef on her.

I get into bed beside her and turn the light on cause I feel like reading. Terry turns her face towards the wall. I pick up the books I got from George. The first one, the one with the red cover, is called *Quotations from Chairman Mao Tse-Tung* and it's got a photo of the guy on the cover. He looks something like Blow Job's cook, except for the wart on his lower chop.

I glance through a few pages and throw it over in a corner. I mean, with quotations like this: "Investigation may be likened to the long months of pregnancy, and solving a problem to the day of birth. To investigate a problem is, indeed, to solve it," how do you expect anyone to read it?

A pregnancy's a pregnancy and the only way to solve it is by not screwing a broad stupid enough to get one in the first place. Or if not, by an abortion. There's an old Indian woman who lives over by Parliament Street who does them for twenty bucks. All the chicks around here go to her cause she's so cheap. They say she does it with a knitting needle.

The second book's something else (green cover). It's called *Tales from the Arabian Nights* and it's about an Arab broad in the Middle Ages called Scheherazade who gets married to a guy called Shahryar. This Shahryar's got a specialty. Every night he marries some little virgin, lays her, and the next morning knocks her off cause he can't stand them once they lost their cherry.

One day it's Scheherazade's turn and she cooks up a plan. Every night she's going to tell this Shahryar creep a story, and just when she gets to the juicy part, she'll say she's sleepy and that she'll finish the story tomorrow. That way she lasts out for a thousand and one nights until the guy finally falls in love with her and marries her sister called Dunyazad. Funny bunch, the Arabs.

I read a couple of the stories (they're supposed to be the ones she's telling him) and they're not bad except for the language: "Hearing these words they marvelled with exceeding marvel," and "Fie upon thee, thou cur."

I'm bending over to pick up my cigarettes that are on the floor beside the bed when I drop the book and a sheet of paper falls out. I open it and damned if there isn't one of George's poems written on it.

It's about this broad, Scheherazade, and what's going to happen to her on the thousand and second night when she's run out of stories to tell. It's a great poem, even though I don't get half the words. Here it is:

Rose Petals

Oh! sidereal sapphires tumbling from the skies
Flash and sparkle in your eyes,
And the shimmering moonlight
Dances on your alabaster thighs.
Dear Scheherazade!

At last! In this quicksilver night,
Cowed by the radiance of your light,
You approach on bended knee
(Your crystalline body flows so gracefully).
Dear Scheherazade!

Yes! A thousand times your tinkling voice
Has made my jaded soul rejoice
With the noble beauty of your tales.
(Oh, the sorrow when I laugh and the joy when I wail.)
Dear Scheherazade!

(Rose petals cover the bed
On which you will lay your head.
And the chains on your feet
Sweetly clanging as you weep
"Come to me my tyrant, for it is you I need.")

O! Exquisite bird of paradise,
A million suns will never rise
That can compare with the grace
Of your ivory breasts; of your liquid embrace.
Dear Scheherazade!

Oh! The impatient terror of your sighs
And the scintillating languor of your cries
Reverberate before my eyes
Like the haunting echo of silver bells
Soaring through the mountains and the dells
Dear Scheherazade!

Then! As you gasp out my name
In the climax of your pain,
I will have reached the source of my content,
For my goddess's will is spent.
Dear Scheherazade!

Come most delicate of flowers,
One last night and the world is ours.
Oh, my dear Scheherazade!

How's that, eh? No doubt about it, George is a real intelligent guy. Hell, he did a year of university. I feel sorry for that guy sometimes, though.

He's a dreamer. He belonged to the Communist Party and dropped out of it cause as far as he's concerned, they're just a bunch of so-called revolutionaries, more worried about holding on to whatever job they got with the Party than going out and doing something.

He switched over to the Trotskyites and left them too cause they weren't democratic enough. Their boss would kick them out if they argued against anything he ordered. About that time he dropped out of the University cause he said that the only way to make a revolution here is by starting with the poorest people. That's why he came to Cabbagetown. (Society's asshole is what he calls it! "Looking at society through its asshole.")

He joined up with some Mao group that were mostly dropouts from other groups and they decided that the only way to get power is through a violent revolution. I guess all that went to his head cause now his big idea is to throw bombs and things to help us out.

Like I said, he's a dreamer. The only thing people around here care about is having some money in their pockets, and a good drunk and a screw on a Saturday night. He lives off pogey and whatever he can bum from his friends, and I feel sorry for him cause he's either going to end up in jail, or a bum. He should have done like me—taken a bartending course and that way have a career. Hell, I got no worries for the rest of my life. Sure wish I could write like him, though.

The third book's called *City of Night* and it's about a guy who hustles queers in bars. Like Ted. It's an autobiography. Like, the guy who hustles is the same guy who wrote the book. It's so interesting that I drop the *Arabian Nights* book and start on this one. Man, can he write! It's one o'clock before I put it down. He's describing New York and it's a real swinging city in spite of the queers. I'll have to go there one day.

Terry gets up and has a glass of water and I ask her for one too. "You feeling better now?" I ask her, not because I care, but because I'm in the mood for a little piece right now.

"Yes," she answers, and falls back on the bed.

She's a real funny broad. Any other one would have had lots to say about yesterday, but her, not a word. Like nothing had happened. But she's thinking about it, you can bet on that. Probably wondering how I'm taking yesterday's information about her. I won't tell her. She can ask first.

August 10

Terry still looks kind of pale around the gills this morning (she drops another coffee cup and wakes me up, but I don't lose my cool this time), so to make her feel better I say, "Want to go to George's tonight? He's having another bash." Her face turns a whiter shade of white and I think for a minute she's going to barf, so I laugh and say, "I'm just joking honey. Come here." She comes over to the bed and I give her a big kiss and later she goes off to work happy as a snake on a sunny day. I wonder what the guy that knocked her up was like? Probably a first class fink with a brushcut and short pants.

Now that the holidays are getting close I'm more pissed off than ever at work. Mrs. Waddling bugs me, Miss Virgin drives me up a rope, and Maggie's giving me ulcers with her mealtime talks. Just twenty days to go.

The woman who thinks my blue eyes are adorable comes up today and tells me my blue eyes are adorable. I want to say that compared to her washed out turd-coloured goggles, anybody's eyes would be adorable. Sometimes work can really be a drag.

I'm in no mood to sit in the room tonight, so I whip over to Blow Job's when I get off the streetcar.

There's about twenty kids standing around in front of the place. About fourteen to twenty years old.

They're a bunch called the Cross Gang cause they've taken some Church symbols like the Cross and fishes and things, and they tattoo them on their arms and carve them on park benches and telephone booths, but there's nothing religious about them.

They're about the toughest gang around. They use filed-down steel combs for blades and some even got razor blades sticking out of the soles of their shoes. Hell, they put the bunch we used to have to shame. I recognize one of them, a little Frenchie by the name of Guy. I guess he's only about five foot two but I seen him one night taking on three guys and cleaning up the sidewalk with them. He could probably even give Spike a good run for his money, except that Spike's in Kingston for the next seven years for knocking off a Mac's Milk store and pistol-whipping the manager. I'd laugh if he was in the same cell as my old man.

A taxi pulls up to the curb as I'm inside getting a pack of smokes, and I don't even recognize the driver until she pushes her way past the gang outside and walks up to the counter.

"Hi, Marilyn," I say to her.

"The name's Murray," she yells at me, but with a smile on her face. That's Marilyn all right. She's still the fastest boot in Cabbagetown, but she's turned butch ever since she got out of Mercer (she'd been in for fighting). Hangs around down in the butch bars near the bus station at Bay and Dundas whenever she's not wheeling the taxi around. We always figured she was butch cause she'd never ball like the other broads. Not even at parties when she was as stoned as everyone else. Dirty Doug tried to get her into a corner once and she yelled at him. "Fuck off creep"—she always yells—and booted him so hard in the knockers that he couldn't walk straight for the next two days.

"Hear you got a real cute number in your place," she yells, winking her eye at me. "Maybe I'll come over and see her sometime."

She has her hair cut short like a guy's and combed into a DA at the end, and wears men's pants, shirt and shoes. Can't say that I blame her for being a butch. If I'd been through what she had, I'd probably be one too.

It was her twelfth birthday and her old man came home from the beer parlour with a couple of buddies and the three of them raped her, singing "Happy Birthday" all the time. Her old woman got home from the factory (she was on the evening shift) just as the last guy was getting off the bed. She heard Marilyn crying, went in and saw what had happened. They started yelling at each other (the other two guys beat it), and she went into the kitchen, got a knife and stabbed the bastard about a hundred times. Didn't stop till there was nothing but a blob left on the floor, and Marilyn lying on the bed, her crotch covered with blood, watched the whole thing without saying a word.

They came for the mother with an ambulance cause by this time she was leaning out the window screaming her head off with the knife in her hand and blood all over her. She'd gone right out of her mind. They strapped her up in a stretcher still screaming, put what was left of the old man in a basket, and took Marilyn to the hospital cause they thought the blood on her crotch was from the knife.

She pushes her way through the bunch outside and races off in the taxi. A couple of them yell "butch" at her, but not too loud cause her boot's still something to watch out for.

"Telly lukie sickee today," Bum Bum says to me just as a cop car drives by and one of the cops turns his flashlight on the guys on the sidewalk.

"Why don't you stuff that frigging thing up your ass, cop?" one of them yells and the car pulls to a stop.

A big cop with a face like a dead mackerel steps out, flashlight still in his hand.

"All right, which one of you little fuckers said that?" Nobody says anything, but they start fanning out in a semicircle in front of the car. The other cop steps out, his hand on his holster.

"You heard me!" the first cop yells, "which one of you's got the mouth?"

The gang moves in on the cop. Something flashes in somebody's hand. Somebody mutters, "Let's get the mothers." The cop moves back a foot, while the other one gets back in the car to call for help.

The cop pulls out his nightstick and the gang stops for a minute. He looks scared. His nightstick's raised above his waist. The other cop gets out again just as a boot goes flying at the first cop. He smacks it with his stick, and the guy hits the sidewalk, swearing and holding onto his leg. The other cop pulls out his gun and points it at them, yelling "Okay, tough guys, get over against the wall with your hands in the air." His gun's pointed at the closest guy's head. Nobody moves.

A motorcycle cop comes blazing up to the restaurant and runs right into the gang, his stick swinging up and down. One guy falls backwards, blood streaming over his eyes, and Guy, who's standing in the middle of the group, whips out a chain and flicks it around in the air trying to catch the cop in the face with it. The cop with the gun comes up behind him and hits him on the back of the head with the butt. Guy crumples up and crashes against the side of the car.

The three cops kick and shove the guys against the wall beside Blow Job's, and frisk them before a paddy wagon takes them away. Guy, still unconscious, is picked up by his arms and legs and thrown in the back of the wagon with the rest of them.

By this time there's quite a few people watching the show and the cop with the flashlight shines it in their faces and tells them to move before they get busted too.

"What for?" an old guy shouts.

"Never mind what for," the cop shouts back. "Just break it up before I bust every jerk here."

A fat woman with curlers in her hair and house slippers on her feet yells, "Who ya think y'are, God or something?" and the cop, sweat on his fish face, yells back, "Go on home, Maw, and take those curlers off your bum," and the peanut gallery laughs and the cop gets back into the car, smiling at his big joke.

I'm reading some more *City of Night*. You got to admit the guy's got guts, writing about the things he's done. Hustling queers and all that scene. I wonder how that book got printed. Christ, some of the things he describes are pretty strong.

Terry's washed her hair. She looks like a drowned rat, sitting there by the window waiting for it to dry. Himmel's thumping around upstairs, but it's her own thumping cause I know the sound of it by now. So she had no luck getting a lover over the weekend. Proves that even bums got their pride. She probably goes at it with a banana or a carrot at nights now.

August ii

I see George today up on Bloor Street while I'm walking to work. Actually he sees me cause I'm busy following this chick with one of the nicest butts I ever seen on Bloor in a long time, and long blonde hair.

"Hey! Mike!" he yells at me just as I'm getting close enough to this chick to see how her front end is shaped.

I'm mad there for a minute.

He's on the other side of the street, in front of the Embassy Tavern with that creep Indian he brought over one night. "Come here a minute!"

I look back at the chick, but she's already disappearing towards the Colonnade, her little tail twitching like a sackful of ants.

I walk over, stopping a couple of cars and getting honked at by the drivers. I love bugging their asses by making them stop. Shows them that they're not king shit cause they've got wheels. I never worry about them hitting me, cause if they ever do, I'll sue them for every cent they've got. And they know it too.

We sit down on the curb and light up smokes. That is, George and his Indian light up my smokes, and we sit there for a while, feeling the sun on our faces.

"How's it going?"

"Not bad, and you?"

"Not bad."

Real thrilling conversation. Is that what he called me over here for?

I'm sitting between George and the Indian. George is on my left. He looks like he's in his own little world, far away from all of us. That means he's thinking and soon we can expect some earth-shattering statement from him. Indian looks like he did the night I met him. Like he's going to kill somebody. Or everybody. Maybe his folks cut his tongue off when he was a kid cause they had nothing to eat one day.

"Well, have you thought about it?"

"Thought about what?"

"About joining RAP."

"If it was RAPE, I'd be with you today."

They both shoot me a pissed off look. Especially Indian. I put my butt out on the sidewalk.

"Besides," I say before they can cut me up for cracking that joke, "the only ones who'll get rapped are us."

"Don't kid yourself," George answers, his eyes flashing, the red scarf round his neck blazing under the sunlight, "we mean business. We were just over at the Colonnade and we've decided to start at the Canadian Handicraft Shop because it's a typical symbol of the white man's exploitation of the Indian and Eskimo people. Stealing their handicrafts off them and selling them at a high price for their own profit."

"Start what?"

"The campaign, stupid!" George roars at me. Goddammit, nobody calls me stupid. Nobody.

He better not say it again, or I'll thump him. "We're going to place our first bomb in the Handicraft Shop at noon hour one week-day when it's full of people taking their lunch break."

"I thought you were going to start at City Hall."

Indian's looking at the Colonnade with a half-smile on his face. "It doesn't matter where we start," George cuts in again. He's starting to get really mad. Maybe he didn't get any tail last night. "What I want to know is, can we count on you?"

"Who's we?" I ask, lighting another smoke. "How many guys you got?"

Both George and Indian look at me like I asked the forbidden question. Nobody says anything for a minute, and inside I'm laughing cause I got them by the balls with that one.

"Well, I'll be honest with you," George finally answers, looking at his feet, "it's pretty hard trying to convince the people in Cabbagetown of the necessity of what we're going to do for them, right John?" The Indian grunts something. At least he can grunt.

"That's why we need fellows like you who are sufficiently educated to start off until the people realize the reason for our actions and—"

"Hold on a minute," I interrupt. "Why don't you get people from the group you belong to?"

Silence again.

"To be frank with you, because there's always the danger of a police informer. We must organize outside the group, as you call it, for the sake of security. We especially need people who never belonged to any political party or organization before. People unknown to the RCMP."

I look at my watch and I see that I've only got half an hour left, so I decide to end all this right here and now.

"Look George, what the hell am I going to get out of this? Is it politics that's going to feed me? Is is politics that's going to keep me in spending money? What the hell do I care if there's poor people in Cabbagetown? There always has been and there always will be. They like it like that, and nothing you or I do is going to change them. All we'll get out of it is a rope around our necks, or the next fifty years in the pen." I stop for a second to take a drag cause I'm not used to talking so much at once. But I start off again before George can get in his two cents worth.

"Politics is for the birds. Who gives a shit what the politicians say? Look at the Salvation Army. They're playing politics every time they come down to Allan Gardens with their drums and bugles, and promise all the winos there a better life if they cut off the booze. But the thing is, they don't really want the winos to stop being winos cause if they did, there'd be nothing for the Sally Anns to do after, and they'd be out of a job. Besides, I like the way I'm living too much to fuck it up by throwing bombs around."

I get up cause I've said my piece and I got to get going. George's looking at me like he can't believe his ears. Hell, what's he think? That I'm a dummy or something? I got my ideas on things. I just don't spout them off too often.

"See you around," I say to them as I turn to walk up the street, dusting off the seat of my pants with my hands.

"Yeah, see you around, Mike." George waves at me with that stunned look still on his face. "Hey, come on over some time next week and we'll have a real talk on this."

"Sure," I yell back, pleased as hell with myself cause I know that George respects me more than ever now. I don't even notice the broads on the street, and at work I smile at everybody, which shakes Maggie up so much, she's got nothing to say about any movie star at lunch.

Happiness is a well-digested meal. Even if it's yesterday's spaghetti.

Hell. I forgot to ask George what 40,000 = 52 means.

August 12

I'm going to walk to work again this morning just in case I can spot that cute little number on Bloor Street again.

I'm walking past the park when I hear a squeal over by the bushes. That stops me cause it sounds like a woman. The bushes move and I walk in their direction to see what the score is. Suddenly a scruffy looking joe with sunglasses on runs out of them and down the other end of the park, where he jumps into a car and races off up Jarvis.

I look into the bushes, opening them with my arms, and spot a bundle of rags. It's one of the little sluts from around here and she's lying on the ground sobbing. She looks up as I get closer to her and squeals again. She's scared.

Her skirt's ripped and she's covered with dirt from head to foot. Her nose is running and there's been a clump of hair ripped from the side of her head.

"What's the matter?" I ask her.

"This guy tried to fuck me," she answers, sobbing. I'd say she's about ten or eleven.

"Just like that?" I say to her, lighting a smoke and sitting down beside her. There's a cut on her left knee, probably from being dragged on the ground.

"He promised me a buck if I'd go in the bushes with him and help look for his lost dog." She blows her nose with her hand and tries to hold her dress together, but it's been ripped right up the front.

"You should have known better," I tell her, looking her square in her snotty little face. "What'd he do to you anyway?"

"The bastard put his hand over my mouth and ripped my skirt— I'll get shit for that at home—and he pulled down his zipper and was going to screw me when I bit him in the hand and yelled. Then he took off. He didn't give me the buck he promised me neither."

"Here, have a drag." She takes the smoke and pulls on it for about two minutes, then hands it back. She wipes the tears off her face.

"Aren't you Arnie's little sister?" I ask her cause I think I've seen them together before.

"Yeah, that's right." Her voice gets hard. "Don't tell him what happened eh? I'll get the ass beat off me, if he finds out."

"What about your folks?"

"Ah, they're stupid. I'll just tell them I got it ripped climbing over a fence. They don't care anyway." She's smiling now, thinking how she's going to fool her parents. Already she's forgotten what's happened to her. She's probably been laid lots of times before anyway.

The guy was something else though. He looked at least forty cause his hair was gray at the sides. What a guy that age wants with a snot-nosed kid that hasn't even got any boobs yet is beyond me. It's obvious the guy's not from around here, cause if he was, all he'd have to do is come up on Sunday and wait for Marie and save himself the trouble of trying to con some kid into the bushes and maybe get a rape charge thrown at him, which is good for twenty years if you got a tough magistrate in front of you.

She asks me for another smoke and when I've lit it for her, she gets up and runs off in the direction of Jarvis Street, holding her dress in one hand and the smoke in the other, yelling at a couple of kids who're playing ball, "Hey Rog, Lennie, guess what happened to me!"

Now it's too late to wait around in front of the Colonnade for that chick, and all I can do is walk by fast, hoping she's coming by at the same time. She isn't and I hop into the Club feeling the opposite of what I was yesterday, which makes Maggie so happy she tells us how Brigitte Bardot does it.

Miss Virgin comes in with her hair uncombed (which is about the same shape as when it's combed) and a bruise on her left arm. Man, that poor skeleton must spend all night battling with her boy friend.

Mrs. Russell's on tonight. The two top buttons of her uniform are undone and I get a good look at her breasts. She sure likes showing them off. Almost as much as I like looking at them.

It's almost empty tonight, only a couple of old dames on their way to a concert or something who've stopped at the Club for a Shooting Sherry and a meal. I grab a magazine from the lounge and read an article about geniuses. It says that most of them had dominant mothers and weak fathers—guess that means I'll never be a genius—and goes on to say that most of them didn't like school either. Maybe I've got a chance after all. Some of them become homosexuals because of their mothers, like Oscar Wilde and André Gide, whoever they are, and I wonder if that's the case with the faggots that hang around the park. I doubt that, though. Most of them look like they were hatched from an egg.

I'm starting to read another article about what a swinging place London is when Mrs. Russell comes and leans over the bar, her arms folded under her breasts so that they'll stick out further, and says, "No very bisy toonight, yah?"

I look at her bouncing boobs and answer, "Nope, it's pretty dead around here." She laughs and her whole body shakes. Man, what I'd do to get her in the back room for five minutes!

She talks for a while and I look at her boobs, and by then its quarter to eight, so she says, "See yu tumoro, hay," and I say good night to her boobs and catch a streetcar home.

You know something? She likes me. I bet that by September I'll be getting a good feel out of her every day. And maybe something else too.

I tell Terry about what happened at the park this morning and she really looks put off. Like it had happened to her or something. "Poor little girl," she says, "she'll probably have that horrible experience on her mind the rest of her life."

I'm not going to tell her that the poor little girl couldn't have cared less, but why spoil her evening? If she's getting her kicks by imagining what that's done to her, who am I to wreck it. Besides, I'm busy reading *City of Night.*

August 13

Terry wants to go dancing tonight. Hell, I didn't know she could dance. But I say no cause I don't feel like it. She's in a real happy mood cause she made three bucks in tips. I'm feeling pretty happy too so I say let's go over to the beer store and get a twelve-pack. She shrugs her shoulders as if to say oh well that's better than nothing, and we walk up Parliament to the store. There's a line-up and we have to wait fifteen minutes, but it's nice out, not too hot, so we don't mind.

About halfway back I give the beer to her to carry cause it's getting heavy and I light up a smoke and think of that chick on Bloor Street and whisper in Terry's ear that I love her. She smiles up at me and says, "I love you too." She's carrying the case of beer in her arms like it was a baby.

The lights are out in Himmel's room, which means she's hitting the bars tonight hoping to get somebody over there. I know just the guy for her. Peckerhead. We've always called him Peckerhead because when he was six, all his hair fell out and he's been bald as a pecker ever since. I can't even think of his real name. He's a real clown. He'll do anything you tell him. Like once we were all over at the park one Sunday when he comes walking up. Spike's with us and we got nothing to do so he tells him, "Take your pants off and go up to Birdie and tell her you want to be saved." (Birdie's this woman who used to be a whore till she got religion and turned up one Sunday dressed in white right down to her ankles with a Bible in her hands and preaching about hell and heaven to everybody in the park. She died about a year ago. They found her in her room dead with that white dress wrapped around her face. Nobody figured out why.)

Anyway, Peckerhead gives his creepy laugh, like a horse farting, and takes off his pants and walks right up to Birdie and asks to be saved. Birdie just about keels over. She closes her eyes and screams something about Satan and falls on her knees, and there's Peckerhead standing there smiling cause he thinks he's being saved. Finally Spike yells back at him, "Come here and put your pants on," and Peckerhead comes back all happy saying, "I been saved, I been saved."

They had to carry Birdie away cause she was rolling on the ground and screaming so hard even the pigeons were looking at her. Man, oh man, the laughs we used to have with Peckerhead.

He's working for a telegraph company, delivering telegrams on a bicycle with a uniform and cap, and he makes forty bucks a week, which his old man takes off him cause he drinks a bottle of rum a day. But Peckerhead doesn't care. He's got his uniform and his cap and his bike and he's happy. He still does what you tell him. Sometimes an old woman, who hasn't got a hope in hell of getting a man cause she's so ugly and smelly, will grab ahold of him and take him to her place and tell him exactly what to do. And Peckerhead'll do it and leave the next morning all happy. The queers get him now and then too. In fact the only person that's never used him is Himmel-witch. Maybe I'll tell her next time I see her. It always helps to stay on the good side of your landlady.

We drink beer and listen to the radio and read (Terry shines my shoes). It's great having a nice quiet evening at home. Especially when you're both in a good mood and there's lots of beer.

After, we have a little burping contest. To see who can burp the loudest. Naturally I win. Poor Terry, she turns red, says she can't do it, and finally after I've shown her a couple of good loud ones, she tries real hard, and comes out with a little peep. I laugh and shake the room with a real roaring one and say I've won the prize, and the prize is you, and that's when we hit the bed.

August 14

It's gone right up to ninety-five today and the weatherman says it'll be just as hot tomorrow. I feel like a chocolate in somebody's mouth. I'm sweating like a pig by the time I get to the streetcar stop, and inside the streetcar it's worse. I grab a seat beside the window but that doesn't help any cause there's no breeze. By the time I get to the Club, I feel like a glass of water, I'm so sweaty. Christ, there'll be people dropping dead like flies on the sidewalks today from the heat. I'm glad I'm inside all day.

Everybody's in a bad mood because of the heat, which doesn't help my humour any. Maggie's going into one of the worst stories I've heard yet, about some singer, and for the first time since I been there I tell her to shut her trap. Her mouth drops down to her feet and it's a full minute before she says anything.

"You've got your nerve, you young hoodlum," she finally gets out. Me, I feel like smashing her in the yap with the cream chicken on my plate, but I keep my cool.

I get up and say, "I'm going up to the bar to eat," picking up the plate and knife and fork. "Well, that's fine with us," she snaps back, "isn't it girls?" The other old bags at the table don't say anything. They're enjoying the whole show too much. Personally, I think they're glad that somebody's finally shut her up.

"I'd rather eat with the pigs than with you," I yell at her, really mad now. "At least they only grunt."

Upstairs I cool down a bit and realize that what I said about the pigs was kind of stupid, but what the hell, she deserved it. If she goes to Waddling and complains about me, I'll just tell her what a disgusting slob Maggie is, and Waddling'll believe me cause like I said before, she treats me like her son. So no worries there.

Virgin comes in looking like something they dragged out of a sewer. All covered with sweat and her hair all over her face and a bruise just above her right knee. At this rate she'll be dead before the month's out, not that it's such a bad idea.

The members have been coming in all day long like they just crossed the Sahara desert. They're drinking Scotch and water, rye and ginger, and Tom Collins down so fast that they're keeping me on the run without stopping. By seven o'clock I'm wishing I had one of George's Molotov Cocktails just to clear the place out.

By the time I leave it's eight thirty because of some late arrivals—the bastards—and it's still hot as hell, although there's a slight breeze which helps some. I've got no change for the streetcar, so the conductor has to change a five dollar bill, bitching while he's doing it. I step on a woman's foot as I walk down the aisle and she starts bitching. You'd think I dropped a five-hundred-ton anchor on it.

As I get off the streetcar, some drunken bum walks right into me and calls me a maggotmouth for getting in his way. Maggotmouth? First time I heard that one. I push him out of the way and walk down the street, smoking like a steam engine to keep my temper down.

A bunch of kids about five years old are throwing rocks and tin cans and anything else they can find across the street at a bunch of kids on the other side, who are picking up whatever's being thrown at them and heaving it right back. A pop bottle whizzes past my face as I'm getting near the bunch on my side. I grab the closest kid—a dirty little five-year-old—and yell hard enough for them all to hear.

"Get the Jesus home before I pretend you're a football and boot your ass all over Cabbagetown!"

That slows them down for a minute, but just to make sure they get the point, I boot the kid and send him flying into his buddies. That stops them. They go running off up an alley and the bunch on the other side starts calling me mother-fucker and other names until I make like I'm going to cross the street and they beat it behind a house. Michael the peacemaker.

As I go up the front porch a rock bounces on the sidewalk behind me, and one of the kids yells, "We'll get you for this, you flaming faggot!" And like I said, they're five, maybe six years old.

I crash into the house, whip over to the fridge, pull out a beer and gulp it down in ten seconds flat. Christ Almighty, did I need that! I open another one and drink it while I'm getting changed. Terry says, "You look mad. Is it because of me?" I answer, "Apart from the fact that I've been beefing with everybody all day long, nothing." And I add, "Don't you start." She comes over to me and says, "Why should I want to argue with you, Michael?" and kisses me. I finish the beer and open another one. It's the last one, but I don't care cause three beers is enough to get my nerves in good working condition again, and besides we're going out for a beer anyway. But not to the Harmony House or the other joint, but to that quiet bar on Sherbourne Street where I was going to take her last week.

She looks real sharp tonight, with her hair combed straight down like Bonnie, and a blue ribbon tied at the back, her blue dress and high heels, and a great big smile on her face cause I give her a wolf whistle as we step out on to the street. A real sharp piece. Her long legs dancing over the concrete and her purse swaying back and forth as she walks. I'm feeling better already. You would too.

It takes us about half an hour to get there, but she doesn't mind. Funny about her, she's on her feet all day, working like a DP, yet she likes to have a walk before going to bed at night. Me, I'm sitting on my can most of the day and my feet ache when I get home. It must be the farm living. Like, chasing after the chickens when they break out of their pen.

By the time we get there I'm just about ready for another beer. Like I said, it's a quiet little bar. Wooden walls, floor and tables like the Harmony and small juke boxes hanging from the walls over each table and an old TV. The juke boxes haven't worked for the last ten years and the TV's always on the blink, so nobody comes here, which is why it's quiet. Tonight's no exception. There's maybe six people in the place including the waiter. We grab a table near the john and the waiter comes over with a beer tray in his left hand. He slops two glasses on the table and says, "I hope Red there's twenty-one."

I look at the guy. He's got straw-coloured hair that falls over his forehead and he's wearing a white shirt with yellow stains all over the front of it. A pair of black pants so low on his ass that they look like they'll fall to the floor any minute. A little bird mouth and tobacco-stained teeth. A real beauty.

"Of course she's twenty-one. Whattaya think I am? A cradle robber?" I answer. All three of us laugh at that. He puts the tray down and leans over the table, "You know, when I came to Toronto I found me a real cutie like yours, she had red hair too, and one day we walked into a bar on Yonge Street and the bouncer stopped us at the door and asked my girl her age. She looked eighteen, but she was twenty-eight. You should have seen the look on his face when she showed him her ID card! Boy, I never laughed so hard in my life."

Just to show us how hard he laughed, he starts laughing now. It sounds like a cross between a barking dog and a kid pissing against a tree.

"Twenty-eight. And the bouncer thought she was underage!" He laughs harder.

Yeah. Real funny. You should be on TV, you clown. Or in the zoo. Hey, that's an idea. I'll take Terry to the zoo tomorrow.

Someone yells for him and he says, "Scuse me, folks. I'll be right back."

"Take your time," I yell at him as he walks over to a table occupied by three of the grubbiest looking grubs I seen around in a long time. Two men grubs and a woman grub. They're so pissed they can hardly sit up straight. In fact the man grub opposite the woman grub has put his feet up on her lap and the other man grub is resting his head on her shoulders. At least she's good for something.

The waiter dumps three glasses on their table and the man grub with his feet up searches around in his pocket for some bread. After about five minutes he comes out with exactly the right amount in coin and throws it on the table saying, "Keep the change, Charlie," and all three of them start laughing. Charlie (it figures he'd have a name like Charlie) says, "Thanks a million, Fred. I'll remember you in my will," and they go into hysterics over that. Strange how beer makes people laugh. Sometimes.

I'm busy telling Terry what a lousy day I've had when Charlie drops his elbows on the table again and says, "Yessiree, she was quite a kid. Looked just like Red here," he points his finger at her, "only not so bootifull." He laughs. His breath smells of beer. I didn't notice it last time cause I was looking at the grubs. Terry blushes and I've had enough. Goddammit, he's here to serve beer, not to tell us his sex life.

"Why don't you get us a couple more brews," I say to him with a nice smile on my face.

"Why surely," he answers and walks over to the counter.

"Isn't he a pain in the ass," I say to Terry, who shakes her head and gives me a you-said-it smile. I'm just about to add that he's probably got his pants pinned to his pecker so they won't fall down, when guess who comes back with two glasses that are half foam.

"These glasses are half foam," I say to him.

"Well, I'll be a mother's son," he says, looking at them like he's never seen a glass before in his life. "Hold on a sec, I'll be right back."

He comes back with the glasses filled right up to the top with beer and only a thin line of white around the rim. He looks proud as a kid that's just had his first piece of tail.

"How's that, nothing but pure malt in them there glasses."

"Great, just great." There he is ready to drop the tray and lean over the table again. I can't take this any longer.

"Hey, your friends over there called you."

"They did?" he says, looking up. "I didn't hear them."

"What's the matter, don't you believe me?"

"Why sure friend. I believe you," he answers, looking hurt. "It's just that I didn't hear them."

"Well why don't you go over and see what they want." I'm really starting to get mad at this stubborn bastard. Christ, at least at the Harmony the waiter, Big Jim, lets you drink your booze in peace.

He goes over to them and I smile at Terry and look up at the juke box. It's got songs marked on it that were big when I was a kid, like "Kisses Sweeter Than Wine." A real swinging joint. Terry's starting to tell me about her day when Charlie comes back and says, "They didn't call me. You weren't putting me on there, were you mister?" He looks kind of mad. But not half as mad as me. I open my mouth to tell him to fuck off when man grub beside woman grub croaks out, "Three beers for my comrades and I." Where have I heard that kind of speech before? I think for a minute. Why sure. It's the guy who was telling me about why he became a bum, last Sunday at Allan Gardens.

As Charlie goes back to them muttering under his breath, I have a good look at him. I guess it's the same guy. His beard's longer and he's dirtier, but that way of talking he has, you'd spot that a mile away. This might be fun. I'll wait till he comes to go to the john and I'll ask him to finish his story. I tell Terry about super war hero and she gets a real kick out of that. That's what I'll do. That'll make for a few laughs and it'll keep that goddam Charlie away too.

Charlie doesn't come round again and he gives us a mean look every time he walks by, which isn't very often cause there's only another couple in the place, so Terry and I talk about this and that and every fifteen minutes or so we order more beer which Charlie drops on the table without saying a word, leaving as soon as he gets paid. I don't leave him a tip. Terry's really learned to drink since she's been with me. The first time we went out she puked after a couple of beers and now she guzzles them down like they were Cokes. At least she's learned that, thanks to me.

We're having a chuckle about Mrs. Himmel when there's a crash behind us and we turn round to see woman grub standing up with her chair turned over on the floor.

"I gotta have a piss," she says to nobody in particular and starts pulling down the zipper on the side of her pants right there in the middle of the bar. She's slobbering at the mouth and her age is anywhere between forty and seventy. War hero gets up kind of shaky and takes her by the arm saying, "Allow me to escort you."

"I don't need nobody to escort me," she mumbles at him, but he gives her a little push towards the john and she smiles at him and says, "Thash wha I like bout you. You got mannersh." The other guy's trying to pick his feet off the floor where she dumped them when she got up, but the effort's too much and he sinks lower in his chair.

She's still trying to pull her zipper down and half her right side's showing. It's black and blue like somebody gave her a good boot recently. War hero opens the door of the ladies' john for her and gently pushes her in. He's standing outside the door waiting for her, swaying from side to side, when I yell at him, "Hey, you want a beer?" He looks at me and comes over to the table and sits down, almost missing the chair.

"Young man, did I hear correctly that you are about to offer me a tumbler of hops?"

"No, just a beer," I answer before he gets into his head that I'm about to treat him to a barrel of the stuff.

"Don't you remember me? You were telling me at the park last Sunday how you became a bum."

He looks at me real hard, his eyes almost closed. He smells so bad that Terry moves her chair back a bit. Then he says, "Why, of course, you're the young university graduate." A smile lights up his grub face.

"Yeah, that's right pops." I smile back. I call him pops, but if it's true he fought in Korea, he can't be that old. Hard to tell with a bum, though.

I pick up my beer and take a good swallow, licking my lips after. War hero looks at the glass long after I've put it down.

"Yes, I thought I'd mistakenly ascertained that you were offering me a cup of good cheer," he says, looking pretty glum. Terry looks like she's going to break out laughing any minute.

"That's not true," I answer, trying to keep from laughing myself. "I just want to hear the rest of your story first."

"Oh, I see. Well—" He looks at the beer again, and at the smoke I'm lighting up. "How far had I arrived in the sad, but true, story of my unfortunate life?"

"Let's see, you were up to where you'd just knocked off a chink and you were feeling pissed off about it."

"Oh yes." His eyes light up. "I had cold-bloodedly murdered that wounded Chinese with a wife and six lovely children in Shanghai due to the death in battle of my best friend and true comrade, Stanley, from Vancouver, B.C.

"For weeks after, and even after my repatriation to Canada, food would stick in my throat and sleep would escape me due to that one infamous act I had committed in a country whose name I don't even wish to remember."

"It was Korea," I say, trying to be helpful, and taking another pull on my beer and drag on my cigarette.

"Yes of course, Korea," he says, smiling weakly and staring at my glass. "Korea, Korea." He sighs and looks up hopefully as I wave my hand at good old Charlie baby. Terry giggles. She's having a ball.

War hero looks at her and chuckles, then he looks at the john door. Maybe woman grub's drowned in the pot.

"Well, what happened next pops?" I say to him so he won't get up to look for her.

Charlie slops two beers on the table and war hero looks like he's going to die cause there's nothing for him.

"I really must see if Hazel is all right," he says, starting to get up.

I offer him a smoke and he sits down again.

"Yes," he says as I light it up for him, "returning to Canada was a terrible shock. Not only did I discover that my dear, dear mother had expired only three weeks before my return, but I also learned that the girl I had promised to marry, the sweet young girl with hair like wheat" (yeah pops, I heard this before) "had run away and married my best friend, Stanley.

"Stanley, the only intimate friend I had in my university years." (What? I thought Stanley was the creep that got knocked off in Korea.) "It was unbelievable. Two deaths and one betrayal in the space of six months." He stops for a minute, his eyes wet and his hands shaking.

I take a good swallow out of my glass so he'll keep on with his story, and just then the washroom door flies open and woman grub comes staggering out with her zipper still open and piss stains on the front of her pants. War hero stands up, takes her by the arm and says, "Pardon me," and walks her back to their table. The other grub's almost on the floor by now and snoring. War hero picks up woman grub's chair, puts her on it, goes over to man grub, shakes him till he's awake, and whispers something in his ear. He fumbles around in his shirt pocket and hands him some change. He calls Charlie and orders three beers. Man grub falls asleep again and war hero takes his beer and puts it beside his own. Woman grub's still trying to pull her zipper up.

"Oh Michael," Terry turns to me giggling, "you shouldn't have. That poor man." She giggles again and hiccoughs and I know it's time to go home. Right then Charlie yells out "last round!"

We walk out arm in arm and I clap Charlie on the back as we pass him, which makes Terry hiccough again and the look on Charlie's face starts me laughing. Outside it's cooled down a bit and the sky's full of stars. I kiss her right on the street and she kisses back hard, her lips moving back and forth. Man, this is life. Walking home with a beautiful broad in your arms and not a care in the world. We kiss again at a red light, and a car honks at us as it speeds by. It's a convertible.

Who gives a shit what people think. I'm happy. We're happy. And that's all that counts.

We get to the corner of Sherbourne and Carlton and we're just getting to the park, where it's dark cause there's no street lights, when a car screeches to a stop beside us.

Terry grabs my arm hard and I turn to the car as the passenger door opens and a skinny guy with sports shirt and sunglasses points his finger at me (he's wearing a red ring on his pinkie) and yells, "Come here buddy, we want to talk to you."

I move back a few steps, pushing Terry behind me and shaking her arm off mine. She's whispering, "Michael, let's go. Let's go," and I'm trying to see who the driver is, but it's too dark. My first thought is that it's the wop I wiped out over at Jerry's place.

One of his legs is on the sidewalk. He's wearing cream-coloured pants. "Come over here boy. This is the police."

Cops, my ass. I can spot a cop a mile away with my eyes closed, and this guy's no cop.

"What do you want?" I yell at him, trying to sound as tough as possible and slipping my hand in my pants pocket, like I'm reaching for a blade.

"Let's see your ID card," he yells at me again. His buddy nudges him in the shoulder and the guy nods his head.

I move up to the car with my hand still in my pocket, get real close till I can smell the booze on his breath, and yell at him loud as I can, "If you're cops, let's see your badges."

The skinny guy looks up at me, his sunglasses catching the reflection from a passing car. He makes like he's going to get out (I poise my leg, ready to catch him in the face before he's halfway out of the seat), takes a long look at Terry who's standing further back, laughs at me, and says to his buddy, "Let's go!" The driver steps on the gas and they do a split turn up Sherbourne and disappear out of sight.

"Who were they, Michael? Oh, the way that man looked at me!"

I light up a smoke and offer one to Terry and take her arm with my free hand. I can feel beads of perspiration on my forehead, and my underarms are wet.

Hell, as soon as that guy looked at Terry, I had them spotted for what they were after.

"They were hoping we were stupid enough to believe they were law. They would have got us in the car, tied us up and taken us out in the country somewhere."

Terry doesn't say anything, but the happy mood she's been in all evening is gone. She looks scared and unhappy. She turns her head as a car passes, as if they were coming after us again.

"Don't worry kid," I tell her, squeezing her arm, "they won't be back. These guys are only good once you're in the car. In the street they're cowards."

Finally she asks what's on her mind. "What would they have done to us, Michael?"

At first I'm not going to answer cause I don't want her any more shook up than she is now, but I figure it won't do her any harm to know in the long run cause something like this might happen one day when I'm not with her, and she should know how to defend herself.

"They would have knocked me out, and then raped you and made you do things to them. Then they would have maybe killed us or beat us up so bad we'd be as good as dead."

She shudders and shakes her head from side to side again. Even under the street light, I can see that she's gone pale. Maybe I could have explained it to her more gently but this way it'll stick in her mind better. I was going to tell her that if anything like that ever happens to her, to yell like hell, but she should know that already. If there's one thing a broad knows how to do, it's screaming. They all do it. Even when they don't have to.

We get home and I look for a beer before I remember that I already drunk them all. Damn it, I could have used one.

In bed I can imagine Terry thinking how lucky she is having me with her when there's so many creeps out in the street and when you come to think about it, she *is* lucky.

August 15

Day of rest, and no beer in the house. I could kick myself for having drunk it all yesterday. Oh well, at least there's coffee in bed followed by some bacon and eggs, and ham sandwiches. Some bananas too.

Already the room's starting to turn into a blast furnace, so I tell Terry to get dressed cause we're going to the zoo, and I step outside to wait for her.

"Oh boy, the zoo!" she exclaims, a grin lighting up her face, and she claps her hands like a little kid. And planting a wet kiss on my lips, she rushes into the john.

Outside, it's just as hot, but at least you don't get that suffocating feeling that you do in a room.

Himmel's sitting on the porch with a six-pack beside her and she's alone. Mrs. Himmel's alone! This you got to see to believe.

She looks at me and says, "Sit down, Mike."

Hell, she must be hard up. This is about the second time she's called me by my name since I been rooming in her shack.

I sit down and she offers me a beer. I'm laughing to myself as I guzzle down half the bottle. Man, hard up isn't the word for it. Let's hear what she's got to say.

"You know Mike, even I get lonely sometimes," she starts off.

"Do you, Mrs. Himmel?" I answer, my voice dripping syrup.

"Yes, at my age," she gulps down what's left of the bottle she's drinking and opens a new one, "a woman wants to settle down. She wants to find a man who'll provide for her in her old age."

She smiles at me. There's foam around her mouth.

"Uh-huh," I smile back at her, showing all my pearly teeth.

"She wants to feel the embrace of a strong man" (isn't she poetic?) "lying beside her in bed, and know that she'll never be alone again."

What's she getting up to, the old scrag? I guzzle down the rest of my beer, and she pops another one in my hand. That's what I call service.

"How're you getting along with your cousin?" she asks with a leer on her mug. Now what in Christ has that go to do with her being lonely?

"Oh, fine. Fine."

"Does she know her way around the city by now?" Leer.

"Oh yeah."

"Has she found a place to live yet?"

"No, not yet. She likes it here." I light up a smoke, and empty the bottle down my throat. The creepy bitch.

"Oh dear," she says, looking at the case of empty bottles, "there's no more beer left." She opens her wrinkled mouth and flashes her decayed teeth. Her housecoat opens a bit at the top, showing her wrinkled tits.

"So I see."

At least I got two beers out of the deal. No sweat involved either.

"But I do have some more inside. Would you like to come in and have a few more with me?"

Man, is she horny today. She must have run right out of men over at the bar. That's not surprising. She's had every available guy in Cabbagetown over here at least once. And I never see them come back for seconds.

"Gee, that would be great Mrs. Himmel, but I promised my cousin I'd take her to see the monkeys."

That's when Terry walks out, looking fresh as a daisy.

"Hi Mrs. Himmel, how are you today?" she says to her, all smiles and chuckles as I get up off the porch.

Himmel picks up her beer case, throws us a dirty look, and walks into the house, slamming the door behind her.

"Did I say something wrong?" Terry asks as we walk up the street.

"It's nothing," I answer. "She's mad cause she can't come to see the monkeys with us. She said she'd like to take one home with her cause she's lonely."

We have a good laugh over that and make our way to Riverdale Zoo.

Riverdale Zoo. Stuck halfway up a hill overlooking the Don Valley. On Sundays it's full of Indians, Wops, Polacks and farmers who've come to see all the strange animals that they've only seen in movies before. Whole families—Mom and Pop and their eighteen kids—all jammed together like maggots on a dead rat, gawking at the filthy animals.

There's a little pool at the entrance and it's filled with half a dozen brats in their bathing suits. The water's about ankle high and so muddy, every time they fall in it, they come out looking like niggers. They're screaming and yelling and throwing water at everybody that passes by. They're having a ball.

We come up to the elephant cage. A ton or two of pot roast walking around in a two-foot circle cause one of his front legs is tied with a rope to a peg stuck in the middle of the ground. He's covered in shit and dirt and he looks about as happy as a hungry Jew with nothing but pork to eat in the house.

The polar bear's dying of heat exhaustion and the only thing he's got to cool himself off with is a six-inch pool of rancid water full of rotting leaves.

The monkeys are something else. They do nothing but screw all day long, and their cage is the most popular. Millions of kids come to see the red-assed little fornicators to learn how it's done. And their parents too. Everybody's enjoying it except Terry, who turns her back and moves on to the lion cage. They're doing it too, and I don't blame them. Their cage is so small they can hardly walk around it. So what else do you expect them to do?

The parrot house. It feels like you're sitting in a giant muffler, and the driver's revving the engine as hard as he can. Man, can those birds squawk! We don't stay in there long. Hell, I couldn't even put up with that one damn budgie she brought home.

At the bottom of the hill there's a grease pool meant for the ducks and geese to swim in. It must be the dumping ground for the city's old oil. They look funny, those birds, their top halves natural, but their bottom halves black and dripping. Two-tone birds.

Seeing those birds makes me thirsty, so we stop to have an Eskimo Pie from an Italian with one of those bicycle pushcarts. Terry's pretty excited about the zoo, but me, I'm fed up. I've been coming here since I was a kid. The place hasn't changed a bit in all those years. It's about the worst zoo in the world.

After, we walk up the other end of the hill and watch a bunch of wild goats. Real wild. They come up to you and take food right out of your hand. We used to feed them the used safes that are lying all over the place. They loved them. Used to come running up every time we came, and for years we thought it was because they had a secret taste for the things, but when they ate used Kotex as eagerly as the safes, we finally understood what every farmer knows: these kooks will eat anything.

We walk past a baboon who's picking his ass for fleas and throwing them at the spectators. Each time he does it, he smiles, his top lip lifting up a foot, exposing buck-teeth that would make Jake jealous. Some little kid throws a stick at him and he picks it up, looks at it, then throws it back at him, hitting the kid's mother. The kid laughs and the baboon smiles. It's obvious that they're in on this together. It's probably the baboon that thought up the whole idea cause the kid doesn't look too smart.

I go into the washroom to empty out the Eskimo Pie I just had. Christ, the place stinks as bad as the monkey house, but then again, that's not surprising. There's the inevitable queer standing in a corner pretending he's drying his hands, and the walls are covered with all kinds of quaint sayings like "I suck cocks" or "Mine's six inches long," followed by a telephone number. But there's one that's a real gas. It's by the door and I notice it on the way out. It says "Dr. Strangelove, or how I learned to stop worrying and love the bum."

That's a gas, like I just said, but I saw a funnier one in a Honey Dew joint. It said "Press here for a five-minute speech by Lester Pearson," and it was written right above the hot air machine that you use to dry your hands. Of course that joke wasn't for everybody. You got to be smart to know what it means.

It's four in the afternoon and my feet are fried to a crisp, so I say, "Let's go." Terry waves goodbye to the elephant as we go past it. He doesn't wave back cause he's too busy going around in circles and picking up the garbage people are throwing at him. Half the stuff he throws back. Smart elephant. That's probably why he's lived so long. He must be at least a hundred years old. He's all wrinkles. One big gray shirt after washing.

The kids are still splashing around in their mud hole. There's so many of them now that there's hardly room for them all to stand in it together. They don't care, at least this is better than playing in the street. Myself, I wonder.

We stop off at Blow Job's for a Coke. He serves us personally (how honoured we are) and says hello to us. We say hello back to him. He asks us if it is hot enough for us. We answer yes, is it hot enough for you? He answers yes. We drink our Cokes. I can imagine all those dead rats turning green with the heat and stinking up the kitchen. The heat and the zoo have got me down, but Terry's happy, so that lifts me up a little.

As we go down our street we can hear the Sally Anns playing "Onward Christian Soldiers" over at the park.

Himmel's inside. Hope she finds some joe by next weekend.

We have supper, but I'm not too hungry. Hell, work tomorrow again. Feels like I just stopped working five minutes ago. Must be the heat. Holidays two weeks from now. I'm going to sit at home every day and drink beer to keep me cool. Ice-cold beer with the perspiration beads running down the side of the bottle.

After, Terry does some washing and presses my pants while I read some more *City of Night*. I don't know when I've enjoyed a book as much as I'm enjoying this one. One day I'm going to write one like it. It's almost too hot to make love. Almost I said. We say I love you to each other afterwards. Nothing wrong with saying it even if you don't mean it. It makes them happy and keeps them doing all the work around the place, Besides I do love her a bit. Let's put it this way, she's stupid but she's nice. Christ, work tomorrow. God, it's hot—I can't sleep.

It's Anti-Vietnam War Day and there's about five thousand kooks standing around in front of the Parliament Buildings at Queen's Park. I'm one of them. Don't ask me what I'm doing here cause I couldn't care less what's going on in Vietnam, but George was bugging my ass for weeks and weeks to come so that the Americans and the Liberal Party could see how many people were opposed to the war. I kept telling him *no* cause it's happening on a Saturday and I'd lose a day's pay if I came, but he kept bugging and bugging, and this morning was one of those typical autumn days with the odour of leaves on the ground and just a touch of cold to the weather, which makes for great walking (autumn's my favourite season), so I decided to come. (I called the Club and told them I had diarrhea.) Besides, he'd told me a lot of cute chicks would be there.

By the way, George's big plan to blow up half Toronto has been postponed. Him and the Indian were practising throwing gasoline bombs over at Cherry Beach one Sunday, and a bomb went off in the Indian's hand. Left him looking like a fried chicken.

Since they were the only two in their RAP (except for a broad who's madly in love with George, and she doesn't count) that was that till the Indian gets out of hospital.

He says he'll be ready by next spring though.

I finally spot George talking to a group of Spaniards who're waving a huge poster that says "Yanqui Assassins Go Home," with big dollar bills painted on either side, and singing something in Spanish in front of a CBC camera.

George is right in the middle of them, with his red scarf around his neck, a pair of Ben Franklin sunglasses hiding half his face, and a blue shirt with half a dozen buttons on it:

Sterilize LBJ No More Ugly Children	Restore Palestine to the Palestinians	Black Power
Stamp Out Imports, Exports and Lamports	Dominicanos, Unios Contra Imperialismo Yanqui	VIVA CHE

INSTRUCTIONS TO MARCHERS

In order to have an orderly and inspiring
demonstration keep the following points in mind.

1. KEEP THE MARCH TOGETHER AS A UNIT – Double file
   on the sidewalk – 3 feet behind the person in front of
   you – avoid large open spaces between sections of
   marchers – maintain a good walking pace – hold your
   banners high.

2. COUNTER DEMONSTRATORS – Ignore them – do not
   respond to provocations – parade marshalls have been
   assigned to give direction and protect the march.

3. LIBERAL PARTY HEADQUARTERS – The map shows
   the route – at Queen and Bay the parade will stop – at
   this point all those wishing to take part in the symbolic
   protest against Canadian complicity will go to Adelaide
   Street and rejoin the demonstration in a few minutes
   at City Hall square for the start of the rally.

4. AFTER THE RALLY – The rally will end about 7 p.m. –
   banners and posters should then be stacked in front
   of the platform so they can be sorted and returned to
   the respective organizations.

   Please turn over for route map and parade order.

MOBILIZATION HEADQUARTERS,
20 College Street, 929-5512; 929-5563

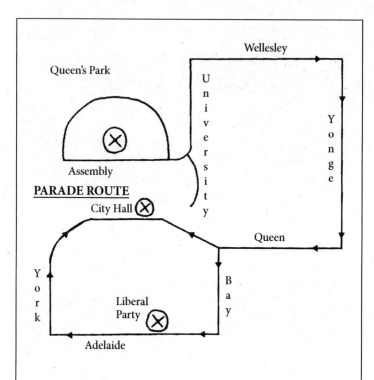

Wellesley

Queen's Park

University

Yonge

Assembly

PARADE ROUTE

City Hall ⊗

Queen

York

Bay

Liberal
Party ⊗

Adelaide

ONT. OCT. 21ST MOBILIZATION COMMITTEE

GENERAL PARADE ORDER

A – Mobilization Committee
    Head Banners, Dignitaries

B – Student Organizations

C – Metro Area Community Committees

D – Out of Town Groups

E – Political Groups

F – Peace Organizations

G – Draft Resistors

H – Trade Unions

I – Others

SCHEDULE

4:30 – Assembly

5:00 – Parade leads off

5:45 – Liberal Party HQ

6:00 – Rally

7:00 – Rally ends

This Che got his head shot off a couple of weeks ago down in Bolivia and George cried for half a day. He put a black border around the poster he's got of him. Big Deal.

The Spaniards are a real wild bunch. They're screaming Yanqui Go Home, and Blow Up the Pentagon. George is screaming right along with them.

"What's the goggles for?" I ask him, tapping him on the shoulder. "So that the S and I boys don't spot me," he answers, recognizing me with a big grin.

"The what?"

"S and I. Security and Intelligence Division of the RCMP. The Establishment's hired gorillas."

"Cops, eh?" I'm starting to wish I'd never come.

"Yeah. Look," he says, pointing at a black-haired guy with a white raincoat and a stogie stuck in his yap, "that's one of them."

I give him the once-over. It's a cop all right, even though he's walking around like he was one of the demonstrators. A cop always looks like a cop, and this guy's no exception.

"They're not going to bust us for this, are they?"

"They better not," he answers, shaking his head backwards to get the hair out of his face. "We got a permit for this, and if they try and stop us, they'll have the biggest riot on their hands since the rebellion of 1837." He spits on the ground.

The whole park is filled with a sea of people and placards. Guys with megaphones are trying to get them organized into some sort of a line. A bunch of American draft dodgers are yelling, "Hell no, we won't go!", the Spaniards are still screaming and singing "Viva Che! Viva Ho Chi Minh," and the guys with the megaphones are bellowing out orders. Little by little, a line is formed. I stick with George and the Spaniards. We're about halfway down the line. Suddenly a bunch of little greasers jumps in at the head of the line with posters reading:

FIGHT COMMUNISM and BOMB HANOI

There's about twelve of them, all about seventeen, and they're joined by a fink wearing a yellow raincoat and a mop on his head, with a sign around his waist saying DRAFT DODGER. The prick. He looks like a goddam canary.

George and the Spaniards are going ape over those guys. They look mad enough to go over and string them up from one of the trees in the park.

"What are they, Boy Scouts?" I ask George.

"They're a group of fascists called the Edmund Burp Society."

The Edmund Burp Society?

"That's a queer name," I say, with a look of surprise on my face.

"It fits them exactly," he says, looking grim.

Just then, one of them unrolls an American flag, and George and the Spaniards look like they're going to take a fit.

One of them mumbles that he'll clean his ass with that rag before the day's over, and he looks like he means it, too. He's about six feet tall and strong as a bull. His name's José. I guess he's the leader cause he yells the hardest.

We start off, with the Burpers at the head, and a line about a mile long following them. Everybody's yelling things like "Pearson, Martin, LBJ, how many kids did you kill today?", "Hell no, we won't go," "Yankee, out of Vietnam," etc.

I'm getting pretty excited about the whole deal and I'm yelling too. A demonstration's a ball.

We turn onto Wellesley and march towards Yonge Street. From there we're going to go to Queen Street and over to the city hall, where they're going to make speeches. I look around. I saw one real cutie when we were lining up, but I've lost her now. But like George said, there's lots of others.

The Burpers break off halfway along Wellesley and climb up the staircase of an old building overlooking the sidewalk. As we go by they yell "Commie, Red, Pinko" and other colours, and a couple of them spit at us.

George, José, and a few others go up the stairs and slug one of them in the yap. He steps back with a scared look. The little shit, if he'd spit on me, I'd have gone up there and cut his tongue out. A motorcycle cop pulls up and George and the guys jump back into line. The Burpers stand there like ants on a piece of sugar. That punch in the mouth has shut them up for a while. They run down the street to the front of the line again.

Somebody's singing "We Shall Overcome" and five thousand voices join in. Man, who do they think they are, the Ray Charles Singers? I'm going deaf.

At the corner of Bay and Wellesley, George and the Spaniards cut off and run down a block so that they can get in front of the Burpers, who're just turning down Yonge Street. I follow them, but that gets me mad. How am I supposed to meet the broads like this?

We make it just in time. The Burpers with their American flag waving in the breeze are just getting to the corner when we come steaming around it like a pack of wild dogs. We jump right in front of them and start singing some Spanish song about Fidel Castro. (The others sing—I listen.) By the time we hit College Street, the Burpers have got over their surprise and run in front of us again.

Musical chairs.

I look behind me. Christ, the line's about two miles long. I never seen so many people in my life, and they're all singing and yelling. You gotta see it to believe it. The cops have stopped the traffic on Yonge Street and we got the whole west sidewalk to ourselves. And the line gets bigger and bigger. We get down to Dundas and still they're turning off from Wellesley where we started. The Saturday shoppers are either on the opposite sidewalk or in the store entrances. Most of them are just standing there with their mouths open, like we're a bunch of Martians or something, but every now and then somebody yells "Reds go back to Russia," or "Commie traitors," and George and the boys hoot at the guy or stick their little fingers up at him.

We're approaching Queen Street when what I been waiting for since we started happens. A Spaniard yells "Nazi bastards" at the Burpers and one of them turns and swings his placard at him. José bashes the guy in the head and George and somebody else jump the flag carrier. Placards and feet are flying all over the place. George has got his arms around the guy with the flag and the Spaniard's trying to pull it out of his hands. Somebody's got a rock in his hand.

A Burper goes flying against a store window. CBC guys are filming the whole thing and I turn my head. Dozens of guys come running up to lend a hand and it looks for a minute like all hell's going to break loose. Somebody hits the ground and somebody else boots him in the gut. The flag's on the ground and one of the Spaniards is trying to rip it up.

This has all taken place in about thirty seconds. That's the time it takes for the cops to come wheeling up and separate everybody. That's right, separate. Not one guy's arrested. Not one. I'm so goddam mad, I can feel the steam rising to my head.

Goddam it, just try to have a fight like this in Cabbagetown and you'll get your head busted in two by the Law, and get thirty days in the Don Jail too. And here these clowns pull off the same deal right on Yonge Street and the cops just pull them apart. That's enough for me. I say "See you around" to George and walk over to the other side of the street. Goddammit. That's justice for you.

I go into a restaurant for a Coke and this cute little chick who doesn't look a day over sixteen, with short black hair combed Beatle style and two perky little boobs, serves me. I give her a big smile and a wink. Just like I thought, she smiles right back at me. A saucy little smile too. She looks like she knows the score. Think I'll stick around and see if I get anywhere with her. If I know my broads, she's probably just ripe for a good-looking stud like me. And like I say, she knows the score. Not like Terry. God, she was dumb!

She tells me one day near the beginning of the month that she's pregnant and that it's my kid in her gut. Says that she'd never used a safe or anything since we were together. I ask her why not and she answers that she wanted to have my kid cause she loved me so much. I say bullshit and then she tells me why she really came to live with me. It seems I look like the first guy that knocked her up and I even have the same name. She's never got over her baby being taken away from her, and since I was a dead ringer for that joe, she thought she could have another baby just like the one she'd had off him.

Crazy, huh?

Naturally I threw her out. But I did it in a nice way cause after all she's a human being, not a piece of garbage. It'll teach her a good lesson that'll help her out in life: don't get pregnant cause when you do, nobody wants you.

Yeah, when she looks back on this a few years from now, she'll thank her lucky stars that she met up with me. Somebody had to show her how to make out in this world.

"Thread Gathered and Tightened"
An Afterword

In the late 1980s I took a creative writing course taught by the playwright Lawrence Russell, who announced one day that the problem with Canada's literary culture was that at no time in the nation's history had we executed a writer for the things he or she had written. Maybe he didn't put it exactly this way. In fact, I can't remember exactly what he said, only the gist—that until we hung or electrocuted or guillotined someone for what they'd done with and to the written word Canadian literature could never properly begin. The comment was met by the class with silence. Maybe the rest of the students were doing what I was doing, thinking of Cicero, More, Bruno, Raleigh, Chénier, Lorca, Babel, and others who, if not killed *exactly* for what they wrote, were killed because they couldn't keep silent in the face of power.

For all I know, maybe we have killed a Canadian writer somewhere along the line, though that's not really my point. Russell was always a provocateur—which is what made him such a likeable and memorable teacher—but the outrageous statements were more important (at least for me) for their nuances than their immediate effect, even if it sometimes took me years to appreciate them. He was saying something about playing it safe, about keeping feathers unruffled, about always being mindful of the status quo. It was worth striving for (metaphorically speaking!): execution. (Not surprisingly two meanings of the word "execution" are equally pertinent here, since being put to death was commensurate with writing well.)

This is in no way to praise those who've made a career writing book after book about how bad much of Canadian literature is, apart from those works they happen to be publishing, many of which, to my eye, don't seem a whole lot different from the books they're complaining about—proving that the best antidote for bad writing is not complaint but rather good writing. What saves Russell's statement from similar charges is exactly that—it was a statement, fifty words or less, and then he was on to other things. The point was only worth spending a sentence on.

Had he lived several hundred years earlier, Juan Butler might have been granted the honour of his own sentence—a state execution, imprisonment in a tower for a while, or exile. As it was, he had to deal with sanctimonious printers:

> Peter Martin, a local publisher, is fuming at Canada's obscenity laws. One of his recent books, *Cabbagetown Diary* by Juan Butler, was rejected by two printers who feared the contents would be labeled obscene and that they could be charged under the Criminal Code. Martin says he knows of no case where printers have been charged, just the publisher or book seller. He finally put it out on his own "uneconomic" press. Martin feels that this is a form of censorship by the printer forced on him by the law. ("Last Word" 23)

The first printer charged such a high price for the work that Martin was forced to go elsewhere; the second agreed to a more modest sum, but then tried to censor the book's contents during the printing process (Fulford 133). From the very start, it seems, Butler had little thought for playing it safe, keeping feathers unruffled, or being mindful of the status quo, though *Cabbagetown Diary*, for all its unvarnished take on what Frank Davey called "the brutality and depravity" of "Cabbagetown residents" (63), was nothing compared to the murder, sexual assault, mutilation (Ross 68), and apocalyptic mayhem of *Garbageman*, the second of his three published novels. Nonetheless, it manages to convey a neighbourhood, citizenry, and mindset without a shred of redemption (well, maybe a shred . . .), with the most salient offence being what a *Chatelaine* reviewer described as the "shattering" and "casual exploitation of [. . .] women" ("Other World" 10). This exploitation, however, does nothing to advertise some kind of down-and-out machismo (as seen in Charles Bukowski), but instead deepens our sense of the heartlessness of the environment Butler is writing about. And other offences abound: homophobia, racism, pedophilia. Butler refuses to indulge in fantasies of agency, where characters denied political, cultural, or spiritual resources from the moment they are born can somehow, inexplicably, step outside of their actions and view them from the perspective of upper-middle-class or ivory-tower morality. They are in the midst of the action, and it is through their actions themselves that we glimpse the corruption they wrestle with and enact.

Two years after Butler's death, Bill Buford, identifying a 1970s and 80s literary movement he called "dirty realism," would identify the politics of this kind of writing: "It is possible to see many of these [works] as quietly political, at least in their details, but it is a politics considered from an arm's length: they are stories not of protest but of the occasion for it" (5). This is exactly right in the case of *Cabbagetown Diary*, since Butler's protagonist, Michael, chooses in the end to return to his tenement, to the life he knows there, rather than become politically active:

> Is it politics that's going to feed me? Is it politics that's going to keep me in spending money? What the hell do I care if there's poor people in Cabbagetown? There always has been and there always will be. They like it like that, and nothing you or I do is going to change them. All we'll get out of it is a rope around our necks, or the next fifty years in the pen. [. . .] Politics is for the birds. Who gives a shit what politicians say? Look at the Salvation Army. They're playing politics every time they come down to Allan Gardens with their drums and bugles, and promise all the winos there a better life if they cut off the booze. But the thing is, they don't really want the winos to stop being winos cause if they did, there'd be nothing for the Sally Anns to do after, and they'd be out of a job. Besides, I like the way I'm living too much to fuck it up by throwing bombs around. (173)

Throughout the novel there is no character or organization that isn't in some way implicated in the practices it wants to root out and destroy. The Salvation Army finds its raison d'être in the very conditions it seeks to ameliorate, in a way that, at least according to Michael, indefinitely prolongs those conditions. George, the communist radical, worshipper of Che Guevara, maker of Molotov cocktails, exploits the apparent naïveté of individuals such as Michael in order to advance his own agenda, choosing the agents for, and hence casualties of, his schemes from among the general population rather than his comrades. And when Michael finally takes part in a demonstration against the Vietnam War (this is the late 1960s, remember), he realizes that even the conditions for and responses to protest are fraught with class politics. Witnessing police intervention in a fight between left-wing radicals and Nazis, Michael notes: "That's the time it takes for the cops to come wheeling up and separate everybody. That's right, separate. Not one guy's arrested. [. . .] Just try to have a fight like this in Cabbagetown and you'll get your head busted in two by the Law, and get thirty days in the Don Jail too" (200). The suggestion here—one of Buford's "occasions" for protest—is that Michael rejects the patronizing attitude of all political organizations toward Cabbagetown and its residents, declaring his independence (whether it exists or not) in choosing the way he's living, and preferring its comforts and certainties (such as they are) to participation in what he regards as an exploitative politics. Butler's vision of Cabbagetown thus involves an extreme atomization, where each character plots an agenda in alienation from those around him or her (and this includes the female protagonist, Terry, who moves in with Michael only because he is a physical substitute for a former lover and a means to get pregnant again), and at the same time a rejection of condescending attitudes toward identifying and ameliorating the misery of "the poor and downtrodden."

This is of course not to say that the novel suggests poverty is a good thing; the concluding line of *Cabbagetown Diary*, where we learn that Michael kicked out Terry, a teenage runaway, on discovering that she was pregnant with his child, more than adequately registers the horror of her fate and of the environment that led to it. Butler's is a harrowing vision, exitless. No wonder some of his favourite writers were Hubert Selby Jr. and John Rechy, whose seminal novel, *City of Night*, first published in 1963, forms the one point of contact between Michael and the possibility of something meaningful emerging from his life: "I don't know when I've enjoyed a book as much as I'm enjoying this one. One day I'm going to write one like it" (193). The obvious assumption here would be that *Cabbagetown Diary* is in fact the novel Michael writes, though I have my doubts, since such a correspondence between protagonist and author would undercut—and I think *it is* undercut—by an unselfconsciousness in the writing that no amateur would permit, and that keys us into the naturalism of Butler's work: namely, that what is important here is the naked confrontation between a milieu and the people who inhabit and are conditioned by it. The style of *Cabbagetown Diary* is, moreover, not at all similar to *City of Night*, with none of the dark lyricism of Rechy's prose, presenting instead, as its subtitle suggests, a "documentary" aesthetic whose straightforward prose is a corollary to the ugliness of the life it exposes. There is no redemption to be found anywhere in this work, except perhaps in the bravery required to face it in the act of writing it down, even as the threads of the story gather into something unsolvable, inescapable. The gap between the narrator's desire to write a book "like" Rechy's and the book Butler actually produced is perhaps the only place where this text offers us the "meaning"—and by this I mean the activity of writing, not a thematic summary—that Michael senses is lacking in his life, and that he dreams of striving for. This is further brought home when we consider that of all the books Michael borrowed from his radical friend, George, it is Rechy's novel, amidst a stack of political tracts and manifestos, that appeals to his sensibility, that gives him an authentic (again, not because of *what* it says, but because of *how* it says it) window on the world as he has experienced it.

The temptation at this point, then, would be to consider Michael a kind of window through which we can see Butler himself. It's an easy trap to fall into, and links him to a long line of writers stretching back to Thomas Nashe, and perhaps further, and includes Byron,

Poe, Rimbaud, and modern variants such as Hemingway, Mailer, Bukowski, even Roth, who have made a career out of mingling their authorial personas with their lived ones. Butler was certainly no stranger to the sort of outrageous behaviour that followed such writers and could sometimes be read in their works. There was, for example, the notorious incident at a literary soiree where he "not only punched out a not unprominent figure on the local scene, but the guy's wife as well" (Snider F7). There was this description of him late in life: "But eventually, Juan became the kind of guy you dreaded to run into, he had worked himself into a place that was so extreme, so far away from the normal run of things, that conversation became near impossible" (Snider F7). And finally there are the sad facts of his death: "Three months ago, at the age of 37, he died in a Toronto psychiatric hospital. He hanged himself" (Dickie 17). This, after a few years of shuttling in and out of psychiatric wards, heavy-duty medication, moves from Toronto to Vancouver and back again, a novella that disappeared, and wild conspiracy theories involving a murdered aunt and the Mafia. The stories of the writer blend with the stories written, and the two mutually reinforce each other, though of course this is not exactly true either, since Juan Butler the writer, and his works, have largely disappeared, the story of his life buried in a dozen obituaries, and the novels in the back shelves of antiquarian booksellers. Such dis- and reappearances, however, are standard tropes in the unearthing of a lost *poète maudit* by literary treasure hunters, and I would not want to defuse the possibility of a Butler myth, necessarily, since there is nothing gained by the loss of wonder and mystery, or the blandness of fact, as long as we are careful to remember the complexities governing myth, literary or otherwise. Myths are, after all, useful in attracting readers to a particular writer, and that a lost writer (especially if they've been lost in the particular way Butler has been) is often an appealing filter to the work itself, informing the reading in potentially productive ways— for instance offering a window on the works' relation to the canon, its period, and the culture as a whole. The very first question to ask is why a myth that has the potential of Butler's was not celebrated in the first place. Why wasn't anyone interested? What does this say about our preferences, then and now? How does it inform our sense of the place of this novel vis-à-vis the Canadian canon?

One answer to this is found the similarities uniting Michael and Butler, and the discomfort it occasioned in reviewers and contemporary authors. Both were residents of Cabbagetown (Butler for a much shorter period of time); both were incarcerated at the St. John's Training School for Boys in Uxbridge, Ontario, for juvenile crimes (Michael for stealing a car, Butler for armed robbery); both were no strangers to fractious sexual relationships and violence. There is a focus on ugliness—even a politics of ugliness, one that continually thwarts amelioration or redemption—that wouldn't have endeared these men, or the text that unites them, to the general public. But the differences are as notable—Michael, from what *Cabbagetown Diary* tells us, lived all his life in that part of Toronto, whereas Juan Butler spent time growing up in Spain, Canada, and parts of Europe, and was therefore better read, more culturally sensitive, and intellectual in a way Michael had no opportunity to be. Butler's story is thus both sadder and richer, and Michael's more instructive not of how Butler lived but of what he saw in the world, the people and places that captured his attention and sympathy. Michael does not escape or attempt to change Cabbagetown because ultimately he does not have the resources—imaginative or material—in order to do so, and certainly the writing of this novel, insofar as it presents Michael in complete unselfconsciousness, warts and all, suggests that change or escape is impossible, not only because Michael has no awareness of the wider world outside but also, and more alarmingly, because he (and I think to some degree Butler himself) glories in refusing to abide by standards other than those he knows—in other words, he doesn't even *want* to change. The last line of the novel surrenders Michael entirely to the heartless world Butler carefully analyzes. This is indeed a documentary, but Michael is not the man behind the camera—or perhaps it would be more accurate to say that he's not the *only* man behind the camera. The carefully orchestrated alienation of *Cabbagetown Diary* informs every aspect of reading the text, including the strange doubling and oscillation that accompanies our attempt to sort out author from narrator.

It is precisely from this—the readers' alienation from Michael—that the novel draws its power, similar to that of *Sister Carrie*, *McTeague*, or the *Studs Lonigan* trilogy. *Cabbagetown Diary* has in common with these works an attempt to make readers recoil from what's on the page, to keep them in confrontation with what they're reading rather than being swept away by it, so that naked representation itself serves to continually highlight and keep us in mind of the complexity of social ills that characters, and even some of the political movements those characters participate in, cannot sort out. Where Butler's work differs from that of Dreiser, Norris or Farrell, respectively, is in a wariness over what comes next, or even if something *needs* to come next, since our awareness of the limitations that surround Michael—social, cultural, political—always runs aground on the furious passion with which he lives his life, his refusal to change, the sense of the wasted effort of those who, like George, believe that Michael needs only to be awakened politically, and who are continually surprised to find that he is *already awake* but unwilling to lend himself to what he regards as compromised political and cultural prescriptions. Thus does Butler retain, at the heart of the individual human, something inexplicable, resistant, unfathomable—a mystery impervious to cultural or political analysis, available, if at all, only to art itself, which is perhaps the only form capable of fusing contradiction into a whole, of taking those disparate strands of story and thought and gathering them into this singular, fatal vision.

Tamas Dobozy

Works Cited

Buford, Bill. Editorial. *Granta* 8 (1983): 4–5. Print.

Butler, Juan. *Cabbagetown Diary: A Documentary*. 1970. Waterloo, ON: Wilfrid Laurier UP, 2012. Print.

Davey, Frank. "Juan Butler." *From There to Here: A Guide to English-Canadian Literature since 1960*. By Davey. Erin, ON: Press Porcepic, 1974. 63. Print.

Dickie, Barrie. "Juan Butler, 1942–1981." *Books in Canada* Aug.–Sept. 1981: 17. Print.

Fulford, Robert. "Delayed Diary." *Saturday Night* 20 Nov. 1970: 133. Print.

"The Last Word." *Toronto Star* 29 Sept. 1970: 23. Print.

"The Other World." *Chatelaine* Feb. 1971: 10. Print.

Ross, Gary. "Juan Butler: Improbable Anarchist." *Toronto Life* Dec. 1974: 68. Print.

Snider, Norman. "A Life Ended Much as It Was Lived." *Globe and Mail* 11 July 1981: F7. Print.